MAIN

ENCORE
TO AN
EMPTY ROOM

An EXILE
Novel

Kevin Emerson

 KATHERINE TEGEN BOOKS
An Imprint of HarperCollins Publishers

For Skip

All photos by Kevin Emerson except:
Hay bale tractors photo by Lori Stone
Stone buffalo photo by Erin Ostrander

Katherine Tegen Books is an imprint of HarperCollins Publishers.

Encore to an Empty Room: An Exile Novel

ISBN 978-0-06-213398-4

Typography by Carla Weise
15 16 17 18 19 PC/RRDH 10 9 8 7 6 5 4 3 2 1
❖
First Edition

ENCORE

TO AN

EMPTY ROOM

THE FAMILY ECLIPTIC

MELANIE FOWLER
Val's Mom

RANDY
Caleb's uncle,
Eli's old band mate

CHARITY
Caleb's mom

THE POPARTS PLANE

ETHAN MYERS
Postcards from Ariel singer,
Summer's ex

KELLEN McHUGH
Allegiance bassist,
knows about tapes!

JASON FLETCHER
Candy Shell Records,
signed Ethan

MILES ELLISON
Allegiance guitarist

THE ALLEGIANCE CLUSTER

All Hail
Minions!

PARKER FRANCIS
Allegiance drummer

JERROD FLETCHER
Head of Candy Shell,
former Allegiance manager

Supreme
Commander

Bait

The
Unfortunatelys

MAYA BARNES
Dating Matt,
Summer's friend,
Candy Shell Intern

Fluffy Poodle and
the #s of Doom!

THE ASTEROID
BELT OF BANDS

Freak   Show

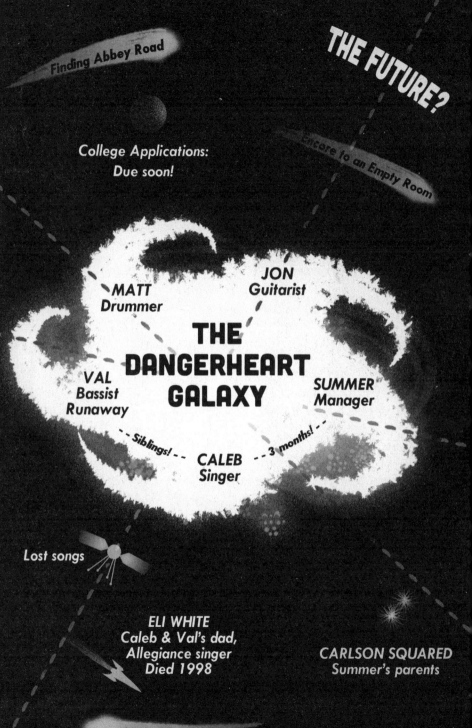

"Hello?"

"This is 911 dispatch. Please state y—"

"Hello?"

A hiss, and the screen goes blank. I stare at the phone, as if it's going to shrug and apologize. All this power, to speak to any other human on the planet via a quick space walk, to like what they're having for lunch from thousands of miles away, and still . . .

The battery goes dead right when you need it.

"Ugh!" I want to throw the stupid phone I—

"Summer . . . ," he groans from my lap.

I bite my lip and squeeze back the tears and shove my phone away in my jacket pocket. It's not the phone's fault, not the phone company's conspiracy to build batteries that start sucking after two years. It's not the 911 operator's fault or the fault of the inventor of the steam engine that made the human dream of long-distance travel even possible in the first place.

It's my fault.

A pack of adults stumbles by. A couple of them eye me mid-laughter. Twentysomethings with liquor-glazed eyes. Their cheeks are rosy above their fashionable scarves.

"Are you okay?" one of them says, nearly serious, her eyes starting to clear.

"Girl, you are *not* getting any there," another says, appraising my situation, and this trips the alcohol-loosened triggers and they all start giggling and leaning into each other and the almost-lucid girl sinks back into the pack and they stumble on.

"Can I borrow your phone?" I ask quietly after them.

He coughs in my lap, a thick sound. I wonder if there is internal bleeding I don't know about. Probably not. But still . . . His body starts to shiver.

I take off my coat and drape it over him. My own shoulders won't stop trembling. My ears and toes are starting to feel numb. My butt is long gone from sitting on this ice-slicked staircase. I should get up and head back to the club, get someone to help, but I don't want to leave him. Or risk hurting him by trying to drag him inside.

I don't want to move at all.

Hasn't there been enough? Three thousand miles of wild plans, lies, and dreams that soared like magical leaps to the stars and back. . . . Maybe my battery is dead, too. We tried, though, didn't we? A for effort? But it doesn't matter. This is what I get, deserved or not. Everyone's gone. Everything's ruined. No band, and no future. Just pain, loss, and a dead cell phone.

This time the tears come. I wipe at the snot on my sore, freezing nose and look desperately up and down the street. Williamsburg at one a.m. You would think there'd be no shortage of people. But not on this street, not in this weather.

Something stings on my already frozen cheek.

A snowflake.

They drift down through the yellow streetlight, large and solitary and sentient-seeming, floating to earth like little paratroopers, making tiny whispering sounds as they land on the pavement.

"Nnnn."

"It's okay," I whisper to him, but once again, I am a liar. Nothing is okay.

3 MONTHS EARLIER . . .

Out of the Shadow: The Son of a Fallen Star Steps into the Light

—posted on December 19 by Nellie Martz

You all remember when the news broke this fall: Eli White, guitarist and singer for famed late-nineties band Allegiance to North, had a son: Caleb, born two years before Eli drowned in Santa Monica. To protect him from the scrutiny and notoriety, Caleb's mother, Charity, kept his dad's identity a secret, finally revealing the truth to Caleb on his eighteenth birthday.

The internet caught on not too long after that, and suddenly Caleb was at the center of a storm of questions: What was it like to be the son of a rock star? To have a ghost for a dad? To find out now? How much did the son resemble the father? And, could Caleb shed any light on Eli's final, mysterious days?

The only problem: Caleb wouldn't talk.

Not. One. Word.

Until now.

Toast & Jam has the exclusive interview with Caleb Daniels right here!

T&J: First of all, what was it like, finding out who your father was?

Caleb: A total shock. I mean, some people ask me

if it's exciting to know I had this famous dad. But I never had him in my life. And now that I know . . . it's strange. On the one hand, I wonder what it would have been like if he'd been around, teaching me guitar and that kind of thing. On the other hand, everything I've read about him says he was a mess. Maybe it would have been worse. Plus, I'm a musician, too, and I don't want to end up like he did.

T&J: Not even the writing-brilliant-songs part?

Caleb *(a rare smile)***:** I guess I wouldn't mind that. But it seems like, a lot of times, brilliance comes with a price: the lighter the light, the darker the dark. Sometimes I worry, like, what if I got the dark part, too?

T&J: When you learned about Eli, you didn't tell anyone. Why not?

Caleb: I don't want to make it on my father's name. I wanted my music to be judged as being by me, not by "the son of Eli White."

T&J: Rumor has it your very first response was to break up your former band, Android Necktie.

Caleb: Well, yeah, I kinda freaked out. Now that I've lived with it a few months, I can see that I was probably overreacting. But the good thing is my new band, Dangerheart, is great. My band mates are the best. It's a better fit for me.

T&J: I read some speculation that you and your bass player, Val, might be an item. Eyewitnesses say you have real chemistry onstage. Care to comment?

Caleb: Ha, no. We're very close, but it's not that kind of relationship. I have a girlfriend.

T&J: We've heard that, too. She's also your band manager. Conflict of interest?

Caleb: Conflict and interest.

T&J: Nice quote!

Caleb: Ha-ha. Seriously, I'd be lost without her.

T&J: Back to the question of notoriety: Wouldn't being associated with your dad's name be helpful in getting noticed? There's a lot of competition out there.

Caleb: It would. We debated that, but . . . the word is out, so it doesn't really matter now anyway, does it?

T&J: You sound disappointed by that. Tell me, if the world hadn't found out, would you have ever revealed the truth?

Caleb: [thinks]

T&J: Is that a complicated answer?

Caleb: Well, it's like, I know maybe this goes against some of what I just said but here's the thing: Everyone knows about "Eli White." He's like a legend. But, what if . . . there's another version

6

of him? Who nobody really knew? Who was
more than what we think.

T&J: Are you saying you know something about him
that you're not telling us?

Caleb: No. Just that . . . I have to believe there was
more to his story. And I wanted to find out
before I let the world in on our family. But, like
I said, it doesn't matter now.

*Next: We get the scoop on Caleb's band, Dangerheart,
and how Dad has already made it into their first hit
song, "On My Sleeve"! [Click Here for Part 1]*

Mount Hope High School

Moonflower Artist Management and Mermaid
Assassin Productions proudly present:

THE HOLIDAY MELTDOWN!

A POPARTS ACADEMY PRODUCTION

Outside under the lights at the
Marketplace Plaza
December 19th, 6 pm

FEATURING:

The Unfortunatelys
HellzBellz (Holiday sing-along!)
Supreme Commander
Freaktastique
All Hail Minions!
Dangerheart

There is no worse time to live in Mount Hope than the holidays. When most of your town is a sprawling labyrinth of factory outlet malls, and every streetlight is decorated with a banner that reads *Mount Hope. Get Your Giving Here!*, it's hard not to feel like your Christmas spirit has crawled into a corner and died.

The constant drone of modern holiday remixes, crazy traffic, no parking, and endless lines at the coffee drive-through because everyone is ordering drinks with eggnog and peppermint and cinnamon and extra froth but then also "skinny." It seems like we're all unhappy and exhausted and jostling into each other, like, the bigger the sales, the more severe the frowning.

Everyone that is, except for me. No time for frowns! Me and my classmate Maya Barnes have work to do. Sure, in one fuzzy-red-fingerless-gloved hand I'm holding a drive-through-stalling venti triple two-pump peppermint skinny mocha (ho ho ho!), but in the other I have:

"Take a break from shopping to see the best new bands in town!"

Flyers.

Maya and I are stationed at a clogged mall intersection. For the last hour and for—I tap my phone, carefully balanced against the side of the mocha—twenty more minutes, our job is to hype up our big first-semester project: the Holiday Meltdown concert. Soundcheck is happening right now. The rumble of bass and drums startles some shoppers out of their zombie shamble. We've been promoting for weeks, and this is our final chance: a search for those last few upbeat souls just yearning for a break from shopping and a dose of rock.

"Great new bands playing right over at the Marketplace!" Maya calls.

The young professional woman whose attention she's trying to woo brushes past her without looking. Her bag even bumps Maya's arm and makes her mocha spill.

"I want to kill them," I say out of the corner of my otherwise smiling face. I'm kidding. Mostly.

"Hate is only wanting someone to love you," Maya

replies, her smile equally plastic.

This makes me laugh. Maya's right. And I know that when I'm out walking anywhere, the sight of people handing out stuff always makes me think, *No! Don't see me!* And yet, now, here I am. Except this is different because what I'm handing out is awesome! A show with great bands under the lights, with a crowd full of scarves and fog from breaths and real cheer! How could anyone want to miss it? They need to know!

And also, I'd rather be the upbeat, smiling version of me, as opposed to the hunched, grizzled veteran who's cynically bah-humbugging the whole thing.

That person is so much less fun.

Maya and I are getting graded for this show, and one of the scores is for turnout. This group project is the biggest grade we get for the quarter. Our PopArts classmates are flyering at other key intersections nearby. We already got a great score on our promotional campaign (poster with fire-breathing snow monster), our grassroots marketing (online blasts and giveaways, plus Arctic Apocalypse costume contest), and our social justice component (a portion of snack and merchandise sales go to support the county's transitional housing program).

We'll also have to present a report on the effectiveness of all this, including statistical analysis of things like actual attendance versus online responses, money raised versus budget spent on promotion. Yes, rock and roll can occasionally involve spreadsheets.

Actually, I vastly prefer that stuff to this moment with the flyers. Here, it's just you and your cheery smile against the indifference of the universe. But these are the final minutes, and I need to bear down and turn some heads.

A young couple walks by. College students home on break? Exactly the listening audience I'm after.

"Take a break from shopping to see the best—"

"Oh, no thanks," says the guy, super polite.

Ugh. Oh, well, I pep up my smile for the next target: a trio of middle school girls. Another perfect Dangerheart demographic.

"Awesome high school bands playing over at the Marketplace tonight," I say. Two of the girls are chatting and the third is buried in her phone. Their eyes barely register me but a hand does flash out and take a flyer.

As they walk away I hear her say, "What's this?" Like the paper magically appeared in her hand. But then she taps it against her friend's shoulder. "Hey, check it out."

Just that little comment fills me with hope. In this sea of stuff, in this planet of seven billion, Dangerheart could be noticed!

The crowd surges past and I pick my spots. It's weird to categorize people. We're always being told that labels are bad, but being selective helps to minimize the cosmic sadness that is finding your flyers crumpled and recycled on the next corner.

Older couple = no.

Thirties-ish solo guy = yes. Takes flyer. Score!

Parents with kids = halfhearted try. Even if they stopped by, would they post about it online? Come back for another show? Doubtful. I've seen parents. Have two of them. The only things they post about are their kids, or pictures of what they're eating for brunch.

"I'm sick of your flyers for strip clubs!" a middle-aged woman snaps at me, brushing away my hand. "I should call the police."

"It's . . . ," I start to say but it is no use. The woman hurries on.

Maya takes a risk on three jock guys walking by. "Oh, cool," the guy taking the flyer says with what might be real enthusiasm. But out of the corner of my eye I see him ball it up and flick it at his buddy's face.

I notice Maya noticing this. "Jerks," I say.

Maya sighs. "We should head over."

Maya is only a sophomore, so she's absorbed a few less blows when it comes to this kind of thing and hasn't quite learned how to shrug them off yet. Not that I'm any pro at it, either, but I've definitely developed a thicker skin. Whenever I'm jaded or sarcastic, it's just to hide the sound of air slowly escaping from my inner optimism balloon. Luckily it's time to just enjoy the music.

I flip through my pile as we walk. "I think I handed out about seventy-five," I say.

"Same here," says Maya. "I hope some people show up."

We weave our way through the succession of shopping quadrangles. The thump of bass hits me in the ribs. I love that feeling like no other. I never played an instrument as a kid, except for a few short piano lessons, so while managing bands may not get me up on the stage it gets me close enough to feel the music seeping into me, to get lost in its loud.

We arrive at the plaza and find the Unfortunatelys up onstage doing their final checks, lit in blues and reds. Strings of large glowing stars extend from the stage out across the plaza, bathing the crowd in a golden aura.

"We should do our start-of-show head count," Maya says, her enthusiasm back. She likes the numbers, too.

We split up to opposite sides of the crowd and gather our data: total attendance, approximate ages, and text each other the results. The crowd isn't bad. I count over two hundred, with a mass of students up in the front, and then a mix of adults, some parents with middle school kids, a few families and grandparents.

"I'm going to find the Commander backstage," says Maya when we reconvene at the back of the crowd.

"Cool, I'm meeting the band for burgers."

"Don't miss our set!" Maya says with a smile, but I hear the note of worry. Even though Maya and I are friends, there is an inequality that comes from me and my band being older and, well, better. It's a subtle thing in music, the way pecking orders work. Dangerheart could get away with eating dinner through Supreme Commander's set. It's acceptable, fits the status quo. But it would also make us just a little bit jerks. You have to keep these things in mind all the time. Because even though it might be okay now, in the long run, musicians are always keeping score.

As I head around the corner to the restaurant, my phone buzzes. A Twitter post:

Toast & Jam @spreaditonthick 1m
The son of Eli White steps out of the shadow.
http://bit.ly/aWrh2 #dangerheart @catherinefornevr
@livingwithghosts

Oh, sweet! Finally, the blog post is up.

After Caleb's identity as Eli White's son was revealed, we had to set up a separate account to deal with all the interview requests. Caleb didn't want to do any of them; he doesn't want Eli to overshadow him or the band, but I finally convinced him that the shadow was there whether we liked it or not. Do a search for Dangerheart and well over half the results are about Eli. It's been driving the band crazy.

And every day that the world has that conversation without us, the less chance we have of owning it. I pored over the different interview requests for weeks, looking for someone who wanted to write about Caleb, not just use him as a vehicle for talking about the tragic figure of Eli. And definitely not someone who would spend the whole time comparing the two, or the two bands.

I've seen the draft of what Nellie is posting and it's perfect. It doesn't hurt that Toast & Jam has a national following. So hopefully it will calm the world down a little bit, which we need for two reasons: first, so that Caleb can relax and be himself and the band can function without weird expectations. And second . . .

So that we can pursue our other, top secret agenda.

Which is the real reason we're eating burgers right now instead of watching the opening bands.

I find Dangerheart in a back corner booth. They look cool sitting there together, shrouded in mystique. Seeing them makes me smile, but only Matt, the drummer, even notices me approaching. He smiles back. Everyone else is hunched over Jon's tablet.

Caleb has his head in his hands. Something's bothering him. Probably preshow nerves. He gets them pretty bad, even though he's really talented.

"Hey, guys."

"Hey," says Val, getting up so I can scoot in beside Caleb. She's frowning, but that's sort of her default position.

What worries me is that everyone else is, too.

"What's up?"

"We're looking at the interview," Caleb mutters.

"Oh," I say. "Cool. It's good . . . right? I thought it was good." I try to keep my energy positive, but it's faltering, being sucked into the black-hole mood at this table.

"We haven't even read it yet," says Matt.

16

"We're still just looking at that graphic at the beginning," Jon adds.

"Graphic?" Nellie didn't send me a graphic.

Caleb finally looks up. For just a second he smiles. "Hey," he says. He rubs my leg. "I ordered you the jalapeño garden burger. Was that right?" He's speaking quietly. It's the tone his voice gets when he's fighting his stormy insides, trying to find his center.

"Always." I give him a quick kiss that makes a smile briefly grow on his face, and when he smiles, his nose wrinkles and his cheeks squint up against his dark eyes and it almost makes me want to look away, like he's too beautiful, and I grip his hand tighter . . . but the smile flames out in an instant. He pushes the tablet toward me. "Check it out."

I see the Toast & Jam header, the title of the article, and between those two things there is a piece of graphic art, and . . . oh no.

It's a giant close-up on Eli White's grizzled face, staring wounded into the camera, a few days unshaven, hair a mess, bags under his eyes. In front of that, small and only reaching up over Eli's chin and mouth, is literally a tiny shadow silhouette of Caleb.

"That's . . . ," I say with a sigh. "Exactly the opposite of what we wanted. She never said she was going to do that!"

I rub Caleb's back, hoping to steady him. He pushes the pad toward Jon then takes my hand. "I mean . . . wow."

17

I feel a surge of guilt. "Are you mad?" I ask.

"Not at you . . ." He sips his already empty Coke.

I quickly send Nellie an email.

Hey, Nellie! We just saw the post. Thanks so much!
Just curious, where did that graphic come from?

"It's definitely attention-grabbing," says Matt. He's our youngest member and often the most optimistic of us.

"And if you look real close I think you can sort of make out your left eye," says Jon, our lead guitarist and resident master of sarcasm.

"Bastards," says Val. Bassist and surliest.

My phone buzzes with Nellie's reply.

Hey, Summer, so glad you like it! Yes, we changed
the header. I know we had that shot of the band, but
my editor thought this graphic would get way more
clicks. And clicks are king, right?

I'm torn about how to reply. I know what I really want to say, that this image totally undermines the idea of making the story more about Caleb, and yet it's already out there, and we can't exactly afford to tick off a blog like T&J . . .

Gotta love clicks! Thanks again, Nellie!

Our food arrives and everybody starts eating quietly. A couple bites of salt, ketchup, and jalapeños renew my strength and I tap the table. "Look, this sucks, but at least the article is good. And things like this are just all the more reason why . . ."

Caleb meets my gaze and lowers his voice. "We need to find the other songs."

"Exactly."

"It's the only way we're ever going to really have our say," Val agrees.

"And know the real him," says Caleb.

"Right. Until we do," I say, "there are always going to be editors like this who are going to screw things up."

"And don't forget the part where we play the songs and get world famous," adds Matt. "I still have no problem with that."

We all check in with each other, a table of conspirators. I notice that Jon is the only one who hasn't joined in. He's still looking at the article, but then he feels our gaze on him and looks up. "The Eli White All-Stars!" he says in an overly enthusiastic radio DJ's voice. Then he makes the devil horns and rolls his eyes. He's joking . . . I think. Of everyone, Jon has been the least comfortable with how every other conversation about Dangerheart now also includes Eli White. But he's on board enough, I feel sure of that.

"All that's great . . . ," says Val. "But what's the point of this meeting? It's been two months and we haven't found

19

a single clue about where Eli might have hidden his next song. I mean, we still have to consider that the two tapes we found in LA and San Fran were it."

"I know." I hate hearing this because I've thought the same thing. All of us have. But as long as there's still a chance of finding the lost songs from *Into the Ever & After*, I feel like we have to try. "There might be clues we missed," I say. "And the internet is too spotty from 1998. That's why we have to talk to people who were there. Plus, remember what Eli said: *More from the next show.*"

"Do we still think that's Minneapolis?" Matt asks.

"Makes sense," I say. "If we could get a solid lead, we could try to book a gig there and go check it out."

"Yeah," says Caleb, "but it would definitely be easier if we'd found *any* more clues since then."

"I know." He's right. We need something, *anything* to go on. We can't just skip off to Minneapolis, or New York, the last two shows Allegiance played before Eli left the band, without a pretty solid lead, for all the reasons that have to do with still being in high school and having parents and everything.

Also, the rest of life has been keeping us pretty busy. Dangerheart has played a show every two weeks, practiced every other night, and is set to record an EP right after the holidays. Like Maya and me with our first semester project, the EP is a huge part of the band's PopArts grade. Not to mention our first chance to release some music.

I'm applying to colleges, too. Well, "applying" makes it sound like I've actually worked on the applications . . . but I will! Soon! I've still got twelve days until they're due.

Plus, Val's living at Caleb's and working to get her GED online. She doesn't want to enroll in school because then her mom might be able to track her down. Matt is helping her with the math bits because even though he's a freshman he is some kind of genius at math.

None of that leaves much time for sleuthing, and with every week that goes by, the doubt inside me grows: What if we're really just on a wild-goose chase?

Val sighs. "I keep thinking about the Eli on that 'Exile' tape. He was already a mess, and that was *before* he ran off with my mom. Good ol' Melanie couldn't even remember to pick me up from school most days. It's just hard to imagine that he really followed through on writing, recording, *and* hiding the other two songs."

"It does sound like a stretch," I say quietly. Val's mom, Melanie Fowler, was Eli's girlfriend at the end of Allegiance. Actually she was Kellen's fiancée first. Hello, band drama! Val doesn't talk much about her, but I know that Melanie was bad enough to make Val run away a year ago, after a fight on Christmas turned violent. And though Val's never said, it seems pretty clear that wasn't the first violent incident.

Add that to a list of doubts about Eli that already includes a heroin addiction, and the fact that he was about to be sued by Kellen and the rest of his band, along with Candy Shell's

boss Jerrod Fletcher, for lost royalties and tour money. . . .
Is there any way Eli really could have come through on the
tapes?

But still . . . "It probably sounds cheesy," I say, "but we
can't give up yet." Finding the songs is such a big opportunity for the band. And for Caleb . . . I think he really
needs it. Ever since he found out about Eli, he's been torn up
inside. I hope it will help him deal with those demons that
have been swirling around in his head since last summer.

That's why tonight, I've called in an expert witness.

"There he is," says Matt.

A wiry figure has entered the restaurant. He walks
with a hunch like he should work in a mortuary, like he
would know dark tales. Both of these things are kinda true.
Slicked-back salt-and-pepper hair, shoulders slumped, hands
shoved into a black jacket that looks like something he's
owned since the 1980s.

This is Vic, the server at Canter's Deli in Hollywood
who knew where Eli's first tape was located.

He spies us and heads our way.

"You ready?" I say to Caleb. He eyes Vic worriedly and
makes this expression that I call Fret Face. "Sure." He gazes
at me and I can see it all there: the hope, the fear, the trust in
this idea and in me that I feel like I barely earned. I have a
strong desire to grab him and kiss him hard, but I settle for
another quick peck on the cheek, and holding his hand tight
beneath the table, as Vic arrives.

"You wanted to meet," Vic says when he arrives at our booth.

"Thanks for coming," I say.

"Sure." Vic looks around, as if he feels the cloak-and-dagger vibe, too. He grabs a chair from a nearby empty table and sits down. "How you holding up?" he asks Caleb.

Caleb musters a smile. "Not too bad."

Vic nods and stares into the table. "So."

"Okay." I open my phone to a list of notes I made.

Vic's bony hand falls on mine. It's crisscrossed with white lines. Not sure Vic has ever seen a bottle of hand moisturizer. "No recordings," he warns.

"Oh, no, I just have questions written down."

"Put the phone away or I'm gone."

"Right, sorry." Phone returns to pocket. "Okay, first I, well, we wanted to say thank you for helping us find Eli's tape."

"It was a tape?" Vic shrugs. "Huh."

"You didn't know what Eli had hidden at Canter's?"

"He didn't tell me what it was and I didn't ask. I just knew he wanted it hidden until you came looking for it."

"Well," I say, "it was a tape. Of Eli playing his song called 'Exile.' One of his lost songs."

With each detail I watch Vic for a reaction . . . and get nothing.

"Now we're trying to find the others. We think maybe there's one in Minneapolis."

Vic keeps staring into the table. Then he checks his watch. "These are the best hours of the night for tips."

"Sure, sorry." Everything he says throws me more off my game. "Um, but the thing is: Do you have any idea where Eli might have hid any other tapes? Do you think we're right that they might be in Minneapolis and New York? Or is there anywhere else in LA where you think he might have left a clue?"

"Look," says Vic. "Here's all I know: Eli came in that day, hid whatever he hid in the back of that booth, made that fancy menu, and told me to help you find it if you ever came asking, but that was it. He didn't say another word to me about any lost songs or anything. And I'm glad he didn't. I don't want to be involved in any of this. So, if there's nothing else, it's been nice to see you all but I need to go make the rent." He starts to get up.

I don't even know what to say. I'm totally flustered, can't remember my notes . . . Suddenly this seems like a huge waste.

Vic is getting to his feet when Caleb asks: "What was he like?"

Vic pauses. "You mean Eli."

"Yeah," says Caleb. "I don't mean that day, but like . . . in general."

I'm so glad he said something, and I squeeze his leg beneath the table, because I know it was probably hard for him in an anxious moment like this.

It's a good question, too. We know Eli was an amazing musician, but I feel like there are reasons to wonder whether he was a good person. It's not just because he was into drugs, or committed suicide while he had young children out there in the world. Those are more signs of someone who was troubled and struggling, I think.

What I actually keep coming back to is something little and random: when Eli made his first video for Caleb, he aimed the camera at the mirror to tape a reflection of himself. It distorted the image in a way that felt almost . . . theatrical. Even though he was playing this honest song, it still felt like a show. Should you be making a show of your first connection to your lost son like that? I can't quite put my finger on it more precisely, but something about it bothers me.

"He was beautiful," says Vic. "And troubled." He sits back down. "You know, he had the gift, for music, for people."

"For people?" Val says.

"Eli really cared about people. It was a problem for him sometimes. People would take advantage of him." Vic sighs. "Some people have too big a heart for this world. And all hearts break eventually. Eli just felt too much and he could get caught up in the flood."

I grip Caleb's hand. This is a little bit of like father like son.

"Eli used to come by back in high school," says Vic, "and he'd sit at the counter and drink shakes while he did his homework. He'd come out back with me on smoke breaks and we'd talk about bands. He never wanted anything except company. After he died, I wished I'd done more to try to help him, but, at the time, I felt like what he needed was someone to just treat him like a normal person. To talk with him and respect his privacy, and not handle him like he was famous or an addict or any of that. I don't know . . ."

"Sounds like you did help him," I say. "He trusted you enough to hide his secret with you."

"Maybe," says Vic. "We had a game where we'd think

about great bands and what might have happened if a little choice went differently here or there. What if John Bonham doesn't choke on his own vomit? Or what if the Kinks aren't banned from touring the US in the sixties? If Lennon goes with his dad to New Zealand . . . that kind of thing. Eli was into it. He'd go on and on about those alternate realities. I used to wonder if that came from his mom dying."

"I read that she passed away when he was young," says Caleb. "Do you know what from?"

"Some nasty cancer, when he was in high school," says Vic. "His dad had remarried a few years before, and Eli hated the stepmom. I think during those early years Eli was living at that manager guy's house. What was his name . . . ?"

"You mean Jerrod Fletcher?" I ask.

"Yeah. Him. They used to come to the deli together sometimes. But it turns out Jerrod was just another one of the bastards that was after his money at the end." Vic stops. He takes a cigarette from behind his ear and starts tapping it against his palm.

"It's nice to hear a version that doesn't make him sound like a mess," says Caleb.

"Huh." Vic gazes into the table like he's trying to find a thought.

"What?" I ask.

"You just reminded me of something he said that day he

hid the tape." For a second it doesn't seem like Vic is going to continue, but then he does. "He comes running in, acting really paranoid. It was dead in the restaurant . . . Saturday afternoon around three. But that's what he said: that he was cleaning up a mess. When he was done with the menu, I asked him if he had time for our usual smoke break, but he said he had some place to be. Some party or something. I didn't press him, but . . . how could I have known?"

"Party?" I repeat. That doesn't fit what we know. "He should have been on his way to San Francisco for the next Allegiance show."

"Why would he have done that?" says Vic. "They'd been broken up for months."

"Wait . . ." What Vic is saying doesn't quite make sense. "When exactly was the last time you saw Eli?"

"The day he died," says Vic. "September nineteenth." He shakes his head. "Wish I'd known . . . but he seemed so *together* when he came in . . ." Vic trails off.

None of us have a reply. I lock eyes with Caleb and I can tell we're both trying to figure out what this means.

Vic is gazing at the floor, then seems to snap out of a daydream and checks his watch. "I should go," he says quietly.

"Thanks for coming," I say.

"No problem. You guys should stop by sometime. Keep me posted." He turns and stalks off.

Nobody says anything for a minute. My brain is spinning. Finally, I break the silence. "We assumed that Eli hid the tape the day right after he made it. Like before he went to San Francisco. It made sense, but . . ."

"What Vic said . . . that means he didn't hide the tape until two months later," says Caleb. "After he was back in LA. And doing better, according to Randy."

"Probably because he ditched my mom," Val adds.

"So," I say, trying to fit the pieces, "Eli hides a tape at Canter's that day. Visits Randy, too . . ."

"Which is when he left his gig bag behind in Randy's car," Caleb adds.

"It's almost like . . ."

"He was planning it out," says Val. "Carefully."

"And then . . . ," says Caleb, "he went to Jerrod's party."

"Where we heard he got drunk and thrown out," adds Jon.

"If he had a plan," I say, my fingers shaking as I hurry to get the words out, "that means he probably had all three songs finished. And he'd had the whole summer to think about where to put them."

"So you're saying Eli really did plan this," says Val. "Set the whole thing up for us to find."

"It sounds like it," says Caleb.

"Yeah," says Jon, "but . . . if all that is true, does that mean he also planned to . . ."

"Die?" Caleb finishes.

"Sorry," says Jon, "but, yeah."

"No, it's okay," Caleb nearly whispers. "We've all wondered if Eli killed himself."

"We should talk to Randy," I say, thinking of what he said in the van on the way back from San Francisco: he worried that Kellen McHugh, Eli's former band mate, had influenced Eli's death by possibly getting him started drinking that night at Jerrod's party. But Randy also said Eli was planning to give up his rights and let them have his money. "That part doesn't add up yet."

"Randy's in Vegas until Christmas," says Caleb. "You can never get in touch with him when he's there."

"But I don't get it," Val says. "If Eli hid the tapes on purpose . . . why haven't we found the next clue?"

"It's got to be out there," I say, feeling more certain than ever. "We just need to look harder. Eli's come through for us so far." I realize how weird those words sound.

"For once," Val agrees. But she smiles and rubs her brother's arm.

"We should get back," says Matt. "Maya's going to be bummed if we miss the Commander's set."

"Good little puppy," Val chides.

"Shut up," says Matt, but he smiles. Matt and Maya have been dating for a couple months but lately I've noticed that he doesn't sound too happy when he refers to her. Actually, he doesn't even mention her that much. Part of it, I think, is that he used to have a pretty obvious crush on me. But it's seemed like more than that lately. Except Maya acts like everything's fine.

"Yeah, we should go see them," I say. "Back to the business of being an awesome band."

"That sounds like a relief," says Jon.

We wolf down our food and head back to the stage.

Formerly Orchid @catherinefornevr 2m
Burgers accomplished! Now to see Supreme Commander! Hurry to the
Meltdown! You don't want to miss a note!

Caleb is quiet on the walk back to the stage. We all are.
"You okay?" I ask.

"Just a far comet," he says, and pulls me closer. "Good
idea, talking to Vic. That makes the whole blog thing a little
easier to take. Maybe that graphic they used is the right one,
after all."

"No, it's still obnoxious, but yes, talking to Vic helped.
Except in the learning-anything-immediately-helpful department. We still need some kind of solid lead."

We reach the plaza just as the Commander is taking the
stage, and head to the back of the crowd, near the sound-
board, where you can always hear everything best.

"Nice, you made it!" Maya says, a little more zealous than I wish she'd be. She throws her arms around Matt and I catch that slight hesitance from him again. The way his shoulders stiffen . . . He probably doesn't even realize he's doing it, but it's definitely there.

"Of course," I say, humoring Maya with a smile.

"How were the burgers?" she asks.

"Fine," says Matt, and as he does our eyes meet for a moment. Because Maya interns at Candy Shell Records, we decided a while ago that we can't tell her about the lost songs. It's not because we don't trust her. More because we don't want to put her in a position where she'd ever have to lie to Jason Fletcher, her boss and our nemesis. But then, maybe 1 percent because I don't trust her not to accidentally spill it.

Still, I always feel a little sucky when Matt and I are around her and there's this *thing* we can't talk about. It's not really a lie. Just an omission. But sometimes I wonder if, in a way, that's worse. It just sits there between us like dark matter, unseen but deadly.

Luckily, Supreme Commander takes the stage and our attention is focused there. They play a great set. They've matured into a solid three piece and are getting tighter all the time.

As they finish, Maya heads backstage but we stay by the board.

"I can't wait to see this," says Jon as the next band, Freaktastique, takes the stage.

RIP Freak Show, Mount Hope's hottest band from September to November of this year. The band that once nearly derailed Dangerheart at the Trial by Fire. They were doing great, rising fast, when one day their electric front man, Alejandro, who'd been living with his aunt, had to move back to his dad's in San Diego. And then Cybil, who we all thought was in love with the bassist, Trevor, quit to form an all-ukulele band with her girl-friend. Trevor and the drummer, Lane, have soldiered on, but neither of them looks happy now.

It's crazy how many things can derail a band. When there's not band drama, there's life drama. Sometimes it seems like half the key to making it in music is just keeping your band alive long enough.

Their first song begins with Lane dropping a pretty deep groove, over which Trevor plays broken glass guitar. It's got a cool feel and a sharp attitude . . . but then the two of them start singing in unison falsetto:

When we are wearing sweaters
Along the banks of the Seine
I wish we could share a bed at the hostel
But you're on the girls' side, and I'm on the men's

"I feel bad for them," says Caleb.

Ooooh ooh ooh you can ride on my handlebars

"It's kind of catchy," says Matt.

We watch two songs and then go for candy cane cookies. By the time we're back to our spot, Freaktastique is wrapping up, and we all get a little quiet. I can sense a buzz in the crowd as the next band takes the stage.

It's a good thing that Freak Show fell apart, because at Mount Hope High, there's already another new band gunning for top status. Dangerheart may be the headliner at this show, but this next band has arrived in a big way, considering this is only their second show ever.

All Hail Minions! didn't even exist at the start of the school year, but they almost immediately became the second-biggest band at school. And the reason is simple:

Molly Inez is really, really hot.

And I'm not just talking about her looks, which are bordering on surreal—she's been on the local modeling scene since we were all in middle school—it's also her singing and musicianship. She's a senior and even as recently as last year, she was one of those strange creatures at Mount Hope: a musician *not* in the PopArts. She was a classical pianist studying composition and theory in the sad, out-of-date music classrooms in the old wing of the building. But then she came out of nowhere at the homecoming gig with All Hail Minions!, trading in the baby grand piano and cocktail dresses for a slick Nord keyboard, pink hair, fishnets, and a leather jacket.

"Evenin', everybody," says Molly in her strangely

effective country twang. "We are . . ."

The crowd finishes for her and she pumps her fist to each word. "All! Hail! Minions!"

Molly lays down a buzzing synthesizer part. The rest of her band is pure adrenaline, too. Nicky, the drummer, is the only boy. He plays with these light-up neon sticks. Deena, on bass, always wears silver jumpsuits. They play to prerecorded tracks of guitar and percussion and space sounds, and when Molly starts to sing it's like she's growling. The whole thing seems like it should be happening on a spaceship to Mars.

We all watch, arms crossed like typical musicians, and yet, I'm a little entranced. Can't help it. Molly casts a spell.

Until I hear Val groan. "Ugh." She's looking past me, and I turn to see a grinning face heading through the crowd, like a shark emerging from the deep.

"There they are!"

Of course, it's Jason Fletcher. "Hey there, Dangerheart." Jason is in his mid-twenties and always has that professionally unshaven look. Older women probably find him cute but to us he's all smarm. Tonight he's wearing a bright pink scarf with his long black coat and a black fedorastyle hat. He waves a hand at the Minions. "So, what do you guys think of my new stars?"

None of us respond to his question.

But of course, Jason doesn't care. "Man, I love signing a new band and then going to see them and they're awesome!"

He holds up a hand as if any of us would high-five him.

"Yeah . . ." He pulls his hand back, unfazed. "I just got word that these guys will be on the Adrenaline Energy Drink Fresh Faces tour this summer." He sighs dramatically. "That's what can happen when you work *with* your record label friend, and not against him."

"I thought you were going to be getting us some opening gigs," I say to Jason. "Not that we even want them."

"Yeah, except that you do." Wow, nothing can slow Jason down tonight. "I know, Kellen wanted me to put you on the next leg of the Sundays on Mars tour, but they all agree that All Hail Minions! makes more sense. Just look at them . . . definitely worth the advance money we gave them."

He takes a second to gaze at the band, and then turns to me, smiling wide. "You want to know how much."

"I really don't." That's a lie, but I am not going to give him the satisfaction of telling us.

"One million," he says anyway. "Nonrefundable advance."

Jon whistles. And I see that everyone else's faces have turned to stone. I feel my heart racing, falling prey to the lure of that number, so shiny . . .

"Well, I hope you've learned something from Postcards," I say, mainly just to say something. I've been watching how Jason treated his last big signing, my ex-boyfriend Ethan's band Postcards from Ariel. Their first EP isn't doing well.

Show attendance isn't great. Of course he definitely didn't give Postcards a million freaking dollars.

"I'm always learning," says Jason. "Speaking of which, anything new I should be learning about Dangerheart? Any lost tapes of Eli White I should be aware of?"

"Not a one," I say.

Jason sighs. "That's a shame. Well, gotta run. We're doing an interview segment after the Minions set for the NewBeat YouTube channel. *Adiós*, Dangerheart. Don't be strangers."

Nobody says anything for a minute. When Minions finishes their next song, Jon says:

"A million. Dollars."

"I hate to say it, but the Fresh Faces lineup is pretty cool this year," Val adds.

I want to say something dismissive about how Jason will mess it up, but it will just sound petty. Besides, a million bucks at least means that Candy Shell is really paying attention.

And it's weird to watch the Minions set after that news. Hard not to judge them, even harder to resist the urge to pick them apart as they rip through one catchy, dancy song after another. I even find myself hoping they'll mess up.

When Molly announces their last song, we head backstage to get ready. Caleb has been quiet. "Don't let it rattle you," I say. Maybe I'm talking to myself, too.

"What, Minions?" he says. "I'm fine. They do their

thing and we do ours. Pluto strong." He smiles, almost fully.

I stop him before we get backstage and pull him close for a kiss. They're not electric anymore, after three months, not shocks to the system, but in a way they are better, like a slow rising wave that you pleasantly sink into, washing away the sounds of the world. Plus, after three months, our kisses tend to lead to other places, and I feel squirmy and warm inside at the thought of those things. It's all I can do to pull back from him now, and pat his chest.

"Just be you." It's what I always tell him, because with all the forces spinning around us, sometimes that seems like the hardest thing to remember.

Once onstage, the band plugs in, Matt adjusts the drums, and they do a quick line check, testing each microphone and instrument to make sure the sounds are working.

Caleb has donned a floppy Santa hat, and it makes his face a little elfish, but somehow his eyes gleam more and that's unbearably cute. Also he's wearing a maroon T-shirt I got him that fits almost too well. It makes his slim Caleb muscles stand out and suddenly I can't believe I let him onstage looking this hot in front of all these girls except then I remember that's a good thing and try to take a breath.

"Hey, we're Dangerheart," says Caleb, and then Matt immediately counts off. They open with a brand-new song called "I've Been Waiting," one of Val's, and it's great because it's high energy and Caleb gets a little breather onstage to warm up. It always takes him a minute to balance his nervous energy with the thrill of being onstage, to center himself in the moment. Val, on the other hand, just flips a switch and she is in full rock mode the second any show starts.

She's at her typical best tonight, bobbing hard while she plays, snapping up to the mic and barking her lyrics like they're a burden she wants to be done with, like she just wants to get lost, to *be* the music. Scowling, clear-eyed, and with that aggression that makes you ever so slightly afraid. She's been the subject of a lot of online chatter this fall, mostly good. A fan favorite for some, and there is discussion about whose songs are better between hers and Caleb's. Sometimes it turns into a Lennon versus McCartney type debate. There's also the talk of whether she's hot, is it sexy how she stands when she plays bass and stuff, and it can get lewd like anything can online, but Val ignores it.

The crowd has grown since we arrived, and they seem really into it. I see heads start to bob, start to move, wave in time with the beat.

The set is great, totally solid. They save "On My Sleeve" for nearly last. There are actual cheers when Caleb starts the guitar part. As they hit the final, triumphant crescendo and slip into the quiet refrain that ends the song, I can hear people singing along. Excellent.

They end to big applause.

"Thanks," says Caleb. I can see he's grinning. "You guys have been great. We've just got one more for you—"

"Allegiance to North!" someone shouts from the crowd.

Uh-oh. I see Caleb flinch at this.

"Woo!" another person calls.

"Play 'The Sound of Your Smile'!" This gets a cheer from the crowd. That's Allegiance's big hit from *Into the Ever & After.*

I can see Caleb trying to decide what to say, and slowly clamping down into Fret Face. I was afraid of this. The other gigs that we've played since the news broke have been on school campus, and kids have been really cool about not doing exactly this thing, but out here, in the wilds of the public . . .

There's a little lick of guitar and I see Jon smirking as he plays a quick snippet of the riff from "Excuses in Technicolor," another of Allegiance's biggest hits.

This gets a cheer from a few people in the crowd. But it also draws a glare from Caleb.

Oh boy.

"Allegiance!" someone starts to chant, clapping to the syllables. A few others join in. It's not too many, but it's enough.

"Ha ha," Caleb mutters. "Hey, you know what—" I can hear the anger in his voice and if there was any way I could leap up to that stage and stop him—

But then Val is right there beside him, whispering in his ear. His shoulders slump, but he nods, and then turns away from the mic. Val returns to her own mic and says, "Hey,

41

everybody, who loves Allegiance to North?" There is a decent cheer from the crowd. The younger kids in attendance probably don't even know who that is.

"All right!" says Val. "Well, if you like them, then shut up because you're going to love this song by Dangerheart. That's us, by the way. The band currently on the stage in front of you playing our asses off. This is our last song. One two three—"

She starts to sing "Catch Me" and the one or two people who react poorly to Val's "shut up" comment are drowned out by her daring, confident first line, and then the band explodes in.

It feels like the awkward moment has been averted, but I'm still worried as I make my way through the crowd.

There's no greenroom backstage, just a square marked out with yellow rope encircling a honey bucket and a folding table with bottles of water. Most are empty and rolling around, or standing half finished. There are a few folding chairs but they're covered by stacks of instrument cases.

"Good set, guys," I say, but everyone's just packing up quietly. Once Caleb has stashed his guitar he glares at Jon's back.

"Hey . . . ," he says.

Jon feels Caleb's gaze. "What?"

"What the hell was that up there?"

Jon's face scrunches. "What was what?"

"Playing that Allegiance riff," says Caleb.

"Calm down, it was a joke," says Jon. "I was just trying to appease the masses."

"It felt more like fanning the flames," says Caleb.

"Actually, what I was trying to do was take some of the heat off you," says Jon. "Besides, they're not just asking *you* to play a cover, they're asking the whole band. Man . . ."

Jon turns and continues packing his gear.

Caleb looks like he's about to say more but I catch his eye and plead with him not to. I know why Caleb is mad, but I also think Jon has a point.

"Hey," says Val, "let's talk more about it at practice. The best thing we can do with all this Eli business is focus on making our statement with our music."

I completely agree, but don't say anything. I don't have to. Val has proven herself as the most intense about practice, and about making our performance excellent. And it's more important these next two weeks than ever. Recording a great EP is the best thing this band can do right now to let people know who we are. And really the only thing we can control.

The band finishes packing without a word and we start lugging gear to the parking lot.

Caleb and I have plans to hang out. "Do you want to join us?" I ask Val. Not that I really want her to. But I feel like I should ask.

Luckily, Val just scowls. "Nope. See you at home," she says to Caleb.

We take Caleb's stuff to his car. "Where do you want to go?" I ask.

"I don't know," he says glumly.

I almost want to tell him to snap out of it, but I know it's been a long night. "Well, the Spritz is closed. We could go to Tina's."

"I'm not in the mood for fro yo."

"Traffic should be almost done. How about we drive up to Portola?"

Caleb shakes his head again.

"Well, then, I guess it's back to the PopArts fund-raiser table. More bake sales are good for my grade, anyway."

About ten steps into our walk Caleb puts his arm around me and I can feel him exhale hard. "Sorry," he says. "I probably shouldn't have said anything to Jon."

"It's okay," I say, "you had a point. But Jon was just trying to help. He probably thought that making a little joke would diffuse the situation."

"Yeah," Caleb agrees. "I'll patch it up with him tomorrow."

I lean into him, and the feel of his arm and the smell of him post-gig swats away all the buzzing thoughts for a moment. I feel warm, and content, and find myself amazed at how often I forget about this feeling. It's like we have so much going on all the time that I take this for granted, *us* for granted. Which sounds like something an old married couple should be saying.

I turn and stop him in his tracks and mash my lips against his.

"Mmm," he says in surprise, like he's been pulled back into the moment, too. We're both like that, lost in our thoughts too much. But as our mouths remember each other, I let my hands fall down his shoulders, and he rubs the small of my back, and the sounds of nearby people and tinny holiday music retreat. I become aware of each inch of our skin that is touching, and even more achingly conscious of which inches could be, want to be, need to be . . .

But it's even more than that. There's something I want to tell him. We've been dating for almost three months, and sure, I was into him the moment I met him, but it's different now. It's more. In a way that is almost scary. I've been feeling lately like I might want to tell him that I love him, and even though it's just a word, it feels like a big deal. And it's scary because is he feeling that, too? I think so. I know so . . . don't I? What if I say it and he doesn't say it back? Or he does but only because he feels like he has to? Would I even know?

"What?" he asks. I realize that my kissing lost its intensity.

"Nothing . . . everything. It's all good." I smile. It is.

We both take deep breaths, leaning our foreheads together.

"Not fair that we can't go back to my house tonight," says Caleb.

"I know," I say. "Why does your mom have to wrap presents on the downstairs couch?"

"She wouldn't if she knew what we did there."

I laugh and punch him in the arm, but leave my hand there and squeeze for a moment, then slide it down to his side, to his waist.

"Stop," he says, taking my hand and spinning me.

I roll my eyes. "Fine."

We make our way to the back table to get hot chocolates and split a candy cane cupcake. A group of girls walks by, and one of them gives Caleb the long stare.

"Did you see that?" says Caleb. He pulls me closer again.

"I most certainly did," I say, sinking into his arm.

"That wouldn't have happened before all this Eli business."

"Um, yes it would have. Don't forget you're still the hot lead singer in a great band."

He smiles and we kiss. "So, should we get back to the top secret research tomorrow?"

That sounds great. Usually research involves lounging on Caleb's couch, half draped on each other, doing a little more searching than just Google. Except then I remember: "I can't. I have the visit."

"Oh, right."

"I know," I say, crashing back to earth with the thought

of my Saturday obligation. "I'd almost succeeded in pretending that didn't exist."

"It won't be that bad," says Caleb. "I expect frequent texts."

I smile but it's a little forced. Thinking about tomorrow just reminds me that Caleb isn't the only one living in a shadow. If there's any upside to his situation, it's that at least everyone knows so he can talk about it freely. The shadow I'm dealing with is more like that dark matter, an omission that seems to be growing. It blots out the free and easy feelings, gets in the way of possibility. It might even be the reason I haven't told Caleb I love him. And with every day of senior year, it feels more and more likely to swallow me up.

Formerly Orchid @catherinefornevr 38m
If you don't want to be somewhere, is traffic a blessing or a curse?

"Some students have a background or story that is so central to their identity that they believe their application would be incomplete without it. If this sounds like you, then please share your story."

"Mmm," says Dad. "Probably not that one. That's your penalty for being part of the bourgeoisie establishment. That and a lack of financial aid."

"Yeah," I say, my finger running down to the next essay question on the common application.

"How much further?" Mom asks.

"Two miles," says Dad, checking the map on his phone. "Might as well be two hours though at this pace."

We're crawling along on the 405. Have been for an hour.

"I know I could use a bathroom sooner than later. You in the same boat, Cat?" Mom asks.

"I'm okay," I mutter. The nickname annoys me as usual, but I let it slide.

We are on our way to UCLA. Dad has a friend, Elaine, who works in the economics department. Her daughter, Stacia, is a sophomore. Stacia's agreed to show me around for the afternoon and evening. My dad set it all up. He is at least perceptive enough to notice that my heart isn't totally in this college application process, so he's hoping this will help give me a boost. I'm going along with it because that's the contract. The more I fulfill their vision of me, the less they pay attention to mine. And yet, the more senior year ticks along, the more the college future and the Dangerheart present heat up, the more I feel like Summer and Catherine are headed for a cage match.

"Hmm . . ." Mom is looking at her phone. "Santa Monica Boulevard is still pretty clear," she reports grimly.

"Of course it is," says Dad sarcastically. They're not fighting. Just calculating their score against the universe. They debated which route to take for like ten miles. When they decided on the 10 to the 405, it was with all the seriousness of two astronauts who'd realized the only way to stop the asteroid from hitting earth was to ram their ship into it.

And yet, Dad's first instinct had been Santa Monica. But Carlson Squared would never make that choice. I feel like pointing this out to them, but I'll just sound like the typical teen who thinks she knows better, but who of course isn't thinking rationally. Instead I just gaze out at the brown outline of downtown.

"What's next?" Dad asks me.

"Umm . . ." I scroll down the list of application questions. I feel like I could easily answer that first one, or rather, Summer could. Summer, who has made music a central part of her identity. Catherine, on the other hand, what's her biggest background story? *That I feel like I'm living a double identity? A sleeper agent in my own house?* But I don't want to write about that because my parents will no doubt want to proofread this essay and that's the last thing I need.

College applications are due for just about everywhere I'm applying on January 2. That includes Stanford, my number one, but extremely unlikely, choice. I'm a good student, really good, but Stanford is uber-selective. I'm also trying for Pomona, UC Berkeley, and Colorado College.

And I'm doing all that while wondering whether or not I even want to go. Sometimes when I imagine how Summer might spend next year, it's completely different.

"*Recount an incident or time when you experienced failure,*" I read from the question list. "*How did it affect you, and what lessons did you learn?*"

"That's a tough one for someone so successful," says Mom.

It's one of those compliments that I appreciate and yet it also makes me want to barf a little.

"What about losing in that debate club freshman year?" Dad suggests. "Or getting cut from JV volleyball?"

"I'm not sure those are going to make me stand out to an admissions committee," I mutter. Summer's stories about Ethan and Postcards from Ariel would. Or the story about how I lied to Dangerheart back in the fall and kept Jason's gig offer from them, how I did that as much for me as for them and how it blew up in my face in a crappy basement club in San Francisco and nearly ended the band. That qualifies.

I mean, even Catherine has bigger failures than my parents know. Debate club! Sheesh. How about two summers ago, the very first time I ever had sex, with my then-boyfriend Todd Forster? My period ended up being late by almost two weeks and I was in a total panic, imagining I was pregnant, having to tell my parents, who I assume realize that I'm having sex by now, but who don't let on if they do. I didn't even tell Todd for like a week, worried about how he'd react, and then when I finally did he freaked out and treated me like some kind of criminal. If nothing else that helped me learn to trust my instincts. I'd always suspected Todd was a jerk.

It turned out to be a false alarm. And I realize now that none of that was actually a failure on my part. Still, it felt like one for a while. I was a wreck for months.

But that's definitely nothing compared to the indignity of being cut from JV volleyball! Except I can't really blame my parents for thinking that's my biggest drama when I don't share the other ones with them.

"Okay, finally," says Dad as we slide into the exit lane. "Let Elaine know we'll be there in about ten minutes."

As we drive onto campus, I read the next common app question to myself: *Reflect on a time when you challenged a belief or idea. What prompted you to act? Would you make the same decision again?*

The question feels like an accusation. Here I am sitting in the car feeling like I live a double life, and yet what am I doing to change that? Meanwhile, the closer we get to campus, the more my nerves ratchet up inside. Even the traffic can't keep me from getting to my future forever. Part of me wants to kick and scream in a tantrum, part of me knows I'm better than that. Part of me feels like there must be some way that these parts of me could fit together, if I was just strong enough, or something . . . but I just don't get how yet.

After a brief visit with Elaine, I am released onto campus. I decline the paper map, just so I don't look like a total newbie, and use my phone instead to find Kerckhoff Hall, where I am meeting Stacia.

I cross two quads, and I like the peace and sound around me. It's Saturday evening of finals week, so there aren't too many students around. The large triangles of grass between pathways are dotted with solitary people reading, or pairs talking quietly and looking over a notebook. Far in the distance, music blares from a dorm room window. A peal of laughter echoes between the buildings.

I'm supposed to meet Stacia outside a lecture hall. She's seeing some special visiting speaker. I enter Kerckhoff and walk down a wide hall. Doors open to classrooms that, even though they are empty, feel busy and somehow more alive than any room at Mount Hope, except maybe the Green Room. I find myself wanting to look around, to read the urgent, multicolored notes on the whiteboards, to study the piles of papers and bookcases. This place feels like a busy hive of learning, inviting me to explore.

I wait outside the lecture hall for five minutes before it empties. I barely remember what Stacia looks like but—

"Summer!"

Luckily, she remembers me. She steps out of the stream of students, slinging her shoulder bag back. She's wearing sweatpants and a cardigan, flip-flops, her hair up in a baseball cap. I was sort of picturing her dressed a little more stylish, I'm not sure why, maybe just because she's older and college sounds somehow more pro, but instead she looks like she's dressed to lounge around on a Sunday. I notice that sweats and hats are pretty common attire for the audience leaving the lecture. I went for fashionable jeans and a black shirt with my hair down and suddenly I feel like I'm trying too hard.

"It's great to see you," says Stacia. We join the flow

heading out the doors. "So, your dad wants me to show you the college ropes, get you excited. Are you ready to *party*?" She throws a fist in the air, bending the last word into a squeal.

"Sure," I say, wondering what I'm about to get myself into.

Then she laughs. "Just kidding. My version of a big night is eating nachos at the café and catching my roommate's a cappella show. If you were hoping for a kegger at a frat house or something, I'm sorry to disappoint you."

"No," I say, "that sounds much better."

We walk to Stacia's dorm so she can drop off her books, and then to a campus café. We pass one roped-off area outside of a dorm where a party is in full swing. Lots of shirtless boys, clusters of girls, everyone with red cups. Other than that, though, mostly what I see is people who look smart, interesting, either sitting and chatting or strolling somewhere. I catch snippets of conversation: everything from movies to literature to politics. There are people entering a hall where stringed instruments are tuning. A pair just behind us on their way to a reading. Clumps headed to a campus bar to watch a pivotal basketball game.

All this happening in the cooling evening, amidst grass and trees. No one checking with their parents. No one getting in cars.

By the time we're sitting at a table at the café, I find that my dad's clever ploy is working. I am starting to picture myself here. And I don't just mean Catherine. Summer, too. More than anything, it's the freedom to think. The whole place feels like an opportunity rather than an obligation. An invitation to wonder about stuff and check it out. It's a feeling that couldn't be more different from high school.

"What's your major?" I ask Stacia.

"International Law," she says, "and I'm minoring in Visual Art. Sculpture."

"Oh, that's cool," I say, and here is another thing: looking at Stacia, I would have thought . . . well, I would have had no idea what she was studying. She's many layers more than how she appears.

It makes me wonder: maybe it's not just me that creates the frustration between who I am and how I have to appear. Maybe that's also just high school. Everyone looks like a specific type there. You pick one and identify yourself by how you act and dress. Here, it seems like you can be anyone, multiple versions even, and that reality is so self-evident that you don't have to show it with your appearance unless you want to.

Stacia yawns. "I also do a jazz radio show at three a.m., which is dumb."

"I think that's awesome."

"What do you do?"

I explain about band managing as we gorge on nachos. I give her what I hope is my most mature-sounding version of how it's not what my parents want me to be doing and how that drives me crazy.

"Ah," Stacia says, waving her hand, "don't worry about that. You think my mom is cool with forking out twenty grand a semester so I can make penises out of clay?"

I almost snort cheese.

"But that's the thing," Stacia says, "once you get to college, it's not about what they want anymore. It's about you. Want my advice?"

"Definitely."

"Smile and nod, and get yourself out of Mount Hope. It will be so much easier to do your thing once you're out of there. It's like you'll finally be able to see straight. I mean, you do need the support of those pesky parents, for tuition if nothing else. But it's worth playing their game a bit, as long as it gets you out."

Stacia's roommate and seven other girls come onstage and start an a cappella version of what I think is an Andrews Sisters song. I don't know what to make of a cappella, but they are making the 1940s sound pretty sultry. They go more modern after that, and we could debate the pros and cons of beat box sounds and lots of doot-doo-waahs, but the bottom line is, just like everything else here, they are doing their thing with not a care as to what anyone might think.

And watching them and soaking it all in makes me wonder:

Reflect on a time when you challenged a belief or idea.

Maybe the belief I need to challenge is my own. Just

because my parents want something for me, doesn't mean that's what I have to want, but maybe that's not even the point. Maybe it doesn't even have to be one or the other. Maybe both of those things, what they want, and what I want, can just be. And the older I get, the less it will matter.

Maybe the feeling of being trapped in a life I don't want is just intense lately because, if I play my cards right, this could be the last six months of my sentence. Of high school, of faking it. My other plan: where Summer stays home? Maybe that's just subjecting myself to more of the same dynamic, to feeling like I have to be two people at once, with the added drawback of my parents being disappointed with me.

Why exactly would I do that?

Caleb, for one. The band, too. Managing a band is an organic process. Sure, I could do some promotion and show booking from afar, but to manage a band you need to be there. Practices, time sitting around discussing the plan, the art, and the little stuff in everyone's lives, these are the real ingredients of growing a band. Stanford is six hours away from all that. Caleb says, when he's at his most supportive, that weekend trips would work, that the band could play gigs up there. . . .

But then there's the personal side. Could Caleb and I really keep our relationship going with that little time together, and with our time apart spent in different worlds? Right now, I feel like we could, and yet, I can't shake this feeling like I should know better.

Looking around this place, I see people living in one world, not two. Being present here and now. Why go to college if you're just going to spend it trying to be somewhere else? Why be here if you can't wander into those inviting classrooms, those lectures and concerts where something new awaits? I think if I'm honest I know that I want to throw myself into what I'm doing. Into the future. The problem is now I feel like there are two futures. And I can't have both.

Plus, there's my parents. Would they even allow Summer's version? Sure, I'm eighteen, but I'm a long way from supporting myself. And if I got a job with enough hours that I could afford an apartment, that wouldn't leave a lot of time for Caleb and the band anyway.

Suddenly it feels like too much to figure out. And I realize that in this very moment I'm doing exactly the thing I just said I didn't want to do: living a double life. I try to focus on what's around me right now. The singers, Stacia, the cool café. This visit is only a few hours long. Nothing has to be decided tonight.

We go for ice cream with some of the singer girls after the show, and meet even more people, and while I introduce myself as Summer, we talk of Catherine things, too. From the finer points of a cappella voicing, to clean water in developing nations, to the best indie bands, Jane Austen, awkward dorm room hookup stories, the upcoming protest about unfair trade in South America . . . and I kind of love it all. I can't remember a time when I've ever talked about all these things at once. And it feels like it could go on and on.

Too soon, I have to meet up with my parents, and Stacia admits they're going to a friend's room to drink some kind of cheap wine that doesn't get you hungover, and even that sounds fun.

When my parents ask me if I had a good time, I say yes, and I am not lying.

I spend the drive home spinning around the conversations. Being smart . . .

Being all the versions of me.

My phone buzzes.

Caleb: How was it?

I want to say amazing.

Summer: Not bad. Fun enough.

It's such a dodge and I know it. Back to my life. Back to faking it. Even with Caleb.

Summer: And a cappella.

Caleb: Ouch!

Summer: :) How are you?

Caleb: Good actually. Feeling better about the article. Did some sleuthing into more old Eli interviews but nothing so far.

Summer: Cool. Let's do more tomorrow. And are we still on for Christmas Day?

Caleb: You are officially invited.

Summer: Yay! Okay more later. xo

I'm giving him the quick sign-off because I am surprised by how strong this sense of guilt is welling up. It almost feels like enjoying tonight was somehow cheating on Caleb. Cheating on a dream we've been sharing.

The feeling makes my heart race. I try to remind myself: nothing has to get decided now . . . right?

And yet, it's only four months until the acceptance letters start to fly. Not that I'm taking getting in for granted. But I've got a range of schools and some acceptances are likely. Which means my future will be determined by April 1. A date that feels far too soon.

Formerly Orchid @catherinefornevr 1hr
Happy Holidays! Go to Dangerheart's YouTube page for a holiday sing-along from our practice space to yours!

Christmas is a small affair at my house this year. Sometimes we've had my mom's cousin and their family over, but that didn't come together, and then my brother, Bradley, announced that he was going to Hawaii with his girlfriend Sonya's family. Mom didn't take that well. So for Christmas Eve dinner it's just the three of us and luckily, Aunt Jeanine.

Normally, Jeanine would be back over on Christmas Day, but she's catching a flight up to San Francisco to see her girlfriend. Things have been going great for her since our secret trip, a fact we gab about every time we go shopping, but one we can't bring up over dinner, because Jeanine is still worried what my dad's reaction will be.

It's a fun night anyway. They are drinking wine, which makes them silly, and we just talk about movies and politics and the latest drama among the extended family and it feels easy.

I do have to field one question from Aunt Jeanine about what is increasingly becoming the only topic in my household and probably on my mind, too.

"So how are the applications coming along?"

"Oh, fine," I say, but I feel a surge of nervous energy. To say that they are coming along implies that I've done anything other than fill out the basic contact information sections. Actually, I did start, and quickly abandon, an essay yesterday.

I've done that three times now.

"I've been thinking about it and taking some notes," I add. And by that I mean mental notes. More accurately: mental notes that I should probably start taking notes.

"I've heard that the essay is just to make sure you can write," says Aunt Jeanine.

I'm not sure that's true but I know she's trying to take the pressure off me.

"I keep telling Cat," Mom says, returning to the table with a dish of green beans, "that the sooner she gets it done, the sooner she can relax and enjoy her vacation."

"Come on, Mom, where's the fun in that?" I smile like it's a joke, but procrastination feels inevitable at this point. I felt inspired after the UCLA trip, but then Caleb and I spent all of Sunday afternoon together and I couldn't imagine being anywhere else. Now I'm back to feeling paralyzed.

It's almost like I need it to be last minute: like I need the fates to be involved, to help take some of the pressure out of my hands. If I wait until the very end, then more hangs in the cosmic balance, and when the decisions arrive, I'll feel some kind of peace. Like it was out of my control.

Maybe I'm just kidding myself.

Luckily, we don't return to that topic of conversation. Dinner is fine and fun, though after a while I wish Jeanine and I could talk for real. In spite of our pact to work on being more truthful with my dad, we're still just avoiding topics around him like black holes.

We exchange presents with Aunt Jeanine after dinner. Our gifts are winks to each other: I got her a book about *Tosca*, and she gives me a gift certificate to Bloomingdale's and a business card for her personal shopper there, Franca. "She says she can't wait to see her Vivien again," says Aunt Jeanine, "but don't worry: I gave her explicit instructions not to go overboard."

Aunt Jeanine heads home after dessert. I collapse on the couch beside my parents, pleasantly too full. They're watching *It's a Wonderful Life*, so I start noodling around online, but there's nothing except people's holiday wishes and pictures of gifts and what they ate for dinner.

Eventually, the movie sucks me in. Mom and Dad know it so well they're quoting lines.

"To Momma Dollar and to Poppa Dollar!" says Dad as George is just putting the last two bills into the safe, hoping they'll make babies.

I texted Caleb earlier and finally I hear back from him.

Caleb: How's it going?

Summer: Missing you.

Caleb: *does math* . . . 667 minutes until you come over!

Summer: !! xo. Hey turn on NBC4.

Caleb: . . . Oh, *this* movie! My mom loves this. Are you really watching it?

Summer: I got sucked in.

Caleb: Why are they talking about banking? I thought this was a Christmas movie.

Summer: Shush.

It's more fun watching knowing Caleb is watching, too. He texts again during the honeymoon scene.

Caleb: Will you cook me chickens on a spit someday?

Summer: Probably never.

And later:

Caleb: So, is this boring?

Summer: No! It's tragic.

Caleb: You mean cuz he tried to kill himself?

Summer: No, because George is never going to hear his three favorite sounds: anchor chains, plane motors, and train whistles! It's about making choices that sacrifice your dreams.

Caleb: Yeah . . . Val wants to watch *Elf*.

Summer: Is it on demand somewhere?

Caleb: We've got a DVD. I think I have to bail on the Baileys.

I'm more than a little jealous of Val getting to hang out with Caleb right now.

Summer: I guess I'll understand. Say hi to Arctic Puffin!

Caleb: :) I like to whisper too.

Meanwhile, our movie goes on, grinding George down, but then ending in song. Mom is crying by that point, and I feel like I might, but for a different reason. Mom's tears are of the heartwarming variety. What I don't understand is why more people don't think this movie is incredibly depressing. How is it the story of the richest man in town, like Harry says? Isn't it really the story of a man who had his dreams beaten out of him, who had to settle for the normal life that he'd always wanted to run from?

And that normal life is so bleak that he tries to kill himself, only we're supposed to be happy for him getting that same life back at the end?

It's all making me feel fidgety, bordering on dread. Maybe it's my slightly nauseous, overfull belly, or the college applications looming just beyond the holiday, or maybe it's the idea of what happened to George Bailey: that the choices you make right now, when you're eighteen, will set up the chain reaction of your whole life. George went from "I know what I'm gonna do tomorrow and the next day and the next year and the year after that," to jumping off a bridge, and it all started with decisions he had to make at this same point in his life. . . .

Maybe I should be writing my essay on this.

I'm just glad when the movie's finally over and we're watching the best of *Saturday Night Live* Christmas episodes.

I sleep anxiously, but it's not all fretting about the future. There's also a little echo of anticipation for Christmas, for the wonder and simplicity of toys under the tree and pajamas all day. Santa came until middle school, even though I'd stopped believing long before that. I think Mom and Dad were just hesitant to let it go. But there's still a little buzz inside me for the magic of the day.

I come downstairs to find that Mom's feeling it, too. She's hidden the pickle ornament in the tree—but without my brother there, it's just me and Dad rooting around in the branches, and he's letting me win. Mom just watches and seems sad. It leaves me feeling grumpy and claustrophobic and glad to finally get out the door and on my way to Caleb's.

Our Sunday search for more song clues came up empty. We reread *On the Tip of Your Tongue,* the collection of interviews and journal entries from Allegiance to North, and scoured the backwaters of the early internet. We dug up an Eli White murder conspiracy page but it was from something called GeoCities and we couldn't get it to load. After a couple hours I could feel the last embers of our enthusiasm from the meeting with Vic fading. Maybe talking to Randy today will yield some results. We can run Vic's conversation by him and see what he thinks.

Unlike the early-rising duo of Carlson Squared, Caleb, Val, and Charity are all still lazing around drinking coffee and eating cinnamon rolls when I arrive. Randy is on the couch. His face is the color of concrete.

"Wild Christmas Eve?" I ask him as he nurses an orange juice in a sunny corner.

He toasts me with the glass. "Drove back this morning. As is tradition. Me and my buddy Pearl take our royalty checks and gamble them away."

"You get royalties for Savage Halos?" I ask. That was Randy's band, back in the same years as Allegiance.

"Yeah," says Randy. "*Sear My Face* was big in Germany and certain Baltic states. Twice a year we get these international royalty checks. It's just enough to have a little fun with, so we do."

"And how did that go?"

He grins weakly. "My Christmas present to you is a high five."

Caleb and I help Charity make bacon and eggs. After we eat, we gather around the tree to exchange gifts.

Deciding what to get Caleb was tough. I'd had this scarf all picked out for him for a month, but then at the last second I panicked, worried it was too girly, and got him a new capo, a cool locking kind because he's been complaining that his slips when he's playing and it messes up his tuning.

"Thank you," he says, kissing my cheek. He rarely does that around Charity but out of the corner of my eye I see that she's smiling. "This is definitely the right kind."

"You sure?" I ask and suddenly I am wondering if he actually likes it or is just saying that. I should have been more creative with a gift! Like more romantic. Except I knew he needed the capo . . .

"It's perfect." He hands me a little box.

It's wrapped in silver paper and feels really light. Inside I find a little hand-drawn Pluto cut out of construction paper. On the back it says:

Tomorrow night. 5pm.

I meet his eyes and smile. He's fidgeting. "Do I need to bring anything?"

"Just you," he says, and his face shades bright red.

"Ugh," says Val, watching us.

I am surprised when a box comes my way from Charity. It's a gift certificate to get a manicure. I can't help glancing at my worn, unpolished nails, the cuticles all torn. They're the first thing to suffer when I'm worrying. There's been no shortage of that lately.

"It's not a statement on your looks," says Charity with a smile. "It's just one of those little luxuries we never have time for, that make you feel surprisingly fancy."

Caleb gets gift cards from his grandparents, and a really nice Bluetooth stereo from his mom. "Randy helped me pick it out," she says.

"Bass in those things is usually suspect but that one's good," he says from his reclined position on the couch, eyes closed.

"Caleb," Charity asks when they are finished. "Where are the presents from Great-Aunt Linda?"

"Oh." Caleb gets up. "I brought the box in the other day."

"Grab the ones by the door while you're up," says Randy.

"I thought you said you didn't bring anything," says Charity.

"Not me," says Randy. "There were two boxes on the front porch when I got here this morning. I moved them into the entryway."

"Huh," says Charity. "That's weird."

"I heard UPS was delivering today because of all the snow delays back east," Randy adds.

Caleb returns with two boxes. "Here's Aunt Linda's, and one of the new ones . . ." He puts them on the coffee table and returns with a third box. This one is really long and flat and at least four feet tall.

"That looks like a guitar case," says Randy.

"Who are these things from?" Charity asks.

Caleb stands the tall box on its end and spins it around. "No label."

"There's one on this box," says Randy. "It's addressed to 'Caleb Daniels and Family.'"

"Definitely the name of our brother-sister project," says Val. She grins at Caleb.

"Looks like it was sent from a UPS store, too. In . . ." Randy frowns. "Princeton, New Jersey."

And Val's smile dies away.

"What." Val stares at the package like it might be lethal.

Caleb and I lock eyes. Val told us her mom knew about Caleb. But Melanie didn't sound like the kind of person to randomly send anyone a present. Unless of course she knows that her daughter is here.

"You want me to open it?" Randy asks.

"I want you to burn it," says Val.

"We should see what's inside," says Charity.

"You do it," Val says to Caleb.

"Okay." Caleb takes a deep breath and puts the smaller box in his lap. He tears at the packing tape and pulls open the flaps. He rustles through packing peanuts and removes a small package. The wrapping paper is red with cartoon Rudolphs and Santas. Seeing this makes Val wince, like she recognizes it. I don't know if she's breathing. I'm not sure any of us are.

Caleb holds up the little present. "You want to?"

Val waves her hand. "You."

Caleb rips open the paper and finds a wad of tissues. Not the kind of tissue paper you'd normally find in a present, but actual tissues.

"That's classic," says Val. Tears have started leaking from her eyes.

Caleb unwraps the tissues and exposes a small stack of photos. He pulls a pink Post-it note off the top and reads: "*Hope you guys like seeing these. —MF.*"

You guys. She must mean Val, too.

The look on Val's face says she's thinking the same thing.

Caleb scoots closer so I can see as he flips through the photos.

The first few are black-and-whites from an Allegiance to North show. They seem like professional shots. There's Eli, in midair as he hits a guitar chord, Parker the drummer slamming his cymbals, Miles and Eli with their bass and guitar aimed at each other. Curiously, Kellen doesn't appear in any of these photos. I guess Melanie didn't feel like saving any pictures of her ex and Eli's nemesis.

The next couple are in color and have a thick white border. They're blurry and washed out. Polaroids. Even back in '98 that would have been retro. The first is Eli, in a suede and sheep's wool coat leaning against a brick wall; the next, looking up from a bowl of soup in a Chinese restaurant;

then a selfie with Melanie, both in giant sunglasses, on some roof deck somewhere. She looks a lot cuter than in the current, bleary Facebook profile photo that I've seen. They're huddled close and behind them the city glows in twilight. The next photo shows Eli at the beach, shirtless, jeans rolled up, ankle deep in the water. Based on the attractions in the background, I'd guess it's Coney Island.

These are scenes from the lost summer, I realize, after Allegiance broke up and before Eli reappeared in Los Angeles, only to die shortly thereafter.

The last picture makes Caleb pause.

"What?" I ask. He hands it over. I see a small boy with a bowl cut of brown hair. He's sitting on the floor, wearing one-piece pajamas, looking up at the camera with a yellow binky in his mouth.

"I think that's you, man," says Randy, leaning over my shoulder.

Caleb nods silently. "And there's this." The last thing in the stack is photo-sized but made of wood. It's white with a small scene painted on it: an impressionistic depiction of a skinny brick building, like three stories high. It looks like a brownstone you'd see in New York City.

"Is that maybe where they lived?" I wonder. "That summer?"

I check with Randy but he just shrugs. "I don't think any of us were in touch with Eli during that time." He looks at Charity but she also shakes her head.

Caleb hands the stack to me and digs back into the box. "There's something else." He produces a small stuffed animal. A little duck. One blue eye is missing.

Val huffs. Her eyes are murderous, and yet she holds out her hands.

Caleb tosses it over.

"Say hello to Bubbles," she says, sounding bitter. "Can't believe she sent that . . ." And yet she rubs the matted, faded yellow creature across her cheek. Bubbles erases any sliver of doubt about who the package was intended for.

We all sit there for a second, no one knowing what to do.

Finally, Randy asks, "What about the big box?"

Caleb stands the package on its long end and starts to pull off the paper.

"Are we sure this one isn't from your grandparents?" Charity asks.

"Did you tell them to buy me a . . ." Caleb peels away layers of paper. "Yup."

He reveals a beat-up guitar case, black with frayed corners. The metal clasps and reinforcements are tarnished. The case is covered in stickers.

"That's . . . that was Eli's," says Randy quietly.

"No way," says Caleb, running his palms up and down the sides.

"The case for his '62 Jazzmaster." Randy sounds reverent. "Man, I remember when he bought that thing. Sea foam green . . . He used an entire summer of money working at In-N-Out. That was on the first tour he and I ever did together, when we were in Poison Pen. Before Allegiance to North."

"Where's the actual guitar?" Caleb asks, shaking the case.

"He sold it," says Randy. "I couldn't believe it when he did. That thing was his favorite, but . . ."

"What?" Caleb asks.

"Well . . . he told me about selling it the last time I saw him," says Randy. "Which was also the day he died. Almost like he knew."

Caleb lays the case down on the couch and pops open the latches.

A strong musty odor wafts out of it, that weird smell of basements and glue. You can see the guitar's outline in the matted red fur lining.

Caleb opens the tiny compartment in the center. "There's something in here." He holds up an object that fits in his palm: it's skinny, a couple inches long, and wrapped in yellow paper held in place by a rubber band. He peels off the band and unrolls a handwritten receipt. Inside is what looks like a piece of circuitry, white with silver dots on one side.

"It's a guitar pickup," says Caleb.

"Let me see," says Randy.

Caleb passes it over, then reads the receipt. "Dylan's

Vintage Guitars. In Denver. This is . . . it's a receipt for the Jazzmaster."

"Dylan's . . . ," says Randy. "Yeah, that's where he bought it on our first tour."

I notice something on the receipt. "Is there something written on the back?"

Caleb turns it over. "Eli's writing."

He reads:

> I've gone back to where I started from
> But I'm still missing you
> Encore to an empty room

We all look at each other.

Lyrics to the second lost song.

Even just those three little lines make me think of the Eli that Vic described, thinking about what-ifs in music . . . and in his own life.

"Back where I started from . . . ," Randy mutters to himself, then he bolts up. "Whoa! I'm an idiot!" He starts counting on his fingers. "LA. San Francisco. Denver . . . I can't believe I never . . . duh!"

"Randy, what?" Val snaps.

"Those are the three cities that Eli and I played on the Poison Pen tour. Well, but we played them in the opposite order."

"One of the things Vic told us," I say to Randy, "was that Eli actually hid that tape at Canter's on the day he died. Same day he gave you that gig bag."

Randy sinks back into the couch, absorbing this. "You mean, like, he was leaving all this for us to find, right at the end?"

"I think so."

Randy rubs his face. "But that makes it sound like . . . him drowning . . ." He doesn't need to finish. "Is that . . . possible?"

Caleb bites his lip.

"I don't know," says Charity. She's crying quietly now, too.

"It was bad enough thinking that it was an accident," says Randy, "to blame it on the drugs, but if he did it on purpose, that makes it . . ."

"Different," Caleb finishes.

"The more we find out," says Charity quietly, "the more I wish I never even told you about him."

"It's okay," says Caleb.

"I wish he'd told me," says Randy. "But I guess if suicide really was his plan, he knew I'd try to stop him." His brow is furrowed, and he stares into space. I know Randy took Eli's death pretty hard. It must be seriously messing with him to consider that Eli planned it.

"Either way," Caleb says to Randy, "I think this

definitely means is that he wanted you to be part of the search. He probably meant for you to find that letter in his gig bag in the first place."

"Some detective I've been," Randy groans.

"Still . . . ," says Val, eyeing the guitar case. "We don't know who sent us the case."

"You don't think it was your mom?" says Randy. "I mean, there was only the one shipping label. Do you think she knew about the receipt in there? Like she's . . . in on helping us find these songs?"

Val actually busts out laughing. "What, you mean like, Eli told my mom sixteen years ago to remember to send this guitar case here for Christmas *this year*? My mom can't even remember to make dinner, or take a shower . . ." She looks down at the little duck and throws it on the floor.

"Maybe your mom sent it because she knew you and Caleb were together and it's a coincidence," I suggest, though as I say it I don't really believe it.

"I never saw that case around our house," says Val.

"Can we call UPS?" Caleb asks. "I mean, they should have a record of our address and the delivery, and should be able to tell us something."

"Their offices would be closed today," says Charity.

"So . . . ," says Caleb, "do we think it's possible this guy Dylan, in Denver, really has the next tape? Should we try to call him?"

I do a search. "His shop still exists, so that's something."

Randy rubs his beard. "I mean, I guess . . . if the tapes retrace our tour, LA, then San Fran, then Denver would be next. Man, this is still blowing my mind. The idea that Eli thought this all through . . ."

"I don't think we should call that guy in Denver," says Val. She's staring hard at the case. "I mean, we already have enough people watching us with Candy Shell and Kellen McHugh. What if we call this Dylan guy out of the blue, and he has some time to think about it and realizes he has something valuable? He might decide that he could make a pile of money selling the tape to Candy Shell, or on his own or something."

"He hasn't said anything before now," I point out.

"He might not even know he has it," says Caleb.

Randy flips the pickup between his fingers. "It could be hidden somewhere. Pickups usually come in pairs. I bet if we find the matching one, we're going to find the next tape. It's got to be Denver."

"So how are we going to get there?" Caleb wonders aloud.

Everybody's eyes turn to me.

"What do you think?" Caleb asks. "A show in Denver?"

It's the first thing that makes me feel like smiling. "Nothing would make me happier than to set that up."

Val makes a little noise, like wind through a crack. She's staring at the pile of photos. The one on top shows her mom, smiling.

She finds my gaze. "I can't let her find me."

"I think she already has," I say carefully.

"Well, then I need to leave. Go somewhere else."

"You're not leaving here," says Charity, wiping her eyes. "I'd say it's more likely that this package is meant to be an olive branch. I mean, that's what I would mean it to be."

Val shrugs. "You two couldn't be more different." She gets up. "I'm going to take a walk."

We are silent for a minute. I find myself reading the stickers on the case. It's like a list of the best clubs you'd want to play at around the country. The Make Out Room, the Paradise Rock Club, the House of Blues, Antone's, the Wax Shop. There's a familiar sticker for Ten Below Zero. Eli had one like that on his gig bag, mostly worn away.

"What are we going to do?" Caleb asks. He's looking at Charity.

"Maybe I should try to get in touch with Melanie," says Charity. "Val is essentially living with us. We're harboring her, I mean not like she's a fugitive, but . . ."

"She's a runaway," says Randy. "Though Melanie doesn't sound like the type to take legal action."

I rub the top of Caleb's hand as he sits there. He's a world away, deep in these dark and familiar waters. It's the essential trap we're in: whenever we do find out anything about Eli, Caleb has to reckon with who his father was, and that's only getting harder the more we learn.

He shakes his head, returning from afar. "We should go find Val," he says. "You think?"

"You go," I say. "I'll help clean up here."

I watch him leave and feel for him, for Val too. No matter how much either of them run, the ghosts keep following them.

But at least now we have a lead.

It's time to stop running and get back to the hunt.

7

We're on edge for the rest of Christmas Day. But the phone never rings. The doorbell never chimes. It takes Caleb some time to talk Val down, and after they finally return from a walk, Val is determined to kill the rest of the day playing video games. When I leave the basement, she and Randy are infiltrating some sort of frat house full of naked coed zombies who have laser eyes. The puddles of vomit are lethal, too? Or something. Randy's sharing a growler of beer with her, which Charity has decided to ignore for tonight.

Before I go, Caleb tries putting his Telecaster into Eli's old guitar case.

"Check out the metaphor," he says when the guitar fits.

"Well played." It crosses my mind that the guitar case,

with its soft padded lining, resembles a coffin. I know better than to try to make a joke about that. But I also know that seeing Caleb's guitar in there gives me a chill.

He closes the lid and runs his fingers over the chipped stickers. "It's the closest I have to hearing his stories, you know? To hanging out with him. I think the thing that's most annoying sometimes is that I actually do want to get to know him. To have him in my life, well, as much as he can be. I just wish there wasn't all the noise around it."

I give him the biggest hug I can, and we kiss until Charity coincidentally bumps something downstairs as if to say, *Okay, that's enough.*

I wake up and send three emails for possible Denver gigs. Then I spend the morning working on my application. And by that I mean I spend the morning re-listening to all of the recent practice sessions that Dangerheart has recorded, taking notes on particularly great moments that we can't forget in the studio, or in Denver. Like the way Matt drove the second half of the second verse of "Catch Me" with that quarter note kick drum pattern. Or that cool rhythm that Val gave to the second chorus of "On My Sleeve" that one time back in October, the one that Jon said would go good with a motorik beat. Except then Matt didn't really know what that was and you know how drummers get when they don't know a reference. I'd been thinking the other night that "Sleeve" needed one more thing. I think this is it.

There's also the way Caleb sang "Chem Lab" one time where it was just the right blend of his smile and his fret. Another time where Val gave a hopeful turn to her delivery on "The Spinelessness of Water" . . .

I've listened to these songs so many times at this point that they feel like rooms, no, not even rooms: scenes that I inhabit. This drum fill is a staircase, that guitar line the blur of traffic lights out the window, this vocal sound the feel of the carpet as I approach the handsome gentleman in the corner (who's Caleb, of course!). The bass line that is a murmur of conversation . . . There are so many times when I want to comment and share all of these tiny nuances, the late beat here, the overtone there, the second or two when the guitar sounds like the color cobalt . . . but how annoying would all those tweets and posts be? And no one would quite get it. Any listener who loves these songs as much as me has their own scenes that the music whisks them off to. That's part of the awesome.

Notes finished, I check my email again, looking for Denver replies. What I find instead makes me forget to breathe:

From: Tessa Cruz (tcruz@jetcityrecords.com)
To: Dangerheart's Mailbox (info@a-band-called-dangerheart.com)

Greetings from Jet City Records!
December 26 at 9:25am

Hello, Dangerheart!
We just read the feature about you in Toast & Jam.
We've checked out your songs and we'd love to speak
with you about working together. We dig what you
have going on and would love to help you take it to
the next level. We realize you may have had other
offers but we hope you'll consider getting in touch!

We look forward to hearing from you,
Tessa and the Jet City Team

Tessa Cruz
Senior Talent Scout
Jet City Records
Seattle, WA

I stare at it for a minute, screaming silently, breathing hard,
and basically just thinking whoa whoa whoa!

Of course I've heard of Jet City. They're small, but
focused. Not a shark. But not a minnow either. And I love
their album designs.

I text Caleb immediately, but he doesn't reply. After a

few minutes I'm too excited to sit still so I head down for breakfast.

"Somebody's got their nose in the phone this morning," says Dad from the table, where he's eating a grapefruit and reading his tablet.

"Sorry."

"I'm glad we're going to see Caleb again today," says Mom, across from Dad, doing sudoku.

Of course I can taste the side of guilt with Mom's comment. They've only met Caleb one time: when he came over on Thanksgiving evening. Bradley and Sonya were in town and we played Apples to Apples. It was fun and easy: even the part where my brother casually belittled Caleb's (and unspoken: mine) music aspirations by referring to how *he was in a band once, too, back in the day. . . . That was a good time, man.*

I toast a bagel and busy myself with sending a text about Jet City to the rest of the band. Everybody else replies immediately.

Val: Cool. . . . Just kidding HOLY SH????T!!!!

Jon: WHAT. *thud* (sound of me passing out) YAAAAAA!!!

Matt: NO WAY!!! When are we shooting the jeans commercial?

I join in the excitement, and try to keep my small worry about how I'll fit into such record label plans at bay. Labels have their own managers, as I've learned all too well in the past. But there's a world of difference, at least in terms of reputation, between a cool indie label like JCR and something like Candy Shell. A record deal with someone like this is way more of a partnership, and usually much better for the band. And for me. I'm sure I could be involved.

Oh, and another huge difference between this time and last time, with Postcards, is that unlike Ethan, Caleb would actually fight for me.

My phone buzzes again. I'm hoping for Caleb—

Val: Randy called UPS. There's only the one box to go with that shipping label. And they can't find any record of delivering another box here.

Summer: Weird. So how did it get on the porch?

Val: Don't know.

I've just put my phone down when it buzzes again.

Caleb: Wow, sorry. Just got back from shopping forgot to charge the phone last night.

Summer: That's ok silly. Are you ready?

I tell him . . .

And he doesn't reply. I'm about to text and ask if my message went through, when finally:

Caleb: Wow. Wow wow wow.

Summer: Yes! Yes?

Another pause, longer than I expected. And long enough to tell me that he's hesitant.

Caleb: Did they hear about us through the article?

I probably knew that was coming.

Summer: Yup. But the email is all about Dangerheart.

Caleb: But it will be a thing.

Summer: Yes, but I think in a good way. These guys are cool.

Caleb: I suppose there is no avoiding it.

I can't resist poking him a little.

Summer: You are about to win least-excited band member award. ;) Everybody else freaked out.

Long pause.

Caleb: Sorry. I am excited. xo

I can't help wondering if he's lying. And just typing xo to appease me. Like I'm the one being managed.

Summer: Well, we'll talk more about it tonight.

My first reaction after we're done chatting is frustration. Is it fair to feel that way? I know these moments are tough for Caleb. And they keep happening before we expect them to. But to any other band this would so obviously be a great thing.

Also, I don't want to feel annoyed with this pattern: where good things that happen to the band lead to bad vibes with Caleb. Still, it takes me a little while to get over it.

I spend the rest of the afternoon poring over the Jet City website. There will definitely be no application writing now. I imagine Dangerheart among these bands, us on tour next year, playing indie festivals. College would have to wait. But today that sounds fine, as long as I don't think about how Carlson Squared might react. And what about Stacia's advice?

But a record label, a chance for the band to be real . . .

I'm pretty sure you can't expect this kind of opportunity to come more than once.

By four o'clock my excitement for whatever Caleb has planned has edged out my frustration with him, so I spend some time cleaning up and getting into a date outfit. The rare skirt comes out of my closet recesses, and a sleeveless shirt Aunt Jeanine got me that shimmers a little. I'd never wear it to school. Earrings? Sure.

Caleb arrives right on time. My dad gets to the door before I do, and when I come down the stairs, he's in the middle of asking Caleb: "How's senior year going for you?"

"Ah, fine," says Caleb, his voice stiff and polite. He sees me over Dad's shoulder and smiles. I notice that he's dressed up, too. A blue collared shirt and this cool charcoal blazer. His hair is combed just one more notch than usual and still wet from the shower and all of it is adorable.

"Catherine says you're taking the year off next year."

"Well, I'll be working," says Caleb, "and working on the band."

"Yeah," my dad says with a sigh, "college is so expensive these days. It's almost criminal really."

"Hey," I say, racing down the last few steps.

"Hi," says Caleb, sounding relieved to be free of that conversation, but then he also says, "You look amazing."

"Oh, thanks." I roll my eyes to play it down, but my cheeks are burning.

I give him a hug, avoiding a kiss in front of my parents.

As we walk out into the evening, I think we must look like we're headed to a country club or out to a fancy dinner and it feels like it's so not us. I can almost hear my neighborhood, the Fronds, nodding in unison. Finally, Catherine has emerged.

And yet I have to admit there is something sort of exciting about being dressed up, going on a proper date. It makes me wonder: What if Caleb and I were grown-ups together? What if we lived in an apartment in whatever the cool part of town is in five years, and went out in the evenings, to spend time, or to *functions*? What if we had money and dressing like this was something we did? What if we were fancy? That wouldn't be terrible. In fact, I think part of me kind of *wants* that. We'd still be doing music, of course, and we'd have kept our integrity and been true to our art and not succumbed to a commercial for watches or detergent or anything, but . . . we'd be adults.

There is something weirdly romantic about that and also Caleb smells like spring-clean deodorant and soap and I think it would also be fun if we got a chance to remove these complicated clothing layers from one another at some point.

"Have fun," says Dad, snapping me out of the trance, and also causing me to boil over for a second once we get in the car.

"I'm so sorry about that," I groan.

"About what?"

"Ugh, about my dad referring to next year as you *taking*

the year off. As if working full-time and doing the band isn't real work. Like all that really matters is how you *won't* be going to college. It drives me crazy how he just assumes everyone thinks the same way he does."

"Oh, well, I didn't really mind. I mean, that's just how he is, right?"

"Unfortunately."

Caleb rubs my leg. "Forget about him." He turns on one of our favorite bands, Cold Hearts Play with Fire, and for a while we just drive and listen and don't talk.

"Still not going to tell me where we're going?" I ask as we get on the freeway.

"Nope."

We drive, and don't talk, and I love this feeling of just being with him, knowing that we are hearing the same thing at the same time, wondering if the words are making the same picture for him that they are for me. I run my fingers over his as he grips the wheel, but then move them back to my lap so they don't do anything rash.

I want this vibe to last our entire drive but soon my annoyingly busy brain can't help getting back to business.

"Have you talked with everyone about Jet City?" I ask.

"Yeah, they're psyched," Caleb says without a hint of emotion.

"And . . . you?"

"I am . . ."

"Liar."

A half smile breaks out. "I almost am."

"They're a good label," I say. "I don't think they'll just make it all about Eli."

"You're probably right."

"Probably?" I raise an eyebrow at him.

He smiles. "I thought of something else, though. The label thing makes finding Eli's songs an issue. Like, what if we find the rest of them, and we're signed to Jet City? We'd be getting them in trouble, too. And then they might drop us and all of that would look pretty bad."

"Well," I say, play-punching his shoulder. "That is a really super good point that I did not consider."

"Sorry."

"Duh, don't be. Hmm . . . well, maybe we should try and stall them, then. Actually, I know: we'll tell them that because we have to do the EP at school for our grade, we have to wait until we're done with that before we could sign anything."

"Does that give us time to get to Denver?"

"I think there's only one chance to get there, and that's February vacation. And that's right after our EP is due anyway. So . . . yes?"

It's also before I'd hear back from any schools. Before I'd have to make any choices about the future.

"Okay, that has to be the plan, then," says Caleb. He hits the turn signal emphatically and we start to exit from the 5. "Now, no more talk about business for tonight."

"I will do my best."

We get off the freeway and head west into Los Feliz. There's excellent food here, and I wonder if this is our destination. A nice dinner? A dessert stop? But then Caleb turns and we start to wind up the twisting road into Griffith Park.

"Intriguing," I say.

"Did you know," he says with a little grin, "that today happens to be a special day?"

"And what would that be?"

"Today is our half-year anniversary since we started dating."

"Um," I say. "We've only been dating since September."

We twist among houses, then through park gates and up into dark hills and overhanging trees.

"September sixth," says Caleb. "It's been 112 days."

"Do we need to have a talk about math?"

"I'll show you," he says.

We emerge from the steep canyon road and arrive at the Griffith Observatory. I haven't been up here since a field trip in fifth grade, and I remember it looking a little bit like the lab of a mad scientist. Since it's dark out this time, the white walls are glowing in soft lights. The observatory's three domes are green by daylight but at night they are shadowy and secretive. It wouldn't surprise me to see lightning jump between them, to find scientists inside wearing white coats and dark goggles, tinkering with their experiments.

We park and when we get out of the car, Caleb opens the trunk and grabs his guitar. Seeing it gives me a nervous flutter. "Can I ask?"

"Nope."

We walk up the gentle incline, past an obelisk ringed by the great old white men of astronomy. The breeze carries a sweet smell of dry hillsides and pine needles. The Hollywood sign glows in the near distance. In the other direction, the city shimmers like a map of constellations, the light blinking and pulsing.

"Check it out." Caleb points to metal rings set in the cement walk: the orbits of the planets. I take a photo of him standing far off on Pluto that I can't wait to post sometime. Or maybe it will be album art? We hop from ring to ring and kiss at the sun.

"This way." Caleb leads me to the side of the observatory, past a bust of James Dean, to the railing overlooking the glittering hillside. He points to the sky above the observatory. "It's our half-year anniversary there."

At first I think he's pointing to the radio towers that blink on a dark patch of mountain, but then I see a bright, jewel-like star just above the horizon.

"Planet?" I ask.

"Venus."

"The planet of love, ewwww."

"If we lived there," he says, "we'd have dated for half a trip around the sun."

"Most people call that a six-month anniversary."

"Well, but then that's tricky, because a day on Venus is actually 243 Earth days, so a month is like 7,290 Earth days, and—"

I put a finger to his lips. "That is so hot."

"Thank you. I spent like an hour trying to memorize it."

I sink into Caleb's shoulder. "We'd be wearing shiny suits, flying in the eternal sunset clouds . . ."

"Steaming up each other's helmet visors," he adds.

"And I bet no one would request that you play Allegiance to North songs there."

"Somebody would find out," says Caleb, but he smiles. He kisses me, but it's light. His hands are fidgeting. Nerves. He points to a bench. "Now, sit please."

He opens his guitar case and gets out his acoustic. People walking by are noticing and I feel my heart racing. Caleb sits beside me and strums a G, checking his tuning. I see his fingers twitching as they dance from string to string.

"Okay," he says quickly, "I know it's been a drag, with the Eli thing. And I'm really lucky, and I never say it enough. I barely even know how to, so . . ."

"Just play it."

"Right." Caleb takes a deep breath. "This is called either 'Love Ballad with Astronomy References,' or just 'Starlight.' And it's for you."

He starts to strum a light, upbeat pattern, chords that

are hopeful, like balloons. Even by the end of the intro I already know it's amazing but I also know that I am pretty much zero percent objective right now. He sings in a high register for him, eyes closed, neck straining, hair catching the breeze, and all around stunning:

I know it's not easy
Being with someone on the run
The starlight arriving seems so new
But it's an echo of a long-lost sun

And when I say I'm doing fine
Just know that what's implied,
Is that I'm always doing better when I'm with you

And you deserve so much more than planet to sun to moon
We can be binary stars,
Spinning together, looking like one from afar

Caleb's voice and the guitar loft on the breeze. Heads are turning all around us, groups drifting closer as they walk by, but I try to ignore them, to turn off the part of my brain that can't help evaluating: Is this song a good single? What could the drums and bass do— Ugh, shut up, Summer! Just be here!

Every now and then Caleb's eyes pop open, like he's

just returned from somewhere far, and he sees me and both of us have to look away. I smile each time but it also hurts.

And when the signals start to cross
To hell with everything we've lost
I'm always doing better when I'm with you

He finishes, and applause echoes from here and there. Caleb looks at me sheepishly, like he actually doesn't realize how incredible that was. I throw my arms around him, guitar and all.

"So, that," he says.

"That."

"And also, Merry Christmas."

"It was amazing." He's a little bit sweaty and I can hear his heart hammering from the nerves and I hold him tighter. I realize that I need Caleb to be as stormy as he is, to not be able to see outside of his emotions sometimes, because I feel like I am all too good at that. At managing myself and everyone around me. Sometimes you need to feel out of control, and overwhelmed, otherwise, will you ever really do anything about where you're at? Will you ever really take the big risks, do the big things?

"Summer," he whispers.

Suddenly I feel sure of what he's going to say. . . .

"Caleb, I love you."

He pulls back, a surprised smile on the corner of his mouth.

It makes me trip. "What. Wasn't that what you were going to say?"

He stares at me a second longer, just enough time for me to hit the panic button—

Then grins. "Yes, you just beat me to it." He rubs his lips against my cheek, toward my ear. "I love you, too."

The words make me freeze up. "Good," I say, barely breathing.

"Good good?" he asks. "Or scary good."

"Good good," I say but I find myself squeezing tight and fighting back tears. Shit! Why is this freaking me out? Maybe because it's a lot. It's this moment, but also you don't say these words unless you're thinking about the future.

And it was bad enough considering next year when it was just about the band, but what if I love him? How can I leave him?

But those thoughts are stressing me out when what I really want to do is not think. I kiss him and try to just be here in this moment, in the cool night hugging Caleb, the song still on the breeze, with no worry of what comes next.

Formerly Orchid @catherinefornevr 2hr
One week until Dangerheart goes in the studio. What song do you want to hear on the EP?

The rest of break is marked by monotony. We spend the whole school year waiting for the vacations but then after a few days being at home is kind of boring. Plus, I'm sorely missing all those built-in times to see Caleb each school day.

The two pieces of news I do get are mixed. One is that I reply to Jet City and Tessa gives me a general sense of the terms of the record deal: a small advance of a few thousand dollars to record an EP, and then marketing and tour support on top of releasing the album. Some research online confirms that this is a pretty standard deal. The band agrees about stalling to respond until after a possible Denver trip, so I let Tessa know about how slammed we are with our school EP obligation and she seems fine with that.

The other news is less good: most Denver clubs are already booked up according to my blogger friends. They say we'd have better luck aiming for the April vacation, but I feel like that's too late, both for the band, and for me. An all-ages place in Boulder does have an opening but it's on the Saturday night at the end of the vacation, and there's no way we could make it to Denver without missing school.

The one great opportunity that seemed like it would pan out was a house concert series called Hanging from the Rafters. They've actually had a great roster of bands and the organizer, Jerin, says she can guarantee at least two hundred people. The only problem is, they don't actually have a headliner for their February show. Not many bands are touring in the winter, and they may cancel the night. But she says if I knew a headliner we could make it happen. Problem is, I don't.

And all of this assumes that our parents even let us go on this trip. That's a huge "if," and while everyone feels optimistic about it, we still won't know until we ask. But then nobody wants to ask until we know about a gig. It all leaves us kind of stuck.

The band rehearses twice to get ready for our New Year's Eve gig at Haven. That's the all-ages music space that's run by PopArts. It's really just a room at the community center next to school, but when the black lights are on and the music is turned up it's pretty great. We also have our first studio session on the night after school starts back up, so we're getting ready for that, too.

It's probably worth mentioning that I still haven't written my essay. Break isn't over yet, though, so I have plenty of time. You know, if I wasn't busy starting an online wall of inspirations for Dangerheart's EP cover art, searching for a Denver gig, hanging out at Caleb's, daydreaming about being serenaded under the stars . . .

Thinking about the L word.

Isn't that weird? Telling someone you love them when it was so obvious already that you did shouldn't make things feel any different except that it does. I mean, duh, I knew I was into Caleb from the moment I impulsively kissed him an hour after meeting him. It seemed so obvious. But now we're "in love." I mean, it feels like the next step in how you look at a relationship. Even the fact that I told him first, as opposed to a year before when Ethan told me, seems to matter. And I'm not worried about whether or not he loves me back. The song pretty much confirmed that. And this version of love feels way more real and mature and valid than last year's version . . .

Still, these thoughts make my heart race. I can't quite put my finger on it. Maybe it's just big.

What I should be doing is just reveling in how amazing that is, except instead I'm thinking about how writing my college essay means actively working toward not being near this very person I'm in love with.

Searching for a gig sounds a lot easier.

◆ ◆ ◆

On New Year's Eve afternoon—essay status = still not written!—I get together with Maya for coffee and shopping in old downtown. She's been after me to hang out all break, and it's not that I've been avoiding her . . . just that maybe I've been avoiding her. With fresh new clues about Eli's lost songs, being around her means lots of *not* telling her things.

We did agree to let her in on the Jet City news, though, so at least we have that to gab about.

"You guys must be so excited!" she says.

"Yeah," I say, "mostly. We're trying not to rush it."

"Man, I'd love to see the look on Jason's face when he finds out that Seattle had poached one of his bands."

"But you can't tell him."

"Summer." Maya sounds a touch annoyed. "Don't worry, I know."

"And we are so not *his* band." I say this with a smile.

"No, of course not," says Maya, backpedaling furiously. "But you *should* be, from a Candy Shell point of view. So can I just squeal for five seconds?"

"Sure."

Maya does a little dance, making foamy drops of her eggnog latte splatter onto the sidewalk. "You guys totally deserve it. I had to harass Matt to tell me. He was all secretive. You must have really put the lean on him!" She's smiling but there's always the slightest note of concern in her voice when Matt and I are in the same sentence.

"I don't know about that," I say, "whether we deserve it, I mean."

We're headed for Kinesha's, a chocolate and bath boutique where Maya has to return some bath salts.

But she stops outside the door. "Hey, um . . ."

"What is it?"

"It's weird to ask you this, but . . . does he say anything about me?"

"Who, Matt? Of course." I try not to squirm. I'm not technically lying, but kinda.

"He's seemed distant lately. Like I annoy him. Do you know what might be up?"

I push back a wave of guilt. I hate this feeling of knowing more than she does and yet if I have to choose sides, it sort of has to be the band, right? "You want me to try to find out?" I say. "You know, in a subtle way."

Maya shrugs. "Maybe? If there's something, I want to know. I don't pretend that we have something like you and Caleb have—"

"Oh, stop."

"It's true! But still. Okay, sorry. Said enough." Maya makes a motion like zipping her lips. "On to the bath salts."

While Maya gets in line at Kinesha's, I wander between the displays. There are so many colors and aromas and promises of relaxation in the bath salt world, it's dizzying. I pick up a jar of "lavender breeze" and gaze at the large, chunky crystals. We're shower people in my family. Quick and efficient. Filling your bath with salts sounds silly, but who knows? Maybe—

"Summer?"

I look up. It takes our brains something like a tenth of a second to interpret what the eye is seeing, but that doesn't account for the denial that you feel when you see something that you don't want to believe.

"Hey. I thought that was you."

Like your ex-boyfriend, standing on the other side of a bath salt display.

"Oh," I manage.

It's been six months since I last saw Ethan Myers. My first thought is that he looks bad. Actually I'm a big liar: my very *very* first thought is hello, hotness, oh no! But then everything else about our relationship comes rushing back, and by everything I mean the bad: how he cheated on me, and how he left me behind when Candy Shell came along.

His hair is longer, a straight mop that now has to be pushed out of his eyes. While he'd always had sideburns and the occasional soul patch, he's finally succumbed to the full hipster beard, but, typical Ethan, he's pulling it off. It probably makes his gray-green eyes more startling. Flak-jacket green I used to call them, because they seem war weary, the old soul behind that young face . . .

And yet don't I also remember feeling, afterward, like his old soul was just another calculation? Like one of those glowy lights that dangle in front of deep-sea fish, drawing you in. Except those occur naturally whereas Ethan's is more like he ordered it from Sensitive-Artist.com or something. Never mind, I am thinking far too much and need to speak.

"Hey." I smile out of habit, but then wish I hadn't.

"Sorry," he says immediately.

I feel a shower of pure adrenaline in my guts. Sorry for what? For Missy, Royce, and that other girl, the one in San Diego? Sorry for feeding me lines about art and our connection when all you were really thinking about was yourself?

"Didn't mean to startle you," he adds.

Oh. That's right. Knowing Ethan, he's probably not even thinking about all those things that are on my mind. Come on, Summer! Think faster! "What are you doing here?" I ask.

He holds up a canister of pink crystals. "Angeline loves hibiscus bath salt." That's his sister. "But, silly me, I got her vanilla. Those for you?"

"Oh," I say, realizing the salts are still in my hand. "Nah." I put them back. "I mean in town. I thought you were supposed to be in Cleveland."

While saying this reveals that I've been tracking Postcards tour dates, which might make it sound like I care, it's the only thing I've got because I am damn well not going to just stand here and make small talk about freakin' bath salts.

"Yeah . . . it got rescheduled." Ethan's face scrunches and as much as I want to categorize that as another calculation, I did know him to make genuine faces now and then and this is one of them. Disappointment is a feeling that musicians never have trouble feeling, especially about their own success. "Actually, the whole winter leg has been postponed."

"Oh." I'd figured as much when I noticed last week that all the dates on their site had suddenly changed.

"Hey," says Maya, arriving beside me. She takes up a defensive stance, angling her shoulder in Ethan's direction. It's funny to see her chipper face try to look tough, but I appreciate the effort. "Find everything?"

"Hi, Maya," says Ethan.

Maya keeps looking at me until I nod.

"Hello," she says out of the corner of her mouth.

"It's Ethan," says Ethan.

"I'm aware of that," Maya says thinly. "Ready to go?"

"Yeah," I say. Maya turns to leave.

Nice, I think to myself. *Don't give him any more.*

Except then I'm asking: "So what happened to the show dates?"

Oh, Summer. Go ahead and tell yourself it's a business question and you're just interested in how Candy Shell operates. More likely it's because you can hear in his tone of voice that Ethan has fallen down a peg or two. Of course, maybe that's how he means to sound. Ugh, whatever! More than not talking to Ethan, I don't want to let him drive me crazy either. There's nothing wrong with me checking in on my former band, and I can still keep my internal shields at maximum power, to let none of his charms through.

"Well . . . ," says Ethan, rounding the table and walking beside me. I smell the musty tinge of his suede coat, the same one he's been wearing every winter now for three years. The same one I wore sometimes, even while Christmas shopping in these very stores. "You'll probably say *I told you so.*"

I make a mental note, more like a vivid spray paint scrawl, not to say that.

"We didn't have much buzz on the last leg," Ethan continues, "and the album hasn't been getting the kind of traction we wanted. Jason thinks we need a fresher sound, so we're actually going back in the studio to do a new EP that will maybe have a bigger impact."

I'm furious at what Ethan has just told me, not that I'm going to show it. "I'd say, just in my *non*professional opinion, that your first EP sounded pretty great"—*though not as good as the version we'd made ourselves a year ago*—"and that Candy Shell didn't put any effort into actually getting you guys some exposure in those towns. No local radio shows or blogs, no giveaways or promo appearances, no spark."

Ethan shrugs. "That sounds like a more professional opinion than anything we've heard lately."

"Is that because Jason is too busy with All Hail Minions!?"

Ethan rolls his eyes. "Don't even get me started on the Minions."

I feel his eyes reaching for mine, and I know that sort of sympathetic soul-mate stare he's so good at so I make sure to avoid it. Still, it bothers me that he's hurting. It also bothers me that it bothers me, but I think as long as I keep shields in the fully on and locked position, I can handle this.

Also, it occurs to me now that Ethan Myers might be of some use to us in his current wounded state. If I play this conversation right, it might help out Dangerheart.

"Who knows?" Ethan is saying as we exit the store. "Maybe the new album will work." He sounds sincere. "Candy Shell hasn't totally abandoned us. Jason says they've lined up Dr. Hans for a track. He's like a hit song-writer guy or something."

"More like *the* hit songwriter," I say. I read an article recently about him, and how he hangs out barefoot all day in his Malibu house just walking around and humming and singing melodies. He has the whole place wired to record his every sound, and then he has assistants go through the tapes of his day and edit them down to the key melodies, which they play back for him while he relaxes in a natural hot mud pit in the backyard. "But he writes for like Candy Stripes and Pearl Thomas and Ashley Bratt. I mean, that's not exactly your sound."

What I really think is that Dr. Hans is sort of the enemy of music. But then at the same time I often find myself singing along to his hooks.

"I know, but apparently he's a genius." It surprises me that Ethan is buying into that line. He's pretty proud of his own songwriting. And he should be. No matter what kind of jerk he can be. He has talent and I hate to hear him doubt it.

We step to the edge of the stream of shoppers. I can tell Maya thinks this conversation should be over. But my work is not done.

"I can't believe that Mitchell is going for that," I say, referring to their lead guitarist, who was always the most defiantly anticorporate. He almost walked away from the band over the Candy Shell deal.

Ethan shrugs. "Actually, he's out."

"Oh. Really?" I'm not totally surprised, but Mitchell and Ethan were tight. They were in the same bands all through high school.

"Yeah." Ethan shrugs. "You know, he and I fought a lot, anyway. When the Dr. Hans thing came along, he decided that was it. So, we're regrouping on that front, too."

Maya taps my arm. "I have to stop by Hair-Brained before we go," she says, still pointedly talking only to me. Her eyes meet mine like *Time's up!*

"You go," I say. "I'll catch up."

"Okay . . ." Maya waves her hand for me to come closer and she leans in my ear. "Are you sure you're not having a relapse? Because according to the girlfriend codebook if I suspect that you are having a relapse I am authorized to use deadly force plus ice-cream sandwiches."

"Ha, yum." I'm glad for Maya right now. And it makes me feel a fresh surge of guilt for keeping things from her. "But come on, no. Relapse danger is at absolute zero. I'll catch up with you in a minute."

Maya frowns at me but nods. "Okay. I will trust you."

"Thanks." She leaves and I turn back to Ethan.

"Gotta go?" he says.

"Yeah, but I have a sec."

"Cool." He smiles, and the late afternoon sun catches his eyes. I try to ignore these things. To just stand there, hands in my pockets. He's probably already getting the wrong idea by me sticking around to talk to him. And I am feeling exposed and weird and maybe nauseous. Come on, Summer! Just focus. You know what you're doing.

"I'm sorry it's been hard," I say, and though I don't like the sympathetic tone coming out of my face, I do legitimately feel bad for the fact that a good band like Postcards from Ariel that had everything going for it—lead singer's jerky tendencies aside—is flailing.

"Thanks, it's okay," says Ethan. "Like I said, you called it. Anyway, the one gig Jason let us keep is Needle-fest in New York in February. I had to practically beg him, but getting an invite to that is a big deal, as you probably remember."

"Definitely," I say. It would be awesome to play Needle-fest. "Congrats." I actually already knew they had that show from their website. That's part of why I'm still talking to him.

"Yeah, a little positive light in the otherwise darkness. Of course, he says there's no budget to fly us there, and so I'm going to have to build a tour out that way myself . . ."

My first thought is: *the otherwise darkness*? Does Ethan even realize that he just quoted his own song lyrics? Ugh.

But this is the moment I've stuck around for: "When's the Needlefest date?"

"It's like the twentieth of February, or something? Whatever that weekend is."

"Huh. So . . . hey, is there any chance you guys would be looking for a show in Denver that week?"

"Why . . . are you?"

"Well, we sorta have one, but the show needs a head-liner."

"Oh, cool," says Ethan. "You have a new band?"

"Yeah, Dangerheart." We should note the time. Eight minutes before he even thought to ask me what I was up to, and then it was only because it involved him. Classic Ethan. I feel the shields top off at maximum strength.

"Cool," says Ethan. "I'm sure you still have good taste in bands. What's the gig in Denver?"

"It's a house party," I say, moving on and ignoring the compliment. "But it's a well-known series. Probably a step below you guys, but it's a pretty big promoter in town. I'm sure they'd love to have you. I could send you the link. . . ."

"Yeah, do that."

"Same email?"

"Just text me," says Ethan. "Same number."

"Oh . . ."—*awkward*—"I deleted it." Check that: awkward but also satisfying to tell him.

"Ah, sure." He maybe misses a beat, but barely. "I still have yours," he says, getting out his phone. "Here. Just sent you my contact."

I feel my phone buzz in my pocket. "Okay. Cool. I'll send you info."

"Awesome." Ethan grins. "I'll run it by the guys. We'll need a guitarist but we have time."

"Cool." It feels like the conversation should end. Any more and it's going to feel chummy.

"I'm glad I ran into you," he says. "I'll have to come check out Dangerheart sometime."

"I think you'd dig them," I say. My next sentence could be *There's a show tonight* . . . but I keep quiet and take my first step away. Time to catch up with Maya. "Let me know about Denver."

"Will do." Ethan gives me a little salute. A move I remember so well. It bounces right off the shields . . . but not without causing an old echo of hurt.

I turn and get moving.

"How was that?" Maya asks when I find her.

"Fine," I say. "Annoying mostly. But maybe useful."

For the next hour, though, I'm kind of distracted and out of whack. Life is easier when I can just pretend that nothing before August really existed. That there never was an Ethan Myers. I think of myself as being so far from that time; so different from that person . . . I don't like having him back around now.

Then why ask him to a gig? Why on earth would you do that?

Because the gig is in seven weeks and we are desperate. Plain and simple. And there was no bigger band that I could have found.

Still, I spend the afternoon wondering if I've just made a huge mistake.

Seven hours later, I'm holding Val's head over a toilet in the
girls' bathroom of Haven, when I first hear Jon and Caleb
shouting.

"Huu—" Val lurches and more sour fluid pours from
her mouth.

"It's okay," I say, "just get it out."

I keep her steady, trying just to ignore my sense of
smell, and listen again for Caleb and Jon. I'm pretty sure it
was them. But now all I hear is the thump of music from the
stage, where All Hail Minions! are playing the headlining
slot, which includes the countdown to midnight.

That slot was supposed to be ours.

When we booked the gig, we were the headliner, but Felix and Samaya, the student producers, decided to make a change. We didn't know until we arrived and saw the switch on the sign.

Their reason? "The Minions are shooting live concert footage tonight to promote their debut single," Samaya told us. "There's a major film crew coming and they want to get the New Year's countdown because they think it will have great optics. It's awesome exposure for PopArts and the school and Coach said it was okay."

By "Coach" she means Mr. Anderson, who's in charge of PopArts, but, no, that still doesn't make it okay.

"So you're saying that Candy Shell basically bought out our slot," I said. "I think that's kinda crap."

"Oh, it's not that big a deal," Felix said dismissively. "We'd do the same thing for you."

"Yeah, right," Jon muttered.

Val lifts her head and gulps in a breath. "I think I'm done."

"What were you drinking?" I ask as I drag her back to the greenroom. This whole space is alcohol free since it's all ages.

"Cassie Fowler doesn't drink," she slurs. Then adds, "I brought schnapps."

"From where? Randy didn't buy it for you, did he?"

"No . . ." Val shakes her head woozily. "From Charity's supply. Peppermint. It's in the back and she never drinks it. I put it in a water bottle."

I help her to a couch. Jon's and Caleb's voices rise again. Where are they? "Here," I say to Val, handing her the water bottle. "Should I ask why you did this tonight?"

Val shakes her head, her eyes lolling shut. "Just stop shouting . . ."

Great. I noticed she was a little sloppy during the set, a couple bad notes, which is really unusual for her, but I didn't expect this. "Drink that water and I'll be back in a few."

Val responds in an unintelligible mumble.

Maybe I shouldn't be surprised. Val's been on edge since Christmas. I *think* this is the first time she's resorted to getting drunk. But I can't be sure.

I head back out into the hall and listen for Caleb and Jon. After a second I pinpoint their voices and push through the boys' bathroom door.

"That's not going to help!" Caleb is saying. He's leaning against the wall, Jon against the sink.

"What's going on?" I ask.

"He's mad because a girl hit on me," says Caleb.

"Who?" I ask, hoping I sound curious and don't show the fiery spike of jealousy I feel shoot through me.

Caleb huffs. "Some sophomore. Don't worry, I didn't encourage her."

"No," says Jon, "but you came over and interrupted

even though you could clearly see that I was talking to her."

"I was trying to be polite," says Caleb. "She was a fan of the band and she waved at me."

"Wait," I say, "are we fighting over a girl? Really?"

"No!" Jon spits. "That's not—" He sighs and throws up his hands. "It's just another sign of how this whole thing is going to go."

"What are you talking about?" says Caleb.

He waves his hand. "All of this. And you know what? When All Hail Minions! are done we should totally call Molly out for stealing our slot tonight."

"Wait . . ." Jon is making my head spin. How did we get from a girl to the Minions? "Let's not. It's never a good idea to make band enemies—"

"This is bullshit, man!" Jon slams the sink. "It's not okay!"

"Jon, whoa," says Caleb, "listen, you're right. But . . ."

"No! Of course. God forbid!" says Jon. "We can't make enemies! Can't tell anyone about Caleb's dad! Can't take a record deal! What's the point of this band if we're not going to *do* anything?"

I don't know how to respond. I've never seen him like this before.

Caleb looks like he's about to say more, but I catch his eye and try to say *Leave it alone*. "How's Val doing?" he asks me instead.

"Wasted," I say. "She had a good barfing, though, so

hopefully she'll feel a little better soon. Jon, please don't freak out on the Minions, okay? It's not even really their fault. I mean, they just took what they were offered. As to the girl thing . . ."

"Forget it. Whatever." Jon starts toward the door, eyes on the ground. "Happy New Year and all that. See you guys at practice."

"Jon, we're your ride," says Caleb. "We came in the van, remember?"

"Just—fine! I'll be out watching the set." He slams the door.

"What was that?" Caleb wonders to the air.

The door opens again and a boy walks in, sees me, looks perplexed at the sign . . .

"Sorry," I say, and Caleb and I head back to the green-room, where Val is snoring.

"Do you know . . . ," I say quietly. "If this has been a regular thing with her?"

"Not that I've noticed. Then again, she's home mostly alone all day, and she's definitely been in a funk since that package arrived."

"We should probably stay with her."

We sit down beside her in the stale light. Caleb's hand slips into mine. I rub my thumb on the back of his hand.

"Weird night," says Caleb.

"The set was good, though," I say.

Over the dull thumping of the Minions we hear a shout.

"Ten! Nine!"

Caleb and I smile at each other. I put my arm around him. "Seven," we say quietly beneath Val's snoring. "Six, five . . ."

And down to a kiss. "Happy New Year," I say in Caleb's ear.

We kiss some more.

"Gross," Val mumbles, eyes still closed.

A few minutes later, Randy hurries in. "Hey, are you okay?" he asks Val.

"Peachy."

Randy's face is wrinkled with concern. "It didn't even cross my mind when I gave her that beer the other night."

"Randy, I'm fine," Val groans. "It's not going to be a thing."

I can't help but doubt that. And the same goes for the blowout with Jon.

We pull into Caleb's driveway around one and unload. Randy and Matt help Val in. Jon leaves with no words other than quick good-byes.

"Just work at our place," says Caleb, once we are alone in the driveway.

"Nah, I'll be too tempted to sleep, or . . . other things." I smile and hug him. We kiss, and briefly our hands explore each other. I can feel my body warming, my brain simmering, thoughts receding beneath waves of impulse . . .

But I push Caleb back to arm's length.

"Come on," he whispers, looking almost hurt.

"Can't," I say. And why not? You guessed it:

It's January 1 . . . and the essay is not done. Actually, that's not entirely true. I did write an essay about, you guessed it, the torture of being cut from JV volleyball, how it filled me with regret, but taught me to value my strengths. My parents have read it, otherwise I would never have been able to be out for New Year's. They think it's excellent. "*Stanford material!*" my dad said. It's perfectly well done. But it doesn't feel true. Even though it is.

So unless my computer crashes tonight and I have no other choice, I am determined to write something else. Something real.

"But it's so late," Caleb says. "You should work here."

I told my parents that I was staying at Caleb's, that the whole band was. All true. And Dad talked to Charity to make sure it was going to be fine. She's asleep by now, so no one will know that I'm not there. And hopefully by morning I'll be sleeping soundly on the couch. Maybe I'll be done early enough that Caleb can visit me before anyone wakes up . . . but I don't mention that.

"I can't work here. Something will distract me." I poke him in the chest. "And I want a chance to revise it with a clear head." I don't explain that this plays into my weird urge to push this thing to the limit, so that the fates have maximum control.

I get in the car but Caleb follows me. "What are you doing?" I ask as he sits.

"Coming with you. No choice."

"I can take care of myself."

"Duh. So can I."

"Fine." I can't help smiling.

We pull out and head for the freeway. There's only one place I trust to help me finish this application.

Forty-five minutes later, we're sitting in one of the small center booths, beneath the autumn foliage sky of Canter's.

"Here you go." Vic places a bowl of matzo-ball soup and small plates of french fries and pickles beside the silver pot of coffee on the table. Then he stalks off. So far, he's acted like we're any other customers.

Caleb eats a couple fries and then lies back in the booth seat. "I'll be right over here," he says. He's asleep in like a minute.

I get cup number one ready and open my computer and proceed to just stare at the essay questions, my face half tucked into Caleb's hoodie sweatshirt. Just like I have for the last month. And when that gets old, I gaze around the restaurant. It's two in the morning and most of the drunken revelers have either gone home or quieted down. I'm one of about thirty people left. The blues band playing up the stairs in the lounge has finished.

I'm getting bleary, and having that feeling again, like there's nothing essay-worthy about me. I say that I don't

121

want to turn in my JV volleyball essay, but what else is there? I don't have a unique family history, a background that makes me different. I haven't failed at all that much, and most of the failures I have had feel too trite. I could take one of the moments with Dangerheart this fall, like my failure in San Francisco, and spin it into a feel-good essay on trusting yourself, or trusting your friends, but then that feels too . . . tidy.

My phone buzzes.

Ethan: We're in for Denver. We'll do an unplugged set.

Summer: Excellent!

Ethan: Didn't expect you to be awake.

Were you expecting to wake me, then? I wonder.

Summer: Filling out college applications.

I realize as I type that this casual texting conversation should not be okay with Ethan. What would Caleb think if he was awake? But it was so easy to slip into that I didn't even notice it happening.

Ethan: Classic.

He's slipping into it, too. The easy back and forth. I remember it all too well. But he got us the gig, and we are now business partners. So, I need to proceed . . . but with caution.

I hold my phone still and count to twenty. Pauses and time lapses are important to convey that I am not rapt with this conversation. Because I'm not. And I have this suspicion that if Ethan still thinks I'm into him, well, he'd probably be into that idea. That's the signal I'm getting from him. Then again I'm pretty sure he keeps that signal broadcasting to any girl near enough to hear it, twenty-four hours a day. I could be wrong. Maybe he has a girlfriend or something. I didn't ask.

Except I know that's never stopped him, don't I?

Nineteen . . . twenty.

Summer: OK back to work.

Ethan: Roger. Happy New Year!

Summer: You too.

Ethan: Good night.

Ugh, see that? Right there. Something ever-so-slightly informal about that text. *Good night* in print can be interpreted so many ways! From formal to friendly to "it's too bad we're not saying good night with our faces."

Once again I hold the phone still. Count to twenty and consider the responses. There is a return good night. A "later." A smiley face . . .

"That doesn't look like essay writing." Vic arrives beside me.

"Oh, yeah, nope, getting distracted." Saved by Vic. I put the phone aside, and leave Ethan with the last word.

Vic takes Caleb's empty coffee mug and pours himself a cup. "So, what are you trying to do over here."

"Get into college."

Vic makes a face like he just tasted something sour and unpleasant. "Okay. If you want to."

This makes me smile. "I think I maybe do. I'm not totally sure yet. But it won't be an option unless I write this essay."

"What about?"

"Here's one question . . ." I read him the first one about having a background story and identity.

"See, this is why I hated school," he says. "So, you must have something for that."

"I don't know," I say.

"What?" Vic actually looks offended. "Your shit doesn't smell?"

"My what? I mean . . ."

"It's a figure of speech: everyone's story is as important as everyone else's. It's condescending to think that yours isn't. Almost as much as it is to think that yours is *more* important. You know what I mean?"

"Maybe?"

Vic shrugs. "What are the other questions?"

I read the list to him.

The fourth one makes him laugh out loud. *Describe a place or environment where you are perfectly content. What do you do or experience there, and why is it meaningful to you?*

"*Perfectly* content?" he scoffs. "Who'd want that? Who even has time? Speaking of which, gotta get back to my tables, which honestly sounds way more fun than what you're doing."

"Thanks," I say.

And another cup of coffee goes by.

And another.

Time becomes blurry. I listen to two short-order cooks talk about their best New Year's kisses. I listen to a married couple bicker about how the corner pool of ketchup on the fries' plate exceeded its borders, and now there is sogginess, and always with him there is sogginess, and disappointment, and also did he just make eyes at that waitress?

It's starting to feel like we are the last island of people awake in the universe. Like Canter's is a spaceship and we are off in the deep, a ragtag collective of Reuben-eaters, no one quite ready to return to earth, to have to admit that it's a new year. Like if we keep moving at light speed, stay awake, we can keep the calendar from turning forever.

And now it's four a.m.

Vic looms over me again. "You want my advice?"

"Um."

"Nobody in the real world wants to hear your feel-good story about learning or self-discovery or whatever. Nobody wants to hear how happy you are, because anyone that happy is obviously faking it. What people want to hear about is your pain and where you are with it. Pick the topic that feels most painful and write some stuff, and when you're done, be honest with me about whether you are awake enough to drive, because a cab will be on the house tonight."

I look back at the list with this in mind. And maybe it's Vic, or the obscene tired of this night, or the sound of that nearby couple escalating to a full-on argument—thirty-two years of soggy fries and ogling waitresses, and always the shitty way she dismisses him at parties—or just my general state of worry about everything . . . I'm not even sure which question I'm going to answer until I finally start to write.

Perfectly content? I feel like the right answer to this question is something like the forest, or my room, the embrace of my family, the soccer field. I mean, there have been places where I have felt content, for a moment.

But that's the thing: it never lasts.

Perfectly content . . . Should we ever be? Even now: I came here to my favorite diner to write this essay, a place that feels like it is too busy being itself to put on an act. A place with an astounding ceiling that isn't part of a theme, or a brand. It just is. Someone's inspiration I guess, long ago.

It feels like it has soul.

The first time I came here I remember feeling like this ceiling said something about the universe, about how we were all together hurtling through space and there was plenty of time and there was magic, because something like this could just be. I didn't need a reason for why it was here. I didn't need to know the history or to identify with it thematically, to know what it repre- sented. I just needed it to be, without explanation.

And I was content.

For about twenty seconds.

But then life resumed. Just like tonight. Wherever I am, I find myself in a constant state of wondering what comes next, fretting about what needs to get done, and most of all, wondering if I am doing the right thing, being the right person. People say that the only person you can be is yourself but that is a real bummer when you realize that who you are is going to let people down.

I have this hope that college will be the place where I am content. Where the different sides of me, like what my parents see and what I see, will both be able to bloom. But why does it matter that my parents' version of me is validated? Or that my version is validated in their eyes?

I'm not sure. I didn't even know I had hopes about college until I wrote that last paragraph.

It's been confusing. How does anyone feel sure of a decision this big, ever? How is it that you are no doubt getting letters from thousands of other prospective students who know exactly what they want? How do they know this? What religion or cosmic plan have they been made aware of that I don't know about? Or are they freaking out, too, and just better at faking it?

Another part of me mistrusts the very idea of contentment. I mean, we live on a temporary conglomeration of molecules orbiting around a burning ball of plasma in a spiral galaxy that is hurtling at six hundred kilometers per second away from the center of the universe and there will come a time when the sun swallows the earth, and our galaxy collides with Andromeda, and our lives are so short.

Maybe the only thing I'm content in is my discontent. Perfectly discontent? Or is that yearning? Because that's when I'm happiest. Not when I feel accomplished or at peace, but when I am out there on the edge, electrified by possibility.

This is the ball of mess that I am. It doesn't feel like it fits in five paragraphs, like it operates in opening statements that lead logically to epiphanies. It feels like so much potential energy that is always spinning and yearning to grow, finding new inspirations like hopping from one stone to the next in a stream, but also I see things through. And maybe the only time I am content is in the hopping. It's not the place. It's the journey to it, the leap through the air, the wonder of the landing, and the sweet tug of sad at good-bye.

If you think this is the material for a promising under-graduate student, please be in touch.

I sit back. Sip now-cold coffee.
Look at the words and sort of wonder what that was.
They swim a little.
Outside it is nearly light.

I take the cab. Leave Vic my car keys to move it to the employee spaces.

"Come on, Caleb."

We walk out and squint at the predawn. "Why did sleep make me more tired?" Caleb wonders, before immediately conking back out in the cab.

I kiss his forehead, and feel a surge of guilt. I don't know what that essay was but there is a possibility that it is the rocket booster of the cosmic ship that will take me away from him.

Or maybe it will get a good, pitying laugh in the admissions offices and keep me in Mount Hope. Either way, it will do something.

I slump against the cool vinyl in my own corner of the cab and stare vacantly out the window at the empty streets, the sunlit hilltops, and the distant glimmer of snow on the San Gabriels.

The essay is done. When I get home, I'll finish the rest of the common application and hit send, and the fates can commence their gambit.

It is a new year.

And after a few miles I find myself smiling at the dawn world outside and it hits me that here, in this cab, in this moment, I am actually content. Perfectly? Maybe. And I think that it sure would be nice if, before I die, I could figure out what that means.

Formerly Orchid @catherinefornevr 1m
Hypothesis: if severed frog leg is shocked with electricity, then said leg will still be slimy.

It's Monday and we are back in school and into the long, formless month that is January. Caleb and I have different classes until biology lab fourth period, where we have taken the severed leg of a frog, skinned it, and stretched it vertically so that we can shock it with electricity and watch the muscles react. This is supposed to be telling us something about how muscles work.

That the electrocution of flesh makes it twitch?

I'm pretty sure I knew this from the movies.

"So, we're going to have to ask soon," says Caleb. "Do you think our parents will go for it?"

I am bent over the lab table, threading a hook through the top of the frog's cream-colored gastrocnemius muscle. "Ah." The hook slips and tears free of the muscle. The little leg splats to the table.

"Just ditch the gloves," says Caleb, who has been handling the raw-chicken-feeling frog parts without the required latex.

"I think," I say, "that they will go for it, but it's going to take the right touch. My parents will think that driving to Denver and back to play a show is the most impractical thing ever. But, we're eighteen, we'll have Randy with us, and there's nothing else to do on February break, anyway."

I snap off the gloves, pinch the cold, moist leg, and spear it with the hook again. "And if we actually find the tape, it will be worth it."

"Even if we do have to play a set with Postcards," Caleb says. He's not thrilled with the idea, but to his credit, he hasn't made any jealous comments about Ethan. Not that he should. But I'd understand if he did.

"How's Val?" I ask.

"Good, as far as I can tell," says Caleb. "She's been more mellow since New Year's. I think with every day that goes by when there's no word from her mom, she feels a little safer."

"And no sign of . . ."

"No, haven't seen her drinking or acting like she's

131

drinking. She's been studying nonstop for the GED. The math is pissing her off but she's working with Matt a lot and it seems like she's finally taking his advice. I think she's more motivated than ever."

There is a squeal from beside us, and we look over to see Callie and Jenna, my former friends, jumping back from their twitching leg. They are making the kind of horrified faces that would easily get you cast on a Disney Channel show.

Caleb readies the wires and we both bend near to our gleaming leg, with its breath-shortening odor of formaldehyde.

"It's so cute."

"It's a severed leg. From a dead animal that no longer has its legs."

"Yeah, but still."

Caleb zaps it, and we watch the twitching.

As we are cleaning up, I sneak a glance at my phone and see that I have a new email. I slip the phone out beneath the table and read:

From: Andre Carleton (carleton.a@legalpartners.org)
————————————————————————————
Scheduling an Interview
January 5, at 9:56am
————————————————————————————

Dear Catherine,

I am writing on behalf of Stanford University. I would like to schedule an alumni interview with you. Please be in touch with your availability.

Best,
Andre

"Whoa." The message makes my heart gallop.

"What is it?" Caleb asks.

"Stanford interview." I try not to sound too excited. I don't even know if I am excited. Except my pulse feels like it just shot off the charts.

"Oh, cool." Caleb says. I can hear him trying to strike a casual tone but he doesn't quite pull it off. Since New Year's, the topic of college has been a giant non-topic. You can practically hear us *not* talking about it.

I write Andre back during lunch and we agree to meet this Friday, just four days from now. It's sooner than I'd hoped, but he is apparently about to start a big new case. I wonder if it's a coincidence that he's a lawyer.

"That means they have their eye on you for the pre-law program," says Dad at dinner, firmly on the overly optimistic side. "It's definitely a sign that they are considering you seriously."

I'm not so sure about that, or I don't want to be so sure.

After all, my only stated interest in pre-law was a check box on the application. And I still mistrust the idea that I could get into Stanford or any school based on a four a.m. essay written in a diner. But of course there are transcripts and recommendations and all those were basically excellent. Coach wrote me a killer letter, too. And I've gotten confirmations from Colorado and Pomona that they received my applications and they're complete, and that I'll be contacted about interviews soon.

When I said I was going to listen to the fates, I guess I just assumed they would deal more in bad news. It is looking less like that now.

While this conversation is making my pulse spike, hearing Dad's optimism makes me realize that a perfect opportunity has arrived. "I hope so," I agree, channeling Catherine, and then add: "Hey, so, um . . . a show came up for Dangerheart in February . . ."

I watch my parents' faces twitch as I explain that I want to leave on the Saturday of February break, drive to Denver for a Monday night gig, and then drive back.

"That's such a long way to go for a show," Dad says, right from the script. "Is it really worth it?"

I swallow hard and press on. "Well, I mean, yes and no. It's a good gig, but more importantly, it's this amazing chance for a road trip. To see some miles of the country I've never seen. And Randy will be with us."

When they are still silent, I add what I know is going to hit them hard. Part of how I know is the lump I get in my throat as I go to say it: "Besides, as of September, I'll be off on my own doing who-knows-what, right?"

Mom smiles and also gets teary. "Please don't bring that up. I just like to imagine you studying quietly in a dorm for four straight years."

They go silent again and I wonder: Am I crazy to be asking them for this road trip? But I've thought about it from every angle and I feel like they should be okay with it. They've let me go on school trips, and also last year they denied oh-so-many of these very requests. Hopefully this is one of those moments when, with the future seeming luminous in the distance, and their pride about the Stanford interview outshining their worry, they'll go along with it.

"Are you going to have a plan for where you'll be staying?" Dad asks. "Locations and contact information you can give us?"

"Yes."

Mom and Dad share a look.

"We'll discuss it later."

Before I leave for practice, they give me the verdict.

Summer: Yes! It's a go at my house!

Caleb: Me too!

Summer: WHAT IS HAPPENING. AWESOME.

Caleb: Sweet! Now hurry up and get here.

The Hive is packed. I navigate the smoke-filled entryway, the stairs still puddled with bleach from a New Year's cleaning, and the thrumming hallway. When I knock, the last person I expect to greet me at Dangerheart's door is Maya.

"Oh, hey," I say. Matt never brings her to practice.

"Hi, Summer." She's smiling but nervous.

And when I step inside I see why.

Matt's not the one who brought her.

"There she is, finally."

I can't hide my surprise at seeing Jason Fletcher standing in the middle of the room. And it's not the good kind of surprise. He's grinning in that shark-like way, and after hearing Ethan's tales about Postcards, I hate the sight of him more than ever.

His curls are professionally sprouting from beneath a black military-style hat. He's wearing a black sweater, jeans, and black boots.

"What are you doing here?" I ask and I glance at Maya because I'm thinking of how I told her about Jet City, but no, she's already shaking her head at me as if to say that this wasn't her idea. And I'm glancing at Caleb because is this about the songs? But he just shrugs at me.

"Happy holidays to you, too, Summer," Jason says. "I was telling the band that you guys made quite a bit of noise with that blog post before the break. And I heard that the noise traveled all the way to Seattle."

I glance at Caleb again, then Val, trying to determine

what our strategy here is.

"Relax," says Jason. "Jet City Records offered you a deal. I heard all about it. I know people there. But that's the reason I'm here now, on behalf of Candy Shell."

"Why is that?" I ask.

"To counter. It's no secret we've had our eye on you guys, and we don't want to let you slip away."

That is such BS, I feel like telling him. And yet at the same time, I can't help being short of breath anticipating what he's about to say.

"Okay, here's the deal." Jason reads from his phone. "We can offer you our industry standard term with North American distribution and an exclusive option for our Asian and European partners. Standard royalty rates, a budget for your first EP, and . . ." Jason lets the moment hang. "You may retain the services of your manager, Ms. Carlson, as long as she is willing to keep me informed of her plans and be a team player."

Team player. The phrase makes me squirm. But I acknowledge this with a curt nod because I suppose on some level, it should matter to me that in a year I have gone from afterthought to someone worth keeping in Candy Shell's eyes. Still, I can't help my urge to be wary of this. "JCR is offering us the indie fifty-fifty split on royalties," I say, though maybe just so that I sound knowledgeable.

"I'm sure they are," says Jason. "How else are you going to get any money? Oh, I forgot to mention one more perk of the deal: we're prepared to offer an advance to the band. To be recouped against royalties of course."

"Okay . . . ," I say.

Jason grins. "Now, I can't give you the All Hail Minions! deal. You're not getting quite the same kind of buzz. But I believe you have huge potential."

He doesn't continue.

"So?" I finally say.

"Soooo," Jason says theatrically. "Ask me how much."

"Ugh, really?" I say. "We're not going to—"

"How much?" Jon asks.

And Jason delivers the kill bite. "A half million dollars. Two fifty now, the other half on the record's release."

The number goes off like a bomb in my head. Everyone else is silent, too. Shell-shocked. It's like the bands through the walls have stopped playing, too.

Our eyes flash around the room.

Money. A lot of it.

Oh, this is going to be complicated.

"Them's the terms," says Jason. "I asked Maya to come along, because we both know her, and I thought we could appoint her as our liaison while you're mulling it over. I prefer to spend as little time in the Hive as possible." He wipes at his coat while saying this.

As he heads for the door, he looks at me. "We can do this right, this time, Summer. Think it over."

I just nod at him. Once he's gone my tongue is heavy

with the snappy retorts about how he's treated Postcards. But I'm glad I held them back. No matter what I think of Jason, this is still a record deal offer. And a huge one. Even in this modern age, it matters.

The neighboring bands bleed back through the walls: metal to our left, prog rock to our right, and thumping hip-hop from above.

"I'm not sure I'm doing the math right," says Jon, "but I'm pretty sure a half million dollars is like, a ton of money."

"A ton," says Val.

"That is the offer," says Maya from the couch, awestruck. "It's pretty rare for a high school band to get an advance like that. Okay, super rare." She gets up and throws her bag over her shoulder. "I have to go intern, but I'm sure you guys have a lot to discuss." She steps over to the drums, and though it's completely obvious she's going for a kiss good-bye from Matt, he doesn't stand up. When she says, "Call me after?" and has leaned so far over the cymbals that it looks like she might fall on her face, he finally leans up and gives her a quick peck.

"Sure," he mumbles, almost like he doesn't want us to hear.

"Bye, guys," Maya says, and as she's turning I can see her willing away a shadow of doubt caused by Matt's behavior and I feel like smacking him. I don't know if this is related to me or what, but he needs to stop being a dick.

As soon as the door closes, Caleb asks me: "What do you think?"

"I—" have no idea what to say. "Um, I think it sounds amazing, I mean I guess, except . . . the way they've treated Postcards . . ."

"Which part, exactly?" says Jon immediately. "Paying for their recording, sending them on tour, bringing in Dr. Hans? How bad does that really sound?"

I guess we know where Jon stands on this. "I mean," I say, trying to stay calm, "the part where they are postponing shows and losing members and floundering."

"Sure," says Jon, "but look at Minions. Did you see the setup they had for that video shoot on New Year's? Totally insane. I mean, for that kind of money . . . I'm not even sure we'd need to find Eli's songs. Caleb, you could just put that behind you."

Caleb stares at the floor. I see the cloud passing over his face, tightening his mouth. "It's never going to just be *behind* me. He was my dad. And now that I know he might have . . . killed himself, I need to know why."

"And finding the songs would make that advance money go a lot further," says Matt.

"Not if it kills the deal because we make Candy Shell mad," Jon snaps.

Caleb looks up, his gaze at Jon lethal. "It's not your call."

Jon's eyes narrow. "No? Why's that? Because you're more important than the rest of us?"

"No . . ." This takes Caleb aback. I know he hates that

140

idea. "It's not that, but finding the songs isn't just for the band. It's personal." He glances to Val and she nods.

Jon rolls his eyes. "Right. I forgot we're like the next great family band."

"Guys," I say, before this goes any further. "I think we can still have both." I wish I could say the same about my own college situation, but I press on. "We have a good plan. We can look for the songs and hold off Candy Shell the same way we're holding off Jet City. And like, even if Candy Shell were to figure out what we were up to: what's the worst that could happen? If they want to sign us, they'd probably want to help us find the songs."

I don't add that I also have a part of me that agrees with Matt, too. Because don't think I haven't considered that finding Eli White's lost songs and performing them like we've planned would be such a huge deal that a girl couldn't be blamed for taking a year or two off to manage her band full-time. Even parents and admissions officers could be swayed by such a narrative. . . .

But I feel like a mercenary for thinking that way. What matters is that Caleb and Val need to find the songs, and the band needs to not break up because of it.

Everyone is silent. "Well," says Val, "we still have to do the EP for PopArts so right now we need to practice, right? Let's talk about this after tomorrow's studio session." She looks at Matt. "Wanna check if that's okay with your girl-friend and Candy Shell?"

She says *girlfriend* with a condescending note.

Matt just shrugs and looks away. "Yeah, I'll check with her later."

Everyone nods and starts to get back to it but the vibe in the room is obvious: we're on unsteady footing. Or maybe it's just me. The band tension, the songs, the offer . . . And how exactly do I fit in? Jason says they'd let me stay involved, and I think I actually believe him, but . . . to do what? If Candy Shell is throwing down that kind of money, they're going to have opinions, designs, plans.

My next thought surprises me: maybe this is my perfect college out. I could be involved as it all comes together, and maybe then they'd be fine without me.

But ugh! I can't even believe that we're considering dealing with Candy Shell, who has stood for exactly what we don't want to be. Or what I don't want. *We can do this right, this time.* . . . Can I possibly believe Jason? Can a shark change? I don't even know how to think about it clearly now, with the money involved.

And I can tell from the mistake-filled run-through of our songs in practice, that the rest of the band is lost in their own version of these new waters, too.

I'm on my way to the studio after dinner the next night when Caleb texts me.

Caleb: Val's not here.

Summer: ?

Caleb: She was supposed to show up an hour ago. Mom says she's not at home. Said she was stopping by the Hive just to get her amp but it's been awhile and she's not answering her phone.

Shit. I hate that my mind immediately jumps to drinking, but I know that's what Caleb is thinking, too.

Caleb: Could you check on her?

Summer: On it.

I was going to take the bus. Now I'll need the car, but my parents don't mind. They're still basking in Stanford interview glow.

The Hive is twenty minutes in the wrong direction. The whole time I'm driving I'm thinking that I don't want to mistrust her like this. Val was the most motivated at practice last night. It doesn't make sense that she would be flaking now. But with Val, despite how much better I know her, I still have this sliver of doubt. I wish I didn't. Unless tonight proves me right.

I arrive at the door to the practice room and listen. At first I don't hear anything, but evening practices are well underway on all sides so really, how could I?

I get out my key. I never use it, always knocking so the band can let me in and it won't seem like I'm barging in on them.

It's dark inside except for white holiday lights that Jon strung in a trapezoid across the ceiling. They hang low in spots where the duct tape came undone.

"What are you doing here?"

Val's voice makes me jump. Now I see her, lying on the couch on her stomach. She's wearing big silver headphones. The cord trails down to a laptop, an old Mac that she inherited from Charity.

I scan the floor for beer bottles or any other sign of what she's been up to. I see a few tissues. Her bass is lying next to the couch. There's a bottle of Mountain Dew. Val drinks it all the time. Then again that green-tinted bottle could be hiding anything.

"The guys are all at the studio," I say. "Why are you here?"

Val pulls the headphones off and I hear a tinny voice. "I've been working on something," she says. She taps the laptop to stop the track. "I didn't mean to, but it started coming out on the way over here, and I couldn't help it." She picks up the computer. "This was the inspiration."

She hands the clunky machine over and I see a message on a Facebook page. I didn't realize that Val was even on Facebook but then I see that the profile name she's using is "Ginger Carmelita," and the profile photo is a silhouette of a house cat.

"It's just so I can keep up with a few old friends," she explains.

The message is from Darren Peters. I recognize the name from a Kitty Klaws post I found on YouTube back in the fall.

Hey Cassie, I'm pretty sure this is you. Your mom thinks you're in Los Angeles with your half brother, which she was glad to know. Is that true? She understands why you haven't been in touch but she'd like to reestablish contact. She won't tell you why, but I thought I should: she's been pretty sick. Liver issues, and something to do with her blood. I think it's hepatitis. I know it's asking a lot, but I hope you'll consider reconnecting. It's been over a year. Hopefully, time heals . . .

"Oh boy," I say.

"I knew it," says Val. "That package was just the tip of the suck iceberg." Her eyes are rimmed red. She picks up her bass and crosses the room, grabbing the mic stand from her usual spot.

"Um," I say, "what do you think—"

"I don't want to talk about it."

"Okay."

She sits on Caleb's amp, and starts bending the mic stand down to her. "Will you just listen to something for a sec?"

"Sure." I sit on the couch.

"I know they're waiting for me," says Val, adjusting the mic and then the knobs on her bass, "but I had to get this out before I fucking exploded."

I feel my phone buzz against my thigh and figure it's Caleb but I'm afraid to get it out, afraid to do anything that might disrupt this strange and fragile moment.

Val gets the mic straight. She looks so small sitting on the amp, her skinny legs in her legging jeans angled up to support her bass. It's bigger than her torso, the neck thicker than her arms. In the meager light her eyes look hollow and her cheeks sharp, too much life wearing away at her too soon. Her usual eyeliner is like barbed wire around her eyes.

"Okay," she says into the mic, like we are live

146

somewhere. For one second she glances up at me, and I feel that usual surge of inadequacy and insecurity that every one of her looks always inspires, but also I think now that some of the pain is my heart hurting for her. It would be too cliché to say that Val is heartbreaking, but she is a painful beauty, an exposed nerve that is all shadows but also searing bright.

She drops her head, recently green hair falling over her face. She starts to play a cycling rhythm on the bass, eighth notes, some of them chords, thirds I think, but that's never been my thing.

After one time through she senses, like I do, that the assault of bass frequencies through the walls is drowning out the tone, and she cranks up the treble, making the bass sound almost like some sort of low, watery guitar.

The rhythm has a tense pulse, but then the intervals she's playing hint at evenings, at cold temperatures, at moonlight (though I wouldn't tell her that because she makes fun of me and Caleb for those kinds of comments).

I slip my phone from my pocket, daring to look away from her, ignoring the texts I see from Caleb. I flick to the voice recorder app and hit record. I rest the phone on my leg, screen safely dark, when Val looks up and sings:

I can feel the skin beneath your anger
I can taste the candy at the pier
I can remember the good day

The one in a thousand when you were here
Right here

They say that you don't deserve me
I don't know what you deserve
I don't fault you the bruises
The blame
It doesn't do me any good
Nobody's innocent
If you give them enough time

I remember the first night
On the highway west of everything
Hiding underneath all my shit in the backseat
Hiding from the shadows looming over the car
I remember thinking I wish you were there
Any version of you would do

But I won't go back, now
And you can't go forward
I'll find my own
I'll find my own
I'll find my own
My own . . .

And you can tell me anything, now
You can let the hurt show through

I know that you're suffering alone
But I know what I have to do

I'll find my own . . .

Her voice breaks with each refrain, the "own" dipping up into her falsetto, each one seeming to disappear like a bird into the sky. She slaps the same note over and over, driving, and you can imagine how the band would create a storm around this. And what probably surprises me the most is how the song is . . . I want to say *inspirational*, but Val would want to punch that word in the face. Maybe more like defiant, or self-reliant, something like that.

Val finishes and I turn off the recording. She looks up. "What do you think?" I'm surprised she's even asking me.

"I think you have to show the guys."

She kind of nods and shrugs at once. "Not too whiny?"

I laugh. "That is never a danger with you." I check my phone. "We should get down there."

"Yeah." Val starts to pack up her bass. "Thanks for coming for me. And for listening."

"Sure," I say. "We thought—" I start to say but then think it's a bad idea.

"What?"

"Nothing."

"You thought I was here getting sloshed?"

I shrug. "It wasn't fair."

"It kinda was, but nope, just getting drunk on *feelings*."

I glance sideways at her—and she cracks up. So do I. Suddenly we both lose ourselves laughing . . . for about ten seconds.

"You want to carpool down there?" I ask.

"Nope. See you there."

And yet after all that, I still linger in my car, waiting until I see her exit the Hive, just to be sure she'll follow through.

She does.

We arrive and find Caleb and Jon sacked out on the studio couch, both gazing at the ceiling in that burned-out, vacant way that studio time can cause.

PopArts has a fully functioning recording studio, designed by a couple PTA dads who used to work at Sound City Studios. The only drawback is that the engineers and producers are students from the audio design track, and so while they're good at what they do, they're still learning. Sometimes they get stuck on things that a pro would breeze right through. From the look on Caleb's face, I'm guessing that's the case now.

"Sorry, guys," says Val as we walk in. "I was working some stuff out."

"What kind of stuff?" Caleb asks. He doesn't sound mistrustful, more just brotherly.

"Just stuff."

"Come on," I say. "She's got a new song and it's fantastic."

Val's face scrunches, but she doesn't deny it. "What did I miss?"

"Hit it again," Alonzo says into the studio mic. Alonzo is the head of the tech crew, and lead engineer on our project.

The monitors explode with Matt thwacking the snare drum.

"Just this," says Caleb with a sigh. "Something's wrong with the drums."

Alonzo turns from his hunched position over the sound board. He's wearing a backward cap, unwashed ponytail hanging from it, and a Led Zeppelin shirt draped over his pale, bony frame. A Red Vine hangs half-eaten from his mouth. He's been known to eat a whole pack during a session, and he never offers to share. "The overhead mics are completely out of phase," he says gravely.

"I thought it sounded fine," says Jon numbly.

"Well, sure, it sounds *fine*," says Alonzo, "but the phasing is definitely noticeable, and could be catastrophic in the mix."

"Are you guys getting graded on phasing or something?" Jon asks.

"Well," says Alonzo, "that's one of the criteria, but either way, you also shouldn't want it on your recording."

"I also don't want to be found mummified on this couch."

Alonzo sighs in annoyance. "Kylie, try another one degree off axis with the left mic."

"Kill me," Jon mutters.

Caleb checks his phone. "We've been waiting to start for an hour," he tells me.

Alonzo ignores the comment. I remember this from the studio last year with Postcards. There's nothing you can say to an engineer when they're fixated on something. God forbid you challenge them on the importance of something like the 80 hertz, for example, or you'll get a treatise on all the different frequencies and the microphone patterns and how Tesla was misunderstood, and so on.

After five more minutes of skull-pounding snare drum hits, he announces: "Okay, it might be reined in enough. Let's everybody get in there."

The band moves into their positions. Jon is at one side of the large studio room. Val at the other. Drums are center. Caleb is on his own in the vocal isolation booth.

"What's that?" I ask, noticing a tiny keyboard on a stand beside Jon's pedal setup.

"You'll see," he says.

"Good luck, guys," I say and head back into the control room. On the way, I duck my head into the vocal booth. Caleb is running quietly through "On My Sleeve." It sounds so different, just his voice with none of the layers I am used to hearing. "Hey," I say.

He turns. Fret Face. But also focused.

"Remember," I say, "no record labels, no Eli or blog posts, just you and your amazing song and your awesome band. Got it?"

"Got it."

I blow him a kiss and return to the control room, where Alonzo is bent over the faders and dials like a scientist trying to disarm a doomsday device.

Kylie selects a bunch of tracks on the monitor.

"Okay," she says, "'On My Sleeve,' take one. Here comes the click . . ."

She taps a few keystrokes and the cursor starts moving across the screen. Sixteen rectangle graphics start to grow, each a different shade of purple and representing a microphone or an instrument line. The click beeps like an old video game.

Through the large glass window, I see the other three band members waiting patiently, and through the monitors I hear Caleb count off: "One two three four . . ."

He starts to delicately strum his acoustic, a pulse with lots of string attack that sounds almost like an old clock ticking. He sings the first verse, and for a first take it's going great.

At the same time, I see Jon sitting down at that synthesizer. I don't remember us working on any new parts at practice. . . .

As Caleb sings the last word of the first verse, Jon strikes a brazen synth tone, like a laser beam through the song. He starts nodding his head rhythmically in Matt's direction, almost like he wants him to thump along on the kick drum.

But everyone's thrown off. The song grinds to a halt.

"What was that?" Caleb asks.

"I wanted to surprise you guys," says Jon. "I think it will give the song some more energy. Can we try it again?"

Nobody answers right away. They're probably thinking what I am: More energy? The song has plenty of energy the way we've been playing it for three months.

"Okay," says Caleb. He couldn't sound less convinced.

Kylie rolls the tracks, Caleb counts, and back in they go.

He sings the first verse and then Jon starts that synth sound again. Caleb and Val press on, Matt waiting to come in. When Jon nods his head like he wants something new on the drums, Matt just shrugs.

As the second verse goes along I can sort of hear what Jon is getting at. It sounds like he wants to add an upbeat pop element to the song.

But Caleb stops again. I hear him sigh through the microphone. "I'm not sure it works," he says carefully.

"We've only been trying it for like a minute," says Jon.

"Maybe we should all chat for a second," I say, heading into the studio.

"I think you guys should give the part more of a chance," Jon says immediately.

"We've been rehearsing this song for months," says Val. "We had it all worked out."

"I know," says Jon, "it just feels like it needs something."

"You mean," I say, "you feel like it needs to sound more like the Minions?"

Jon scowls at me. "That's not what I was going for."

"That's exactly what it sounded like," says Caleb. "And we're not them."

"Besides," says Matt, "you already had a great part for the song, Jon. Your guitar line is really cool."

Jon shakes his head. "I just don't think it's enough."

"Enough for what?" Caleb says. "To get us the other half million? Is that what this is about?"

"No! I wouldn't . . . You guys don't get it."

"What don't we get?" Val asks.

"I just think," says Jon, "that right now the song is thin. It's just basically Caleb and his guitar and his wounded heart—"

"Whoa, wait," says Caleb. "How come this feels like the same thing as New Year's? Jon, come on, man. You're the lead fucking guitarist. People are going to notice you."

"That's not even—" Jon gazes at the ceiling. "We need to make sure we sound right, you know? If we're going to be on a major label, and the world is going to hear us . . ."

"Then we should sound like *us*," says Val.

"Yeah," Caleb agrees, "we're not throwing a synth on the song at the last minute. Sorry."

Jon shakes his head and stands up. "I can't take this anymore."

"Take what?" says Caleb.

"You! This is what I was talking about. Your band, your songs, and we have to play them the way you want and then we're going to drive halfway across the country chasing after your dad and why? So everything can be even more about you!"

"Jon, I don't think that's the whole story," says Val.

"You're his sister! You don't count." He points at me. "You don't either."

"So," says Matt, "I guess I'm the only one who can tell you you're being a dick?"

"Okay, fine. I'm done for tonight." He starts out.

"Jon, we need to track the song."

"I'll overdub," he calls over his shoulder. "Or you can just play what you want. I don't even care."

Caleb is about to follow him but I hold him back. "Let him cool off. I'll talk to him tomorrow," I say.

"That sucked," says Matt.

"Guys," Alonzo says over the intercom. "Time is getting short. Should we try to get some tracks?"

Caleb looks from me to Val to Matt. "Let's keep going, maybe? Try to at least get something done tonight."

They return to their instruments and try "Sleeve" again. They do a few takes and it sounds great, but empty. Like a story missing a chunk of pages, without Jon's guitar.

"We can find a makeup time," says Alonzo when we're done. "I'll check the calendar and let you know tomorrow."

"I don't know what we're going to do about him," Caleb says to me after, as we're drowning our post-studio blues at Tina's frozen yogurt.

"We'll figure it out," I say. Except I have no idea either.

Formerly Orchid @catherinefornevr 3hr
First day of recording in the books! Things are going so well I can't even show you the footage . . . yet.

Jon's a junior so we don't have any classes together, but I have his schedule, so that I know what times I can text him if there's band business. He'll be in Amp Lab when I have calculus, last period, which is my best shot. I check the top of my binder, where I have twenty *t*'s written: the maximum number of tardies you can get without losing credit. I've crossed off nine. Two of them already have a *c* for calc written below them. I'll probably get a warning for this one.

I'm at lunch with Caleb when Alonzo gets in touch with us over school email.

Things are crazy with the end of the quarter. We are completely booked but just had a cancellation this Friday afternoon. Might be the only time we can do. Also rest assured we have corrected the phasing dilemma in the overhead mics.

"I'm naming my solo act the Phasing Dilemma," says Caleb. "That's cool about the makeup date. Wait, you're frowning."

"That's when I was supposed to do the Stanford interview."

"Ooh," Caleb winces. "It's totally fine if you miss the session."

"Or . . . I can probably reschedule." I know I shouldn't. Not with something this important. And yet, I'm also technically an adult with a life, and plans change. And I need to be at the next session, especially given the drama with Jon. Andre should understand. Before I can overthink it, I email him.

"Okay," I say as lunch ends. "Wish me luck."

I find Jon alone in the Amp Lab. He's sitting on a single stool in the center of a trapezoidal room with carpeted walls. About ten feet in front of him are wide shelves stacked with fifteen different amplifiers, from classic Fender tubes to solid-state Marshall stacks. He has his guitar plugged into a switcher box by his feet, with pedals that correspond to each amp.

He shreds a complicated riff I've never heard, hits the pedals, and does it again. Each new amp changes the tone, the body, the growl.

He hears the sucking of air as I close the sealed glass door. "Oh, hey."

I step up next to him. He keeps playing.

"Which tone do you like better? This . . ." He plays the riff. "Or . . . this." He stomps the pedal and plays again.

"Um, that was really subtle," I admit.

"Little more body in the first one," he says.

"Jon . . . can we talk?"

He hits the mute switch on the pedal board and turns to me, but his fingers keep flicking over the strings.

"So about—"

He cuts me off, his fingers pausing. "Look, here's the thing: remember when the Toast and Jam blog came out?"

"Obviously."

"Well, did you know that wasn't the only blog post written about Dangerheart that day?"

"Um, no?"

"Yeah. A blog called Six String Fire named me the most promising new guitarist on the unsigned scene."

"Wait, really?" I say. "That's awesome!"

"It's a pretty small blog, out of Minneapolis."

"Still, that's so cool, Jon. I wish I'd seen that. I'll have to find it and post it around. Why didn't you share it with us?"

Jon shrugs. "It didn't really compete with the big Caleb

news. I thought someone might notice it later, but after a couple days went by, I realized that if you did a search for Dangerheart, that guitar blog didn't even show up until page six of the results. Page freakin' six. I mean, if you search for Dangerheart, do you know when the first mention of my name, or Matt's, for that matter, shows up? Page three. Even Val's name is barely mentioned in anything that makes the first page for the band. It's all Caleb and Eli."

"It will blow over."

"Yeah, but that's the thing . . . when, exactly? When we sign a record deal that we got *because* of Eli?"

"The record label offers are also happening because Dangerheart is really good," I say. "And that's as much because of you as anyone else in the band."

"Maybe?" says Jon. "I know I sound egotistical, but still . . . page six. It's one thing to be part of a team. It sucks to feel like an afterthought."

"Jon, you're not. No one in the band feels that way."

"You say that, but everybody shot my idea down yesterday after like two seconds."

"Well, yeah, but 'On My Sleeve' has been set for weeks. It's not surprising that a last-minute change threw everyone off. Plus, it sounded really different."

"I was just trying to put my stamp on it."

"But your stamp was already on it. The guitar parts were already great."

"I don't know," says Jon. "I just . . . I think the band

rocks. I like playing in it, but, if I'm never going to be noticed, hell, if I can't ever even talk to a girl at a show without it being about Caleb, then I just don't know if I can stand it."

We're both quiet. Jon's fingers start racing around the fret board again.

"Don't leave the band," I finally say. "We'd be done without you."

Jon laughs. "No, you wouldn't. But thanks."

"So, what do you want me to do?"

"Not sure? I'll see you guys after school. We have to talk about the label stuff, right?"

"We do. Okay." I rub his shoulder. "See you later."

I hurry to the Green Room as soon as the bell rings, and grab what has become our usual table in the back corner. The rest of the PopArts kids have recognized by now that this is Dangerheart's territory—every band has their unofficial spot by this point—but I want to be sure it will just be us and the conversation-obscuring hiss of the nearby espresso stand. Once I claim it with my hoodie and books, I get in line and grab drinks. I know everyone's order, and they all keep me supplied with cash for this very thing. You might think this makes me the coffee gal, like I'm a glorified roadie, but it's actually really satisfying to get everything set up just right, and to know you're getting people exactly what they need. Plus, then no one screws up my order.

The band filters in. Caleb first. Matt and Val come in from the back doors by the rehearsal space. They were having a math meeting outside during Matt's free period, studying limits. Jon is last, but at least he's here. He stalks over to the table and sits down, guitar on his lap.

"Is Maya coming by?" I ask Matt.

"Probably," he says with what seems to be his standard lack of enthusiasm.

"Okay, well, let's talk about the labels and Denver before she gets here. We're all very familiar with how Candy Shell operates, who their bands are and all, but did you have a chance to check out those links I sent with Jet City's roster and album art?"

Everyone kind of nods and shifts in their seats.

"Their stuff is really cool," Caleb offers. It sounds like he's trying to please me.

"We're not really considering Jet City," says Jon, getting right to it. "Are we?"

I guess I should have known.

Matt: "The money's amazing. I mean, my drum set is a piece of crap. And like, my parents have been trying to save for two years to go on a vacation."

Jon: "I'd basically want to barf every day knowing that we said no."

Val: "If I could afford a lawyer, I could pursue emancipation from my mom. And have rent for wherever I'm going to live. Not to mention some new stuff."

I meet Caleb's gaze. He raises his eyebrows. "I don't think we even have a choice."

"Okay, then." I'm not sure what I was hoping for. One part of me wants to make the argument that going with the smaller label would be better for our songs, for our sound. But I have no idea how to make it or even if it makes sense. What could be better for our music than the chance to work on it all the time? Money would help.

I nod to the group. "So, I guess the only problem here is my gut screaming that it's a bad idea to work with Jason."

"You're not the only one who's worried about that," says Val.

"But what about Denver?" Caleb asks.

"I still say we're not breaking any laws or doing anything wrong by following some clues and seeing what we find," I say.

Okay, then. Jon taps his finger around the fret board, eyes down.

"I don't know," says Jon. "It seems like a bad idea to piss off the very label that's making us an offer. Maybe they'd help us find the songs."

"I don't trust them with Eli's songs," says Caleb. "That's the one thing I know."

"So . . . can we all agree that we'll try the EP cover story and at least see what Candy Shell says? If Jason agrees, it can't hurt to stick to the plan and see if we find anything. Then we can decide what to do."

"Here comes Maya," says Matt, eyeing the door.

She's entering on the front edge of a swell of people. They all keep turning and looking over their shoulders and then I see why: Ethan is at the center of the vortex, like the hero home from war.

He's carrying on a conversation with five kids at once, and there are at least ten more who are just sort of orbiting, sucked in by the gravity. Amanda Phillips, a junior and a killer guitarist, is nearly hanging on his arm, batting her eyes and smiling at every word. Coach emerges from his office and makes his way over, beaming. Nobody cares about Postcards' tour troubles: they are still doing great by any PopArts kid's standard.

Ethan has already spotted me. "I think he's headed this way," I say with a tone that should ward off any jealousy from Caleb.

Coach drags him past us, to show him the new sound system on the auditorium stage. Maya drops into a chair beside Matt.

A few minutes later, Ethan strolls back in and stops at our table.

"Hey," he says, looking right at me.

"Hey," I say back, making sure I don't sound too friendly. That's not for Caleb, it's for me. Then I take Caleb's arm and say, "Not sure if you guys know each other, but . . ."

"Ethan from Postcards from Ariel," says Caleb, sticking out his hand. "What's up, I'm Caleb."

"Hey." They shake, and Ethan says, "I remember you from that band . . . The Androids. Guitarist?"

"And singer," says Caleb.

For a second, Ethan's eyes sort of gleam like he's having some easy fun with the idea that I'm dating another band singer, and I tell myself to just stay there holding Caleb's arm because I am not going to give a crap what he thinks. "Nice," he finally says.

"I thought you guys were on a big tour," says Caleb. I wonder if he's trying to sound interested, or if he knows that comment stings.

"Things got canceled." Ethan's tone is suddenly detached, in that no-big-deal way that is how musicians posture. "But it's all right. We're back to do a new EP."

"Cool, man," Caleb replies.

That's posturing, too. *Cool, man* is the musician equivalent of "That's great, and also fuck off."

"So, hey, you guys ready for the big Denver adventure?"

As the words are coming out, I can't believe I didn't see this coming. I should have thought to intercept him or something, but we had so much other stuff to think about and now—

"What Denver gig?" Maya asks.

Ethan answers immediately, in full social mode. "It's a house concert."

"Oh," I hear Maya say quietly. I'm afraid to look over at her. I hear all the air escaping from Matt as he turns to run damage control.

"How's the guitarist search going?" I ask just to change the subject.

"Slow," says Ethan. "From what I've read, Dangerheart already has Mount Hope's best guitarist."

I expect Jon to deflect this compliment with some kind of funny accent. Instead, he has to restrain a smile. "Oh, thanks."

I feel bad, too. Here's Ethan referencing that blog post that none of Jon's own band mates even saw.

"Yeah, well, anyway." Ethan senses a couple other students hovering behind him, waiting to talk. "I'm gonna go see a few teachers. We should chat soon, about gear sharing and stuff."

"Sounds good," I say, avoiding his smile and keeping a hand on Caleb's arm.

"I'm sorry, it just hadn't come up yet," I already hear Matt saying as Ethan leaves.

Maya is getting up in a hurry. "I'll see you later."

"Maya," Matt says, nearly whining.

"Maya, wait." I flash Matt a look. I feel like this is my fault as much as anyone's. Better if I take the fall. "I'm sorry," I say as she steps around the table. "We obviously wanted to tell you about Denver but we wanted to protect you."

Maya spins around. "*Protect* me?" She glares at Matt. "And so you just do whatever Summer says? *That* shouldn't surprise me."

Whoops.

"I don't," Matt says weakly. "I mean, I didn't . . ."

"Not helping . . . ," Caleb warns under his breath.

"Maya," I say. "We just didn't want to put you in an awkward position with Candy Shell."

"Oh, really?" Maya can't quite look at me. She aims her glare instead at the table. "Because you've never put me in an awkward position before, asking me to sleuth around for information on Val's mom, which totally could have gotten me fired."

"I know," I say, "that's why I didn't want to add to it."

"No, you'd rather just make me look like an idiot. Thanks, Summer. I'll be a really impressive liaison to the band when Jason learns that I didn't even know your gig schedule."

"Nobody knows our gig schedule."

"Why not? Are you keeping it a big secret, or something?"

"Yes, for now."

"Why?"

"Just . . . because, we are." I know I'm being vague, and now a touch abrasive, but I don't know what else to do. "We didn't want you to have to lie."

"Well, now I have to anyway, don't I?" Maya snaps. "Even Jason makes me feel like I matter more than you do."

She storms off.

"Maya," I call after her, but it's halfhearted.

Matt is just sitting there. "This is gonna suck."

Val cracks up.

"Hey . . . ," says Caleb.

"Sorry."

"Matt, we'll figure it out," I say.

"No, it's . . . whatever," says Matt. "I thought it was the right choice, too."

I feel terrible about Maya. I also wonder if in her anger, she'll tell Jason about our Denver plan. And if she does, will he be able to connect the dots from Denver to Eli?

But she texts me about fifteen minutes later.

Maya: I'll keep your gigs a secret. But Jason will find out eventually.

Summer: I know. I'm still sorry.

Maya: Tell Matt I'm still mad at him.

Summer: ok.

We sit quietly for awhile: Caleb and I working on our lab report, Matt studying drum fills on YouTube, Jon noodling up and down the fret board.

My phone pings and I find an email from Andre about the interview:

Sorry for the delay. That's too bad about Friday. Cases are piling up and the next few weeks will be impossible. The interview has to be complete by

February 22 and it looks like the only days I have free are Presidents' Day and that following Thursday. Do either of those days work? I hope so!

Crap. Presidents' Day is when we're on our way to Denver. It will have to be that Thursday. Cutting it really close. I'm anxious just thinking about it. A flat tire somewhere in Utah, and I won't make it. But I tell him it will work and hope for the best.

As it turns out, the studio session on Friday goes great. I'm sitting on the couch as the band tears through "Catch Me" when an alarm goes off on my phone, reminding me of the interview I could have had. I forgot to delete it, and it makes my gut flood with guilt.

Everything is rocking, finally. Jon abandoned the keyboard track in "On My Sleeve," and he and Caleb came up with a piano part that ended up making the song even better. Val is totally on point with "Catch Me." The band is a blur of energy through the window. Jon added synths, this time in a good way, and now this song sounds like a chase through a futuristic city by hover car.

All that is great, but it means I easily could have slipped out for the interview.

We also got good news from Jason: he's fine with us finishing our school EP. His response is so breezy that I don't trust it.

But at least now we have things set up just like we want.

I've even warmed up to the idea of signing with Candy Shell. The more time I spend with Caleb, and especially with this recording sounding so good, the more I imagine that this, right here, is how I want to spend next year.

And yet . . .

Two hours later, when I walk in the door and my dad looks up from the couch and asks how the interview went . . .

(Because I never actually mentioned the reschedule . . .)

I clench my gut against a wave of nerves or guilt or both and reply:

"It went great."

Formerly Orchid @catherinefornevr 4hr
Winter break! Taking a road trip to see cousins. Now taking your playlist suggestions. See you in a week!

Calculating Route
Mount Hope to St. George, UT: estimated travel time 5 hr 30 min

summerc this has to be the name of #Dangerheart's alter ego band.

summerc don't blink?

Calculating Route
St. George, UT to Denver, CO: 9 hr 15 min

summerc all the erosion happens in Utah.

summerc my window as a future national park
caretaker and recluse.

summerc the view from Mars.

summerc Hay bale tractors=YES.

summerc "We must go through the mines!"

West of Denver

This has maybe been the greatest two days of my life. There has been so much of everything, too much coffee, and somehow no time to spare even though we have been in the van for fifteen hours at this point. Other than posting pictures under the guise of taking a family trip, I haven't been able to share the details because of the top secret nature of our adventure. And I have been considering whether that makes it all feel more or less special. Less special because if a band shares a single woolly mammoth ice-cream cone in the wilds of Utah and doesn't post a picture of it, did it even happen? Or more because these experiences are mine, and only mine, and no one gets to know?

My parents enjoy the pictures I send. I got word over the last month that I will have interviews at Colorado College and Ponoma, both a couple weeks after I get back. Carlson Squared is at peace. But all that feels like another life, forever from now.

Here in the moment there is only me, Caleb, and our band. We all share these smiles sometimes that almost hurt my heart with how personal they feel. It's just us.

It's almost my shift to drive again, but before I forget:

Things to Remember:

-The way Las Vegas looked like a moon base from a distance

-When it was Jon's turn for music and out of nowhere he put on *Fearless* and we were all horrified because, yeah, we knew every word

-The way our new EPs look. We finished the recording, mixing and mastering with little drama as January slipped by, and we got the box right before we left. I like to run my finger over the slippery shrink-wrapped spines. The cover is this awesome logo that my friend *SarahFromTheValley* drew, where "Dangerheart" is written in this cool font across a big red heart. There are flares at the beginning and end of the word, with stars and planets in the swirls. It looks like a tattoo that a swashbuckling pirate, or a mercenary, would have on his upper arm, the one he wouldn't show you until a quiet moment around a campfire, or something.

-There is no smell quite like the smell of Cool Ranch Doritos mixed with six bodies in a van.

-The sound of four boys through the wall when they discovered that the pay-per-view channels in the Creek Edge motel ($59 a night!) were unblocked

-Val and I flossing together. The clicking sound. HILARIOUS. Why? We'll never know.

-Moonrise at a roadside canyon rim with Caleb. He's

been the quietest of us on the trip. Now that we're back on the hunt for Eli, he gets lost in his head. But on a canyon edge in Utah we held each other and picked out the constellations and kissed in the millennial yawn of the wind over sandstone, kissed atop cliffs that were once beneath a sea, kissed until it became pointless because we were getting oxygen starved, becoming impulsive . . . and also needing lip balm. (Pro tip: desert air is dry.)

—The sense of leaving the world behind. No practices, classes, or obligations. No routines that you sleepwalk through. Everything is vibrant and new. And we could literally be going anywhere. But we're not. We're on a mission. And nothing can change the indescribable magic of that. All the jokes the same, all the stories told, and the extra intangible of being the "band from LA." Like that would be written on the side of our spaceship. Like astronauts. Like great explorers. Like rock stars.

—I don't know what awaits us in Denver, or in the future three days or three months from now, but I don't know how it could ever get any better than this.

The snow starts when we are still three hours outside of Denver.

"It's fine," says Randy. "I've driven in it plenty of times. Let's stop now and get supplies so we can make tracks."

Our plan is to get to Dylan's Vintage Guitars before we go to the house party. Snow was not included in our thinking.

We pull into a rest area and crawl out of the back of the stalker van. A day and a half of travel spent sitting around and between our gear has us all walking like retirees. We've been rotating drivers, and also who gets to ride in the precious padded shotgun seat, which we have taken to calling *the Spa*.

We shamble through the convenience store, probably all looking as bleary as we feel. We all talked big about trying to eat healthy but really it's been pretty much just chips and soda and candy.

"Peanuts are a health food, right?" I say as I pick out a Snickers. Matt is standing beside me, surveying the options in the nougat food group.

"Yeah," he says but gets distracted by his phone buzzing. He sighs as he checks it.

"Maya?" I ask.

"Uh-huh." As he says it, he glances across the aisles and catches Val's eye. She gives him a little eyebrow raise, like, *What?*

This trips my radar. I can't even say why. Intuition? But also, there have been little things, here and there, ways he's been acting, that have made me wonder, just a little, about all the time these two have spent together the last few months. . . . "I know you've been helping Val with her math," I find myself saying. "Is there anything else you want to tell me?"

"Like what?" Matt says quickly. His face gets red.

Intuition confirmed. Uh-oh.

"Matt, it's okay if you have a crush on Val. There's nothing wrong with that, except that you're, you know, dating someone else." I realize, too, that on one level I'm relieved, because it means he no longer has a crush on me.

"Nah," says Matt like the world's worst liar. "But you're right: I'm not sure how great things are going with Maya."

"Have you told her that?"

"Not really?"

"Except in your body language," I say.

Matt seems surprised. "It shows?"

I roll my eyes. "Duh. And if I can tell, she can definitely tell."

Suddenly Val pops up between us. "Got it!" she says excitedly to Matt, holding up an enormous fountain soda. "Fanta for the drummer boy!"

"Nice," says Matt with a genuine smile. "Should we do Three Musketeers or Milky Way?"

"Both," says Val. She punches him in the shoulder.

"Yeah . . . ," I say, raising my eyebrows at Matt and heading for the Little Debbie display. "I'll be over here."

Back in the van, Randy keeps driving and Jon's got the Spa. Caleb and I are on the floor behind the seats, and Val and Matt are together beyond the wall of amps and guitar cases. And now that my radar has been tripped, I realize that they've been in that spot all day. Sitting close, too. Like heads nearly touching. Which probably means shoulders are touching? Oh boy.

Caleb dozes off for a bit, and I am hoping to do the same when I hear a clinking of glass and then Val: "Oh shit!"

She and Matt bust out laughing. Actually it's more like giggling.

I lean over the drum cases. "What's going on back here?"

Val looks up innocently over the giant soda cup. She's trying to suppress a smile. "Nothing, *Mom*," she says, sounding annoyed but then she barely holds back another laugh.

"Hey, Val," Matt says in this weirdly low voice, "can I have some of your soda?"

This makes them crack up.

Oh. Now I think I finally get it. "Did you spike that?"

"Relax," says Val. "It'll be hours before we get to the gig; we'll be fine."

I don't know how to react. I don't want to give in to the immediate mistrust I feel. But playing it too cool undermines my real worry: we can't have two drunk band members at our big show.

"Is it the schnapps again?" I ask, going for something in the middle.

Val toasts me with the soda and lowers her voice. "Peach flavored."

"Sounds delicious." I hope my slightly sarcastic tone isn't nagging but does convey a sense of the stakes. I hate this conversation already and just want to get out of it. "Just be careful, you guys. Okay?"

"You're not going to rat us out to Randy," says Val, "are you?"

"You're not going to screw up the gig, are you?"

Val starts to glare at me but bursts out laughing instead. "We'll be *fine*. Now, go away, please."

I sit back down, feeling like, for the moment, there's nothing more I can say. If they really get worse I'll tell everybody else and we'll intervene.

I guess I shouldn't be surprised. Val's been in better

shape since New Year's, and none of our worries about her drinking have seemed to be substantiated. But now I don't know. If she's had a stash of booze with her, there have been many opportunities while we've been on the road. I think back to last night, laughing over flossing, and now I have to wonder if she was sober then. Ugh, I hate this feeling!

She erupts into giggles again. Dammit. I want to trust her, but I don't. And I'm stuck as to whether to say anything to the others. Caleb is napping or I'd tell him. Maybe after we play tonight. We're in the Red Zone after all. Don't want to mess with the delicate balance right before a show.

Our drive is slow with the snow, and by the time we get to Dylan's, we're worried that maybe it will have closed early. The parking lot of the small strip mall is completely empty, pristine with the inch of snow . . . but the store lights are on.

We all hurry across the lot through a biting wind. The streetlights make the air sparkle with flakes. As we duck through the snow I can see a middle-aged man at the counter inside.

We enter and pick our way through a maze of stacked amplifiers. Guitars hang in tight rows along both walls and down the center of the store. The man behind the counter is rail thin with frizzy gray hair. He's holding a screwdriver to the innards of a guitar pedal. The glass case he's working over is full of them. There are stacks of parts behind him: circuit boards and dismembered guitar necks and head stocks.

"You guys look like you're in town for a show," he says without glancing up at us.

"Are you Dylan?" Randy asks.

He looks around the empty store. "Who else would I be?" Dylan squints at Randy. "Do I know you?"

"Randy. I toured through here with a band called Poison Pen a long time ago. My band mate bought a sea foam Jazzmaster from you."

"Eli White," says Dylan. His eyes trace over us and land on Caleb.

"He was my dad," Caleb confirms.

"Well, I'll be damned," says Dylan. "You're like a ghost of him . . ."

Caleb shifts and holds out the receipt. "I think I'm supposed to show you this."

Dylan squints curiously and takes the receipt. He looks it over for longer than it seems like he should need to. Glances back at Caleb. Back to the receipt.

"It's for the Jazzmaster," Randy prompts. "Sea foam green. You sold it to him in '93?"

"I remember it . . . ," says Dylan. "It was just a long time ago. But this . . ." He seems puzzled, like he's trying to remember something.

I nudge Caleb.

"He also left me this." Caleb holds out the slim white guitar pickup.

Dylan looks at it and his eyes seem to register. "Whoa. Man, that's it, isn't it?" He takes the pickup and turns it over in his fingers. Glances back at Caleb. "He told me you might come by someday, looking for this. I never . . . I mean, I forgot I . . ." He heads into the back office.

We crane our necks and see him deep in a crammed narrow space, rummaging through stacks of those plastic units with lots of tiny drawers, like for art supplies. "Every once in a while I'd stumble across that old thing, and I'd have to remind myself why I still had it. Ahh."

Caleb fidgets beside me. I grip his hand.

Dylan returns and holds out the identical pickup. And wrapped around it, held fast by a rubber band:

A small plastic case. A DV tape.

Caleb takes it and carefully unwraps it. He opens it, confirming there's a tape inside.

"I think Eli told me it was an old bootleg or something," Dylan says. "He wanted you to have it. I didn't understand really what he was getting at. And then of course he passed. Just a couple days afterward. Made me wonder if it was a coincidence or what. The timing seemed so odd."

"There's a note in here," says Caleb.

He removes a small scrap of yellowed journal paper that's been folded neatly inside the tape case. It's from Eli's old journal, the same weathered paper we found in his gig bag. Caleb unfolds a square scrap with neatly torn edges. I can tell immediately that it's Eli's handwriting. Caleb's eyes flash from the words to me.

"Read it," I say.

Caleb nods and swallows hard.

Hey, Far Comet,

If you're reading this, then you're back at the start. I don't know if the clues I left will be enough of a show to get you through to this encore, but if they were, you're holding the keys to my final words. Writing this now, I feel like I'm lost between two worlds: one bed in the hole in the road, the other on the news of the world. There was no more going forward, when you're torn apart like that. Backward was the only way out.

But enough about me. This is about you, little man. Hopefully you're far enough away from those Candy Shell crooks that we can talk safely. And then you can wield your silver hammer and have the last word.

This tape is the Encore. For the final note, all you have to do is look inside the start. Right where I'd like to be, under the sea. Waiting for you. The peace that I found. That I know means you'll be all right.

No far comet should be alone.

—E

"It sounds like he's saying the other tape is . . . here?" I say.

"That is typical Eli," Randy says, sounding frustrated. "Still, let me see that . . ." Caleb hands over the letter. Randy starts to run his finger down the lines. "Lots of weird little Beatles references here," he says. "Lyrics. All from *Abbey Road*, I think."

"Isn't that the third missing song?" I say. "'Finding Abbey Road'?"

"What does he mean the final note is right here under the sea?"

Caleb and I share a glance. "Sea foam green," I say.

We turn to Dylan. His eyes are wide and he's nodding. "I was going to tell you, this receipt you brought . . . It isn't from when I sold Eli the Jazzmaster. It's from when he sold it back to me. The same day he left that tape."

"So the third tape is inside the guitar?" says Caleb.

"Whoa . . . ," says Dylan.

"Where is it?" Randy wonders, looking around the store. "You must still have it . . ."

"Um . . ." Dylan shakes his head, looking horrified. "That's the thing . . ."

"Holy crap, you *sold* it?" Randy nearly shouts.

"No! I'd never do that, but I . . . I donated it."

186

"Donated," Caleb repeats.

"Yeah, to the Hard Rock Cafe. Years ago now . . ." Dylan thinks to himself. "I know it was on display in their New York store for a while. . . ."

"Oh, man," says Randy, rubbing his beard.

"Here it is," I say. It's so easy to find Eli's guitar that I can't believe we never saw it before. But then again, we were never looking for it. I hold out a picture of it from the Hard Rock's site. It's right there, on the wall in New York.

"I . . . I had no idea," Dylan stammers.

"We should get to the show," Randy says, checking his watch.

"Wait," I say, trying to make sure we've put all the pieces together. I turn to Dylan. "So, are you the one who sent us the old guitar case?"

Dylan cocks his head. "Oh no. Eli . . . I don't think he sold it to me in a case. Which I maybe thought was weird at the time . . . Man, it was all so long ago."

Caleb turns over the tape. Val is reading the letter to herself. "Okay, well, thanks," Caleb says to Dylan.

Dylan nods. "Sure. It was the least I could do for Eli. Hey, can I just ask . . . what's on that little tape?"

"Probably just a bootleg, like you said," Caleb agrees. "I never got to see him live."

Dylan nods, still awestruck by the whole thing.

Back outside, the snow is still coming down, slanted by the wind and freezing our faces. We get in the van, nobody speaking yet, but I am already sending a text. An idea is exploding in my brain but I want to see if it's even possible before I mention it.

"You brought the DV recorder," Caleb asks Randy, "right?"

"Indeed," he says, revving the engine and putting it in drive. He's hunched over the wheel, hands in the ten and two positions. "Even brought a cable so we can watch it on a computer."

The van slips in the parking lot but feels more steady once we're out on the main road.

"It's great that we got that second tape," says Val. "But how are we ever going to get the third one?"

"Another tour," says Caleb. "Another time, I guess."

I listen to him say this, and feel tight inside. Because what if there isn't another time? The future is coming fast, whether it's the record labels or graduation . . . I watch my phone for a reply to the text I just sent.

Everyone is quiet. My phone finally buzzes with a reply.

Ethan: You are IN if you can make it.

The message nearly makes me scream. "Guys," I say. "What if we *did* have a gig in New York City?"

"What do you mean?" Caleb asks.

I try to play it cool but a smile cracks through. Excited? Scared? I'm both. "What if we had a gig there on Friday night?"

"Are you serious?" Jon asks.

I hold up my phone. "Ethan got us a slot at Needlefest. They had a cancellation. We wouldn't be on the promo. But . . . as cover? As a reason to check the guitar . . . Randy, if you could, we could keep driving, we could go get that tape now, and we'd have them all. I mean . . . we're already halfway there."

"I'll do it," says Randy. "How far?"

"On it," says Jon.

"We'd have to check with our parents," says Caleb. He looks around the van.

"I could talk to each of your folks personally," says Randy.

"Twenty-five driving hours to New York City," Jon reports. "And . . . two days to get back home? That's if we're driving like, nonstop."

"That sounds completely insane," says Caleb. But he's grinning.

So is everyone.

Except Val. "If we do this," she says, "we can't post about it at all. It has to be completely secret."

"Definitely," I say. I'd already been thinking it would be, since we can't arouse any Candy Shell suspicions. But seeing the way Val's eyes have widened, the way she's biting the corner of her mouth, I realize she has a bigger reason:

New York is awfully close to her mom.

And it's only a few minutes later, after we speculate more about what our parents will say when we call to ask them in the morning, scheme more about how to contact the Hard Rock, and how we'll actually get our hands on that guitar to check inside it, when I realize what this change of plans means for me:

If we go to New York, I'll be three thousand miles in the wrong place for my Stanford interview on Thursday.

"You think your parents will go for it?" Caleb asks, leaning over the seat and massaging my shoulders.

"They just might," I say. After all, they already think I had my interview. And I remind myself for the hundredth time that it's not required for admission anyway. Funny how that worked out. . . .

I don't have to lie to my parents because I already did. And they have no idea that right here and now, Summer just took the wheel and pointed her future in the opposite direction.

15

It should take us about twenty minutes to get from Dylan's to the house party, but with the snow we are crawling along. After forty-five minutes, I text the host, Jerin, and also Ethan, to update them on our progress.

"Idiots!" Randy shouts at the slowpokes in front of us. "Why is everyone in Denver driving like they've never seen snow?"

"Probably for safety," Jon groans.

Ethan: You're good. Everything's starting late anyway. You close?

Summer: Thanks. Yeah we're getting there. See you soon.

Ethan: Excellent. Can't wait!

"How's Ethan?" Caleb asks, looking over my shoulder. I feel guilty that he sees that text and furious at Ethan for the *Can't wait!* On the one hand, it doesn't mean anything, and yet on the other hand it suggests that we're pals.

"He says the first band hasn't even started yet and——"

Val cuts me off from the back of the van. "Tell him there's *snow* way we're getting there tonight." She and Matt dissolve into laughter.

Caleb and I share a worried glance. I mouth the word *schnapps* to him.

He rolls his eyes. "Val," he says carefully. "You're gonna be okay for the show, right?"

"Yes, brother." More giggling.

Caleb leans over. "Give me the bottle. We go on in an hour."

"I told you we stopped," she says in a sulk. But she hands it over anyway.

It takes fifteen more minutes until we are finally pulling up outside the large, glowing house. We've been able to hear the thumping from inside for the last block.

"I don't know where I'm going to park," says Randy, surveying the tight lines of cars on either side of the street. "Let's just unload here." He clicks on the hazards and Caleb yanks open the side door.

As I'm gathering my stuff, I hear more bubbly conversation from the back of the van.

"Does she really?" Val is saying. "I just figured she was too innocent."

"Sometimes yes, sometimes no," Matt replies. "Is that something you do?"

"Always."

That doesn't sound like conversation between two sober people.

"Come on, you guys," I say, leaning over the drums. "We're here. Big glasses of water for you both—"

"Okay!" Matt sort of jumps away, and in the glimpse I had, I feel sure that at least one or two hands were in very curious places.

"Guys . . ."

"Summ-er!" Val says. "We're good. Back off."

"Right." I have to remind myself that we're in the Red Zone, and to not say more.

The back doors pop open and a burst of snow and cold rushes in. We pile out into the biting wind, pull our coats up high, and start hauling gear toward the house. It's narrow and three stories tall, with a porch on each floor. Each is packed with people and the firefly lights of cigarettes.

We have to push our way through to the front door, and find it even more crowded inside, the biting cold exchanged for sweaty hot, but the vibe is pretty cool. The main living room is open through the second floor. Stairs lead up the wall to a balcony. Someone is working a light setup that's painting everything in spinning colors. People are packed tight on the walls and up the stairs and along the railing. The band is set up in the far corner. There's a sea of heads between us and them. Currently it's the act before us, Tender Habits. They are loud, the drums, bass, and guitar a wash of busy noise, but the lead singer has a brittle voice that cuts through, a haunting sound that has nearly everyone in the room captivated.

"Hey, are you guys Dangerheart?" A tough, older-looking girl leans into Caleb's ear. She has gray-streaked hair in two playful barrettes with big plastic kittens on them.

"Yeah, hi!" says Caleb.

"Cool okay hey I'm Jerin. You guys have perfect timing! You're on next! Right after this song! So just stay right here!"

We are stuck there in a line in the doorway until Tender Habits finishes. As they shuffle off, we shuffle on, barely having a chance to exchange hellos. Matt squeezes behind the minimal drum kit. Caleb, Jon, and Val are standing almost shoulder to shoulder, and keep bumping one another as they try to get their pedals laid out and their instruments plugged into the house amps.

I catch Matt staring off into space. "You okay?" I call to him.

"Sure," he mumbles.

"Snacks?" I ask him and everyone.

"Sugar," says Val.

"Got it." I push out of the living room and make my way to the kitchen. There's a long table piled high with a disorganized array of snack foods that's already been ravaged by the partygoers. Closest to me are two large trays of brownies, which seem like the ideal high-energy food preset. I grab a stack and hurry back to the stage. Everyone shoves them down, including Randy, who's adjusting mics for the band. Val takes the last two, leaving none for me.

"Oh, sorry," she says, actually noticing.

"It's fine," I say, grabbing the small brown suitcase we use to carry the merch. Before I leave the stage I rub Caleb's shoulder. "Good?"

He nods and kisses me between brownie bites. His eyes dart around the room. He seems nervous, but he smiles. "This is cool. See you after."

Not only are people standing mere feet from him, but they're leaning through a window from the kitchen, hanging over the balcony above. It feels a little like we are in a prison or a zoo. The age of the crowd varies, from clumps of kids our age to twentysomethings to the occasional older person. Some are chatting and laughing but most of them are staring at the stage expectantly.

I make my way back to a small table by the little sound board, where I can put out our CDs and buttons.

I hear the quick notes of Caleb and Val and Jon checking tuning. Matt hits each drum a couple times. I see them check with one another, and just before Caleb turns to the mic he glances at me. It's the last second before he will become a performer, and when our eyes meet I feel a surge of tingly energy in every part of me. I don't know if this comes across in my eyes or what but Caleb smiles brighter, like somehow we are making a connection through the ether between us. He knows me. And I know him. And it seems extra special when there are all these other people around who are about to see his thing, our thing, from the outside. I mouth *You got this*.

He nods. And they start. And they do have it. Even our half-drunk rhythm section. The set is tight, sweat-laced. They feed off the press of the crowd and at points everyone in the room is moving at once, a common pulse, the floor shaking.

When they are finished, I am mobbed for CDs. I sell a pile, give away buttons nonstop, actually get a few signatures on the mailing list, and it's fifteen minutes before I can make my way back to the kitchen to find the band.

They're all crowded by the snack table and chatting with the guys from Tender Habits.

"Photo!" I gather everyone close and we snap a selfie. Red faced, hair dripping with sweat, and big smiles. It's one of those pictures that, the moment I see it, almost makes me sad with how perfect it is, how perfect we seem right here and now.

"Hey, Summer," Jon says, sweating and smiling and looking the happiest I've seen him in weeks. "Which ones did you give us?" He points to the brownies, and I now see that there were little signs beside each of the two trays. One says *Muggle*, and one says *MAGIC*.

"Oh crap," I say. "Does 'magic' mean . . ."

"Pot?" says Randy. "I'd imagine."

I rack my brain trying to remember. I was in such a hurry but . . . "I grabbed from this first tray," I say. The bottom, Muggle one. "I'm like ninety-nine percent sure."

"Bummer," says Val, though she's smiling. "I love when someone makes a bad choice for me."

My pulse returns to normal and I start two-fisting the Cheetos like a zombie bent over a torn-open abdomen.

"Here we are." Jerin arrives, pinching the rims of three red cups in each hand. She starts to hand them around and I see that it's beer.

"One each," says Randy. "I'm going to be your annoying chaperone tonight. We have too big a day tomorrow. Whoa, not you guys though." He intercepts Val's and Matt's cups.

Val's eyes narrow. She glares at Randy like he's betrayed some code. "What the hell?"

"You two are well on your way," he says.

"Great set!" Jerin says. "Everybody raved about you." She gives Caleb a big hug. Lead singers get the most hugs. I try not to mind.

"We should definitely—" Jerin begins. "Oh-oh." Something catches her eye and she moves to the snack table. "Somebody's being naughty. I hope you guys hadn't moved to dessert yet."

She proceeds to switch the two brownie signs.

"Oh, man," Randy groans.

I don't lose Caleb for the first hour. If anything, he's trying too hard to prove to me that he's not feeling any effect from the pot-laced dessert.

"They take at least an hour to kick in," Randy informed us, like a doctor delivering terminal news. "We'll have to stay here until at least . . ." He checks his watch. "Two or three a.m. before I'll be able to drive us to the hotel."

"You could just have one, too," Caleb says to me as we lean on the balcony railing, waiting for Postcards to start. "Then we'd be in the same place." I know he doesn't mean it to sound pressure-y but I can't help feeling that anyway. I've tried pot once and I didn't love it. And maybe had my timing been different and I'd accidentally had one tonight, then sure, I could have just gone with it. But now I feel like I need to be the responsible one and that leaves me feeling left out. I know nobody intended it that way, and I know I'm sort of dooming that to happen by being withdrawn right now, but I can't help it.

I've already traded my allotted cup of beer for soda. Even that feels like too much pressure now.

"Gonna find the bathroom," says Caleb, kissing my ear. "I'll be right back."

Fifteen minutes later, he's still gone when Postcards starts. And so I end up watching the first half of their set alone.

It's a cool vantage point, looking down at them crammed into a corner, surrounded by people. It's weird though, too. They sound decent, even if their acoustic set has robbed some of their urgency. Ethan is as strong as ever. Maybe better in a way. I might just be applying what I know about how his last year has gone, but he sounds more wounded. Mark, the drummer, is solid and understated as ever, and Pete has always been the glue on bass. Also, I am having flashbacks to how much I used to like these songs. Some of them connect to memories of the better times with that band, with Ethan . . .

And then even though Caleb isn't around, I still feel guilty thinking about this, enjoying the set, and UGH—is there any way to ever be in the moment and relaxed when it involves the past? I'm sure I'm over the Ethan/Postcards thing but if I really was then I wouldn't be overthinking it now.

My phone buzzes against my leg.

Maya: Please tell me you know what's up with Matt.

Oh, crap.

Summer: What do you mean?

Maya: he says he can't make it to my grandmother's birthday party on Thursday, now. I feel like he's avoiding me.

Hello, complicated. Even though she knows about Denver, we still decided not to tell her about New York yet, to keep Jason off our scent. I know it's not cool to be keeping her in the dark like this. What should I say back?

Maya: It's Val, isn't it? Just tell me.

Hello, double complicated.

I should tell her. I shouldn't tell her. I feel torn in two. It's none of my business when it comes to the Val-Matt situation.

Or, it's totally my business.

But this is the reddest of Red Zones. I can't risk our mission to New York. I just can't. Maya will calm down. I'll talk to Matt and we'll tell her that we've got a surprise show. That we don't want Jason to know but it's not about her. We'll tell her all that . . .

Tomorrow. For now:

Summer: Hey! Just finished the set in Denver. Um, ?? I haven't seen Matt in a bit. The party is packed. I'll track him down and see what's up. But I don't think you need to worry.

Maya: Thank you! I don't know though . . . Things have been weird. Tell him I really want to hear from him tonight . . .

Summer: Will do. I think it's okay though! Will you be up late? We have to load out soon so it could be a little bit before he has a chance to text.

I know I'm managing her, and I hate it! But I don't know what else to do.

And when Maya doesn't reply, I wonder if she feels that, too.

I could ask her. But no, right now, I gotta find Matt.

I push through the crowd, still rapt with Postcards. They're playing "Never Leaving You," which I bet is their last one. I don't want to hear this one anyway. It reminds me way too much of the worst parts of last summer.

As I make my way downstairs, I suddenly have a creeping sense of being completely alone, like all these people know each other and I'm the weird alien who doesn't fit.

They all seem to eye me sideways as I push past their shoulders, like they're annoyed by my presence.

"You looking for your boys?" Jerin asks when she sees me wandering across the kitchen. "Try the basement."

I descend a rickety wooden staircase. The sound of the band is muted down here. There's a tinny stereo playing and the telltale tock-tock of Ping-Pong.

I find Jon and Caleb on one side of the table, taking on Randy.

"All right, ready?" Randy has become a fluid, bendy version of himself, crouched and glaring across the table. Jon and Caleb are dancing back and forth on their toes. Randy slams a serve and Caleb makes a flourish of trying to return it but the ball shoots up and bounces off the rafters. It lands back on the table, bouncing straight up and down. The three guys stare at it and burst out laughing. I guess I could find the upside here: Jon and Caleb are getting along better than they have in months.

Randy sees me first and his eyes clear up. "Hey, Sum. Don't worry, I got this under control. No better way to pass the high time than Ping-Pong."

"Hey." Caleb looks my way and his eyes swim to find me, like we're separated by fog. He steps toward me but it feels more like he's coming at me. His too-big smile, his red cheeks and lurching steps, and yet I might just be imagining that because I know he's high. He wraps me in a hug and kisses my head. "I was wondering where you were."

I don't even want to deal with him right now, but I can't help saying, "I was where you left me. When you said you'd be right back." I know I sound like Summer the bitch. But I also don't have the energy to hide it.

Caleb pulls back and looks at me quizzically. His eyes swim. "Oh, right, you told me you'd be right back."

"No, actually—"

"Come on, game on!" Jon shouts.

"Go ahead." I give Caleb a shove back toward the table. I could say that I meant it to be playful but I know I deliver it one notch too hard and he stumbles.

"Whoa." But then he and Jon just crack up more.

"Do you want to join in?" Randy asks. He's laughing a little less hard.

I honestly wish I could just say yes. Just relax and roll with it, but that isolated feeling has become overwhelming, claustrophobic in its emptiness. "No. Have you guys seen Matt? Or Val?"

Randy's brow scrunches. Every move he makes is cartoonish. "Not for . . ." He counts on his fingers. "A while? Oh!" He slaps his pockets like he's remembering something. "Val came and got the keys to the van. She said she needed to get something."

"Where's the van?"

Randy consults the ceiling. "Two blocks . . . that way." He points toward the wall. "Or that way." He points in the other direction.

"Perfect."

The sarcasm goes completely over Randy's stoned head. "I could help you find it— Oh yeah!" Jon, not listening to me at all, had served the ball and Randy hits a vicious return.

"That's cool," I say, already heading up the stairs. "I'm on it."

I struggle through the crowd to the merch table to get my coat. A DJ has taken over and the room is engulfed in dancing. She's really good, but the way the beats are vibrating the house and the crowd is all wrong for me right now. The lights have gotten darker, and I feel like everyone I push past is leering or judging as if with every second that I am sober and they are not, the further they devolve into late-night zombies, the more likely they'll eat me alive.

I push my way to the front door, and am relieved to feel the cold air and space on the front porch. There are fewer people out here now. Clusters smoking and talking softly. I zip my coat and hurry past them, down the steps.

A gust of wind buffets me and sideways snow strafes my face. I wrap my arms tightly around myself and dig my chin into my collar. People really live in this weather by choice?

"Summer!"

I turn to see Ethan disengaging from one of those porch groups and running after me.

He throws his cigarette down in the snow and pulls up his collar. "Where you off to?"

"I've gotta find our van. The band got stoned and there are two members who are maybe hooking up in it." As I say this, I flash back to a year ago, when Ethan and I used to spend considerable alone time in his station wagon after sets. Man! When did life become a minefield?

Ethan stares at me seriously for a second and I wonder if that's what's on his mind, too, but then he bursts out laughing. "Wow, you guys are really embracing the true spirit of tour. Well, let's go." He starts up the sidewalk.

"You don't need to come with me."

"It will be fun," says Ethan. "Plus, I heard there's a gyro place nearby that's open late."

When I hesitate for another second, he says: "I won't make it weird. Promise."

"Fine." Also, a gyro sounds like heaven.

We head up the street. Everything is coated on its windward side with an inch-thick crust of snow. The edges of the world are curved and softened. By the time I am a few steps into the street, the tinkling fragments of conversation have been muffled, the thumping of bass seems distant, and there is only a sort of wide silence and the papery patter of flakes.

Ethan pulls out a pack of cigarettes and starts lighting up. "Want one?"

I shake my head. "No. I'm little miss abstinence tonight."

"That's a good thing," he says, blowing smoke.

"I thought I got you to quit last year," I say.

"Yeah, you were weird like that. Trying to get me to behave in ways that were actually good for me." He nods to the cigarette. "Last few months have been a ride, what can I say?"

This statement immediately makes me want to ask him to elaborate. But this is Ethan: isn't that exactly what he's going for? "Your set sounded good," I say instead.

"Thanks, it was okay. This was a cool gig." He says it with a sigh.

"But . . ."

"Ah, I just thought our days of playing house parties were over. If you told me last summer that I'd be here tonight, I'd never have believed you."

"Yeah, well, that makes two of us."

"It makes me feel like even more of an idiot than I already did for losing you."

Oh boy. *Checking shield integrity . . . still intact, sir!* "You got a good offer," I say.

"Maybe. Your offer from Candy Shell is better."

"You heard about that?"

"Enough." He blows smoke away from me. "In spite of what we've gone through, if you wanted my advice I'd say to take the deal."

"Hmm," I say, not sure how else to respond.

We turn onto the next block. There is no sign of the

stalker van. There is, however, the tiny gyro restaurant on the corner. "It must be a mirage," Ethan jokes. "Mind if we stop?"

I squint through the snow looking for the van. Meanwhile, my stomach growls. "If it's quick."

"You guys caught a break with that Eli White connection," Ethan says inside, as we wait for our order.

I busy myself brushing snow off my hat and shoulders. This is not a conversation I want to have. No comparing the two bands with Summer in the middle. Besides . . . "It's not really a break from Caleb's point of view. But it is a good thing for publicity and stuff." I have to stop there. Can't tell him about the lost songs. Then it occurs to me: he may already know about them. What if the reason for this walk tonight, hell, for Denver and Needlefest, is because Jason told Ethan and has recruited him to gather information?

But I don't think so. I know Ethan well enough to know that he always has some other agenda, but I don't think that's it.

We get our sandwiches, sit in a booth, and start wolfing them down. I didn't realize how hungry I was for something not from a rest area.

"Summer," Ethan says, and I don't like the weight of him saying my name. Too many ghosts associated with that sound. I don't even want to make eye contact with him, but I force myself to.

Ethan is making a face that I remember, his *I'm-about-to-be-honest* face. I made up my mind afterward that this was always a calculation by him, except now I have to say, it feels real, just like it always did. He is either some kind of Jedi . . .

Or maybe we are all just complicated.

But then I wonder: if not the lost songs, maybe his real motivation is some kind of rekindling with me. Except it hasn't really seemed like that either. It's possible that I should cut him a little bit of slack.

"I'm really sorry about last year," he says. "I wanted to tell you that before now, I just wasn't sure if you'd even want to hear it."

He's probably right about that. But I'm surprised to find that while this is causing all of my nerves to ring, it is maybe because I'm relieved. "Thanks," I say.

"I'm glad Caleb and the new band are good. And I'm glad we're doing this gig together. Maybe we can be friends going forward?"

I don't quite know how to respond, and he adds: "Business friends?" He sticks out his hand.

"Business friends. Sure." We shake. I keep it short.

We finish our sandwiches and head back out into the snow. We are three blocks away from the house when I finally spot the van.

The windows are dark.

"They're probably already back at the party," I say. But

if I really thought that, I wouldn't be feeling short of breath.

I grab the back door handle and yank it open.

"Oh fuck!"

There is a flurry of movement as orange streetlight floods in, and in the blur I see Matt lying back against a drum case with his shirt unbuttoned—and then there is Val, her bare shoulder and her bare back and I have a second to feel this weirdly parental relief that their jeans are still on—

I also see the peach schnapps bottle nearby.

And I notice that my bag, along with the others, has been used as a sort of pillow and YUCK.

"What the hell!" Val shouts, pulling her hoodie across herself.

"You guys!" I say. I don't even know what to do with this. "God, get dressed! Matt, Maya has been texting me about you."

"Why?" he whines as he pulls on his shirt.

"Probably because she's your girlfriend!"

Val leaps forward into the van and gets herself organized. I reach in and grab the schnapps bottle. It's only about a quarter full now.

"Classic," says Ethan, grinning at the show.

I look at the bottle and just smash it on the street.

"Hey!" Val snaps, giving me a lethal glare.

"What's going on with you?" I shout. "You have to stop."

"You have NO IDEA what I'm dealing with!" she screams, and suddenly tears are springing from her eyes. She throws open the side door and stalks back up the street, no coat, snow sticking to her sweatshirt.

"Val . . ." Matt slips out the back. "Give her a break," he says to me. "She needs our support, not a nag." The words would sting more if the delivery wasn't slurred by alcohol and pot, but I still feel their impact.

Matt stalks off, too, and I find myself standing there.

"Well, that was worth it," says Ethan. He flinches and pulls his phone from his pocket. "Ah," he says, "my guys are loading out. You ready to go back?"

I look into the van. "Damn, I don't know if Val has the keys or not." I can't lock the van if the keys are inside. And I can't risk leaving it unlocked. Our bags are still in there, and our amps. And when I picture the crowded party, my stoned band mates . . . "I'm just going to stay here."

"What?" says Ethan. "Nah, come back."

"No, seriously. You go. I have my phone."

Ethan's mouth scrunches. "Am I allowed to say I'd worry about you?"

I shake my head. "Not really."

"All right, then. So you guys are really going to drive to New York?"

"We have to clear it with our parents," I say, yawning. "But I think so. I'll let you know by tomorrow afternoon."

"Cool. Okay." He pauses like he thinks we might hug. I

209

don't move. "See you soon, then."

He turns and heads back up the block.

Watching him go, I feel a mix of things. Maybe one part relieved. The part of me that's been huddled in a cell these last nine months, that part that simply cared for him, is allowed a few hours out in the prison yard now.

Another part is exasperation with Matt and Val and really everyone. Even Caleb. I want him around right now and it's not his fault he's stoned but I'm annoyed anyway.

But stronger than all of those is the wave of exhaustion rolling over me. I close the back door of the van, slide the side shut. I lock all the doors and crawl into the Spa, then text Caleb and Randy.

Summer: I'm in the van. Val has keys? Or not. If you need me I'll be here catching a nap.

None of my stoned companions reply.

I stare out the frosty window. The wind has kept the glass mostly clear. Flakes are running in herds diagonally through the orange cones of streetlight.

I shiver at the cold, but weirdly I find that, worrisome dramas aside, I feel the best I have in the last hour. Being solitary suits me right now. Just a girl in a car on a random street in Denver. And the gig was a success, at least from a playing-music-to-people perspective. Everything else might be a mess, but I don't want to think about it until tomorrow.

16

It's almost five a.m. when the band returns to the van. We drive to the Holiday Inn, nobody speaking, and crash, agreeing to reconvene at ten.

I wake up to knocking on the door. It feels like only a second has passed.

"You guys decent?" It's Randy.

I throw on my clothes. Val is still dead to the world.

"Everybody's a go," says Randy. "Amazingly, the parents all trust me. Did you call yours yet?"

"No," I say. I grab my phone and when I open it, I find three texts waiting:

Maya: So . . . never heard from Matt.

Maya: And I have reason to believe you guys are keeping things from me again.

Oh no.

Ethan: Mornin' sunshine. Get any sleep?

Sunshine? Ugh. This all feels like way too much to deal with.

I call my dad at work. I've been sending him and Mom photos from the trip, so they roughly know how it's going. After a couple minutes recapping the safe details about last night, I launch into it.

"We had this amazing opportunity come up," I say. "One of the bands last night offered us a slot at this huge pop festival in New York called Needlefest. It's happening this week, and we were thinking since we're already on the road . . ."

"You want to drive to New York City for another show? Isn't that kind of far?"

"Yeah, but, it's worth it. I mean, since we're off school, anyway. Randy's game to go. The other parents said it's okay. You can talk to him if you want . . ."

"No, that's okay. We trust you, Cat . . ."

That makes me queasy. If they only knew that right after this I'm going to email Andre and cancel the interview they think I already had.

"I mainly feel bad for you," Dad continues, "spending that many hours in the car, but I suppose you think that's fun. Let me call your mom and talk it over, okay? I'll get back to you in a minute."

"Okay, thanks, Dad."

"Think they'll bite?" Randy asks.

My phone buzzes thirty seconds later.

Dad: Ok. Have an adventure! Keep sending us pictures and updates.

"We're good," I say. And though I'm excited, I can't quite smile when I say it.

"Rock and roll!" says Randy, though he sounds exhausted. "Okay, wake up Valerie. We need to be on the road ASAP."

A half hour later we are back in the van and waiting in a McDonald's drive-through and the email I've composed on my phone reads:

Dear Andre,

I am so sorry to say that I can't make the interview on Thursday. I'm on tour with my band and we just got a show opportunity that's too good to pass up, so we won't be back until Sunday, which I realize is too late to meet. Thank you so much for your time! Hopefully I'll still have what it takes to get into Stanford, but if not, at least I'll have this adventure.

Thanks again!
Catherine

In a way, it feels like the most honest I've been to anyone about the choices I'm making. I guess I'm hoping that somehow this will spark Andre to say something nice to the admissions office about me, or maybe just cause the fates to smile more kindly. That is, if I want them to.

I don't know! So I hit send before the nervous energy in my gut makes me second-guess it.

I take a shift driving in Kansas. My nap in the van last night has left me slightly more awake than the others. But after a couple hours, the road gets blurry and I trade with Randy for the Spa. He keeps driving and driving. Everyone else is sacked out hard in the back. Jon is snoring.

"How do you do it?" I ask groggily.

"Lots of years, lots of miles," says Randy. "And lots of band mates too wasted to drive."

I doze on and off as the miles of flat, frost-covered white roll by out the window. The sky is a featureless gray from one end of the horizon to the other. Eventually, the guilt that I feel about the email to Andre, about deceiving my parents, fades, and I start to feel excited again. All of that worry belongs in a world behind us, and now we are on a new map. Like we have left our known galaxy by making this choice. The rogue drive to New York City is a trip into another world, and now anything is possible. We don't know where we will eat next, where we will sleep next, any of it.

It's kind of amazing.

I drift off again, and when my eyes open, dry and sore, I see that Caleb is driving. And I hear Randy behind us saying, "Okay, Thursday at three. That will totally work. We'll see you then." He puts away his phone. "The Hard Rock still has the guitar on display," he reports. "The

214

curator, Lara, said she'd let Caleb pose with it if they were allowed to use the photos."

"What about looking inside it?" Caleb asks.

"I figure we wait to ask until we're there and it's in our hands, and then we explain how we want to open up the back and take a look. That way, no time for a supervisor to mull it over and say no."

"We're getting really close," I say, reaching over to hold Caleb's hand.

"Yeah," he says, and almost smiles, but not quite.

Two hours later, Matt lurches up from his coma. "Stop the van," he grunts.

"Emergency?" Randy asks, changing lanes.

"Yup," Matt groans. "Quick."

"One sec . . ." Randy veers to the breakdown lane and pumps the brake. We shudder over the snow and ice and slide to a stop.

Matt tumbles over Val and Jon, waking them both, yanks open the side door, and stumbles out. He hits his knees on the plow pile, doubles over, and pukes. The brown liquid steams and seeps into the snow like alien blood.

He hurls again, then goes to wipe his mouth with his sleeve.

"Use snow," I say, joining him. He rubs a handful across his face. Then he staggers to his feet and leans against the side of the van, breathing hard. "You okay?"

"Better."

Wind whips at our sweatshirts. The reflection of sun off the snow makes it nearly impossible to see.

When Matt has gathered himself, I say, "I got texts from Maya. She knows something's up."

"Yeah, she's pissed."

"You need to call her."

He nods. "All right."

"No, dummy. Now," I say. "You seriously need to call her right now."

"What am I supposed to say?"

"At the minimum? That you're sorry. Whatever else you want to say is up to you."

"Right." Matt gets out his phone and trudges around to the back of the van.

I get back in. We can hear the muted sounds of him talking. When his voice starts to rise, Randy turns up the radio.

Ten minutes later, he climbs in. "Well, that was easy," he mutters, pale and shaking from the cold, and hungover.

"Everything okay?" I ask.

"We broke up." He collapses back on the van floor.

On cue, my phone buzzes.

Maya: You know, Jason told me about those lost songs months ago, but I would totally have kept your secret if you'd trusted me. I guess we were never really friends. You were just using me.

My stomach drops out.

Maya: Have a great trip.

My first instinct is to defend myself, to defend anything, but . . .

Summer: I am so sorry. Maybe we can talk when we're back.

Maya doesn't reply.

We reach Indiana before everyone is too bleary to keep driving, so we check into this highway-side motel called Relaxation Depot. Randy doesn't mind putting these rooms on his card and we promise to pay him back with gig money.

We eat mealy food at a Cracker Barrel and collapse in our rooms.

Caleb knocks on our door around nine. "We've got the video camera set up."

We gather in the guys' room and Randy plays the tape from Dylan's.

Just like on Eli's earlier tapes, there is a blank blue screen with a date in the top corner in white numbers: 7/30/98.

"This is later in the summer," Randy says. "Post band breakup."

As the seconds pass I have that same worry that nothing will happen. That we are chasing nothing . . .

But then there is a wash of light, the screen becoming pure white and then darkening. There is Eli, backlit by a sunny apartment window. At first, the camera adjusts to the outside light, making Eli a silhouette against the brownstones and the fire-escape bars out the window, but then it finds him. When it brightens, we see that he's grown a scruffy beard. His eyes are rimmed by dark circles.

"Hey, far comet." His voice sound more raspy and beaten than last time. He coughs hard, the camera shudders, and then he turns it so we can see that he's sitting on a couch in a small, disheveled apartment.

"Welcome to the Summer Soho sessions," he says over the rattle of the air conditioner. "There is where I've been—*cough*—hiding out. . . ." His eyeballs dart around the room and he makes a weird half smile. He's jittery. He looks thinner than on the first tape.

"Okay." He grabs his guitar from the couch. "This one . . . This is from the great beyond." He starts to strum, dark and fast, and sings, eyes closed:

I made the hard choice
I took the easy way out
Either one or maybe neither
Doesn't matter now

Cause I'm on the other side
I've been memorialized
The painted picture is so much more beautiful
Than the mess inside

But when I say
I'm all better now

There's no one to hear
And when I announce
I've got one more
No one applauds

So replace my circuitry
With memories of you
And I'll play an encore
To an empty room

Replace my broken memories
With a message to you
It's just another encore
To an empty room

We're quiet when it's done.

"Well, that's a beautiful song," Val says bitterly. She stands. "I'll be in our room."

"You okay?" I ask her. I know it's a dumb question.

"I will be." She heads for the door.

"Want to talk about it?" Matt asks.

"Not really."

A few minutes later, we hear the slap of her bass strings through the thin walls.

I feel a touch of Val's anger. Why would someone end their life when they could write things this beautiful? But that's so often how it goes. The light is made more brilliant by the intensity of the dark behind it. We wonder how that beauty could not be enough . . . and yet we'll never know what Eli was going through. What it really felt like to be him on the inside. All we know is that he couldn't live with it.

I stay with Caleb afterward. For a while, we just stare at the sports highlights that Jon turns on.

Then, slowly, Caleb comes back from inside his head. "It's so weird to hear him," he says. "And I don't understand how the guy in that video ends up killing himself like two months later."

"I don't either."

I see Caleb's brow working. Then he adds, "I feel like the lyrics he writes, I could have written them, sort of."

"Is that a good thing?"

He shrugs. "Kinda. I mean, it makes me worry about me. I don't want to end up like him. It's hard to see him in these videos. Like, having a real person to miss is worse. But hearing the songs makes me feel like we're connected. I think that's a good thing. I don't know. It all feels so mixed-up inside."

I run my fingers through his hair. "Can I tell you a secret?"

"Sure."

"I think your songs are better than his."

He shakes his head. "Nah."

"Yours have the same emotion, but with more . . . hope,

I guess. I know you worry about being like him, and you are, but you're also like a better version of him."

He kisses me. "Well, if you want to think that, it's okay with me."

I put my head on his shoulder, and he lays his atop mine. We knot and unknot our fingers. I feel like we are closer than ever, and yet also like he is still distant, still lost in his head. And a surprising thought crosses my mind, now that it's too late: maybe finding this second song is enough. Maybe we shouldn't continue the search. Because the further we go, the closer we get to Eli's death. And I am starting to wonder if we really want to know what we'll find.

It's nearly eleven on Thursday night when we finally roll into New York City. All of us perk up at the sight of the long, glowing skyline. Maybe we catch a whiff of the possibility this place holds.

We had plans to go look around the sights in Midtown, to get pizza, but everyone's too tired.

The boys are staying with Randy's cousin Dave. Val and I are staying at her friend and former band mate Neeta's apartment. The boys drop us off in the East Village on their way to Brooklyn.

"I've got to put in the family time," says Caleb. "I'll miss you. We'll hang out tomorrow, though. Right?"

"Definitely." We kiss until everyone is annoyed, and then Val and I get out.

Neeta goes to NYU and lives with two other girls in a studio apartment with a loft. Two of them sleep up there and one on the couch in a rotating cycle. When we arrive, the three girls are deeply immersed in a multiplayer video game where they are sexy Amazonian-style warriors mowing down some thuggish male army.

Val, who may not have spoken a single word the entire day, brightens up when we arrive and jumps right in with them. We order pizza. There is small talk. Mostly about bands and former boyfriends. Also I learn that Neeta is a freshman and thinking of a major in International Relations.

Val grabs a beer from the fridge, and catches me watching her. "I'm good," she says. "I'm over it."

I don't know if I believe her, but she's nursing the same one an hour later when I start to fall asleep in my seat. I excuse myself to my makeshift bed on the floor, leaving Val to bond with her old friend.

My head feels full of thoughts about Denver, about tomorrow and learning more of Eli's dark past, about the interview I'm missing, but I'm so tired, I fall asleep almost the moment my head hits the pillow.

"Summer."

I roll over and find Val lying beside me, propped on her elbow. She's wearing a tank top, her hair just-showered wet. It hits me in a fuzzy, just-waking way, that Val is pretty hot. Or more like . . . primal? Elemental? Neither of those are quite right. It's something, though.

Also, she's just staring at me.

"What?" I roll over, my back aching. I slept on a yoga mat, huddled under a meager blanket. I tap my phone. "It's only eight."

I'm aware now of the layers of snoring from around us. From the loft, the couch. There's a lump in the kitchen, hugging an enormous killer whale pillow.

"Are you awake?" Val asks.

"Um, now that you woke me up. What's going on?" My mouth tastes like the arm of a couch.

"We need to go."

"Where?"

She's still gazing at me, her eyes sideways, and except for my assumption that she's human, and given that humans blink on average every ten seconds, I can't be sure that her eyelids have actually moved.

"Princeton," she finally says.

I sit up. My head swims with fuzzy exhaustion. "Wait. Why?"

"There's a couple things I forgot when I split. It's okay. Mom and the boyfriend will be at work."

"Isn't that really risky? Aren't we trying to be sure they don't know you're here?"

She nods. "Please."

I shiver. This apartment is frigid. "Okay. But I demand a quality New York bagel and coffee."

I dig into my bag for my toiletry kit, then shuffle into the bathroom. In the clinical fluorescent light, I don't like what I see. The dark circles under my eyes. Hair matted and brittle with the winter dry. My cheeks and lips seem limp, like I've aged two decades on this tour.

I sit on the ice-cold toilet, brushing my teeth. A spear of yellow hits my face. The sun cresting the craggy line of rooftops outside, the light splayed by ice crystals in spiking patterns on the glass. It's beautiful and alien. Deodorant, water on my face, can't find soap anywhere. Oh well.

"There's a nine forty-five train we need to catch if we want to meet the boys at the Hard Rock," Val says as I get on my coat.

I glance at my bag, feeling the urge to bring it, but also not wanting to lug it all day. "We're coming back here, aren't we? I need to shower and stuff."

"Definitely. Come on."

We slip out. Our breath makes clouds as we descend the flights of warped stairs. Outside, I check my email and realize my battery is at about half. Forgot to charge it overnight, and . . . damn, just left the charger back in the apartment.

"I need to go back," I say.

"We don't have time. Unless you want to skip the coffee."

Coffee or guaranteed battery life? No one should have to choose between these two things, ever . . . "Coffee."

We file along with the swift pace of the sidewalk crowd, then wait in line for bagels that don't disappoint and coffee that does. Val goes for the lox and onions, I just stick with plain cream cheese. The bagel is somehow crispy and chewy and well worth needing to ration my battery usage all day.

The sky is frigid blue, too cold for clouds. The steam billowing from vents and building tops has a cottony weight, its edges aglow with the bright, angled sun. We pass through gusts of hot-dog smell, pretzel smell, shawarma smell, through packs of tourists and schools of commuters. The wind gusts between the buildings and each time I shiver and hunch over further and just try to keep up with Val, who is like a mole burrowing through the woolen shoulders.

We duck into a subway station and grab the 6 uptown. We sit on the smooth seats and Val's head lolls back against the window, sunglasses still on, her skin corpse gray.

"How are you doing?" I ask her.

"Ugh. I feel like death."

"Did you drink more last night?"

"Don't get all after-school special on me, Catherine. I've had friends who were in rehab at fifteen. Do you know what it's like to drink a fifth of vodka before first period?"

"No."

"Neither do I. But I know what it's like to drag that person to the car and the ER. I also know what it feels like to be too late. . . ."

She sits up, clasping her hands and staring at the floor. "Neeta is one of my good friends from back in those days. And yes, I am aware that ever since Christmas I've been drinking too much and acting out, and any good shrink would say that this is due to the mounting psychological pressure of proximity to my mother. My mother with a drug problem. Does Val have her mom and dad's same weaknesses? Will she succumb to those same vices? Find out this week on *Children of the Dead and Negligent*."

I smile. "Yeah, well, you've given us reason to worry, don't you think?"

"I'm not proud. So, how's Ethan?" she asks, as if she'd actually answered my question.

"Still Ethan," I say. "Why?"

"You two had a romantic stroll after hours in Denver, that's why."

"I was looking for you. And also avoiding a contact high and not fitting in."

"See, this is exactly my point," says Val. "You had your reasons. I'm going to respect those reasons."

"I respect yours."

"Actually, I believe you. Just tell me you didn't . . . with Ethan . . ."

"Ugh, no! You mean like what you did with Matt?"

Val smiles devilishly. "I know, I'm terrible. But you know what's even better at reducing stress than drugs . . ."

I shoot her a look of feigned shock. "Caleb and I have not had nearly enough time for that this week with Randy around."

"Ugh." Val wrinkles her nose. "You are talking about my brother."

"Yup. And this is what he likes." I do a little shimmy.

Val completely cracks up. I'm pretty sure it's the first time I've ever made her laugh.

Then she says, "But Ethan's into you."

"He's only into me because he can't stand to have

anyone hate him. And because I'm around. I can handle it. And being business friends with him is better than being enemies."

"Business friends? That sounds hot."

"Shut up. It's so not hot. What's hot is when me and your brother—"

"Okay, okay. Fair enough."

I can't believe Val and I are dishing about boys, but then a cloud crosses her face and she sighs and slips in her earbuds without a word.

We change trains and get to Penn Station. Val hustles us to a ticket machine, and we run for the Princeton-bound train.

We settle into higher backed, softer seats, and as the train pulls out and shuttles through a dark tunnel, I succumb to dry-eyed sleep.

My phone wakes me, buzzing against my leg. I pull myself up from the sweatshirt pillow I'd propped against the window. Outside the world is bright and white and brown. Old snow and bare trees.

Val is wide-awake beside me, staring at the scenery. I wonder how it feels to be coming home. I'd ask her, but her earbuds are still in, the music loud enough that I can hear its tinny echoes.

I get out my phone and find the screen full.

Caleb: Good morning in New York! Are you guys up yet?
(1hr ago)

Caleb: Slept like the dead last night. We're going for food. What are you and Val up to? Holler if you want to meet us. Randy knows all the diners. *(44min ago)*

Ethan: Welcome to the big city. Up to anything fun today? *(33min ago)*

Caleb: Hello? Did Val and her friends kill you? At a cool spot in Park Slope. *(19min ago)*

"Don't tell him where we are," says Val. She's looking over my shoulder. "He'll freak."

I glance at her. And so we are bonded by secrets.

And I know she also saw that Ethan text.

Which I am not replying to. I do write back to Caleb:

Summer: Ah, sorry I missed these! We just got up and walked for coffee. Left my phone charging. Val says it's like an hour out to where you are. We feel like lounging. Girl time. They have lots of Us Weeklys here.

Summer: Just meet at the Hard Rock? Is the plan still 3?

Caleb: Hey! Sure, that's cool. Funny to imagine you and Val reading gossip mags.

Summer: It is the midpoint between us.

I feel a little sick typing this.

Caleb: Randy thinks we should do HRC at 2, to be safe. We're going to drop off our gear at the club first.

Shit. It's already 10:25.

"Just tell him I'm grumpy about that," Val says, still reading along. "That will buy us the extra time."

Caleb: Ha. Well tell her to deal.

Summer: Will do. See you soon. xo

I resist the usual social media business I would normally attend to. Have to save battery. Not that I can post any photos from this clandestine trip anyway. A secret journey within a secret journey.

Instead, I lean back and watch the yards and houses sliding by.

We have to transfer to another train, and after a fifteen-minute wait in the paralyzing cold, we are nearing our destination.

"It's about a fifteen-minute walk from the station," says Val quietly. Her eyes have gotten clear and wide. I don't know if I have ever seen her nervous before.

"Now arriving, Princeton station."

We cross the platform, use the bathrooms, and then walk along the icy sidewalks through tree-lined streets, the sun on the snow blinding us.

"Are you worried anyone will see you?" I ask.

"Nah." Val walks hunched into her coat, just looking straight ahead. "I didn't hang out with that many people. Just band mates."

"You were on the cross-country team," I add.

Val looks almost impressed. "Spying on me, huh? Here,

I'm hungry." She ducks into a Dunkin' Donuts.

"You know," I say as we stand in line, "for a few weeks there, I thought you had come to join Dangerheart so you could steal the lost songs. That you were actually teamed up with your mom."

"That's hilarious." Val orders a dozen chocolate Munchkins. "Like my mom could be counted on to remember anything."

We keep walking. Past an idyllic school, kids playing on the plowed blacktop. Through more quiet streets. Finally Val stops.

"There."

Based on the stories, I guess I'm surprised to see a fairly average-looking suburban house. One story and white and cute. The mailbox has cardinals painted on it. There's still a Christmas wreath on the front door.

But there are other things: the driveway hasn't been shoveled, just a crosshatch of icy tire tracks. The garbage cans beside the house are overflowing with bags. One lies punctured on the ground, a spill of trash crusted in frost.

Val glances up and down the street of similar-style houses. "Most everybody works," she says. "Probably least conspicuous if we just go in the front door."

"You sure about this?" My heart is pounding.

"I'm sure that this is the last time I'm ever setting foot in this house."

We walk up the driveway, then an unshoveled path to the front door, our shoes punching holes in the crusted snow. Val taps the wreath. Brittle needles rain down on the icy steps. "I think this is the one we put up last year."

She tries her key and it works and we step into the warm house, the light dim through drawn blinds.

"Jesus," says Val, her nose wrinkling. The house smells like body odor, Lysol, and other chemicals I don't recognize. We're standing in a living room. Two brown recliners are aimed at a large TV perched on a rickety stand right in front of the fireplace. There are folding tables set up beside each chair, and there is crap everywhere. Newspapers and magazines, clothes, unopened mail. A particularly large pair of gray sweatpants hangs over the near recliner. There are dirty plates, empty beer bottles, an artificial Christmas tree still set up in the corner.

And there are other items on the little coffee table between the two recliners, things that likely have a drug purpose. Glass and lighters and bags.

"This way." Val is breathing in short, quick bursts.

We head into the kitchen. The counter is a junkyard of dishes and takeout boxes. There are blackened bananas, a brown head of lettuce. In the corner there's a cat box that hasn't been changed in far too long. Val pulls open the fridge and finds it nearly vacant. More takeout. Wilted frozen pizza boxes. Four large bottles of Fresca. The shelves on the door seem to be filled entirely with jars of olives.

Val peers deeper and reaches in, retrieving a prescription bottle. She reads the label. "Expired by nine months. Mom . . ."

"She has plenty of others over here," I say, noting a line of pill bottles on the counter.

Val eyes them. Likely evidence that the message she received about an illness was true.

"Fuck." Val stalks out of the kitchen. I follow her down a hallway lined on both sides with cluttered stacks of boxes, packaging, crooked stacks of magazines, lumpy piles of clothes. We pass a bathroom, its counter overrun with junk. The hall ends at two closed doors. Val opens the one to the right.

The room is surprisingly pink. The walls are striped with pink accents and there are bunches of balloons painted near each corner. The rug is lime green. There was probably once a cute set of kids' furniture in here but now the desk and dresser and bed are super basic.

Covering every surface like an angry scribble are black T-shirts and jeans and bras, books and notebooks and guitar magazines, band posters affixed to the wall at intentionally cockeyed angles, bottles of mascara and nail polish in every shade of black and purple. Like teenage Val graffitied over her child self.

It looks like she left for school this morning, like her room has been frozen in time. Except for a thick layer of dust on everything. I think of my parents being on my case to clean like every week. How could her mom let over a year go by and never pick this up?

"God, I hate it here," Val says quietly. Her eyes dart around, like she's taking it all in, or like she's trying to avoid memories. I can't imagine what any of this would be like. To have run away, to be back, a visitor in your own house, in your old life.

She sighs and heads for the desk, where she opens a drawer and starts rifling through a mess of pencils, photos, tape dispensers, and trinkets. She stuffs a few things in her coat pockets and then moves to her dresser. She rummages and yanks out a black T-shirt. She holds it up to me: *Kings of Leon: Only by the Night Tour*.

"First concert I ever went to on my own," she says.

"Weren't you like ten?"

"Eleven. Mom dropped me and a friend off. I think the other parents thought she was actually going in with us. One advantage to having my mom."

"It still fits?"

"I bought it big and ripped the sleeves."

Something catches her eye on the bed. She picks up a small journal, lying open. Just stares at it.

"What's that?" I ask.

"This is what I was doing . . . that night." Val holds out the notebook to me. The paper is graph-lined, which I almost comment on.

The page contains a black ink sketch of a waifish girl

with anime features. She's wearing a leather dress and has bat-like wings half folded behind her. Shading on her arms, legs, and face makes her look almost like she's made of stone. Her fingers are curved, claw-like, with long nails.

A wild scribble of ink slashes diagonally over the figure, and also, here and there are small drops of dark red. Dried blood, I think. They almost look intentional.

"That's Garr," says Val quietly. "I was taking a graphic novel class. She was my hero. Stuck for eternity as a gargoyle but she could be unfrozen by pure sorrow. Once she was alive, she'd be bonded to help the victim who awakened her, except as soon as their sorrow lifted, she'd be sentenced back to stone. She's like a thousand years old but she's only lived like forty days since she was cursed at sixteen."

"Wow," I say. "That's so completely cool."

Val seems stunned by the drawing, as if she'd forgotten it existed.

"You're really good," I add. "That drawing is amazing."

She shrugs and runs her finger over the outline of Garr's wing.

"I know a kid back at Mount Hope, Miley, who runs an online comic site. She could help you get it posted somewhere."

Val raises an eyebrow at me. "Is this what Caleb means by how you manage him?"

"Oh, I guess. Sorry."

"Don't be. That sounds cool." Her gaze drifts to the

hall. "There's one more thing I need." She heads out the door, across the hall, and carefully opens the door to her mom's room.

"Val," I hiss, but I stop in the hall. I don't want to go into that dark room. It feels too private. I can hear her footsteps, and the squealing of a drawer. A light sound of rustling paper—

And then a whoosh of cloth. Sheets.

And a deep, groggy voice: "Mel, is that you?"

I freeze. Afraid to breathe.

There is a second of silence, and then feet padding fast over carpet. Val appears in front of me, face white, locks eyes with me, and bolts for the door.

"Mel . . . hey," the deep voice of the boyfriend is followed by more rustling and heavy footsteps on the floor.

We race through the kitchen, not bothering to step lightly anymore.

"Hey, HEY!" he calls from behind us. "What the hell?"

The bedroom door slams open.

We're back in the living room. Val pushing out the front door—

When I notice something on the wall behind the easy chairs. Every nerve is telling me to run but is that—

I dodge over and peer closer.

It's that image again, the painting of the brownstone building that was in Eli's guitar case. Only this is a photo. That house. It *has* to be the same one, on a street, an

236

intersection in the background.

Eli's never left us anything without it having a purpose. This photo might help.

"Come on!" Val is hanging onto the door, halfway down the front steps.

I can't make out the details in the gloom and scramble to get my phone out of my pocket.

"Who the fuck is there?" Footsteps lumber down the hall.

I open the camera, aim the phone, and tap at the shutter button. There's a click and the flash even goes off.

"Hey!"

I don't know if I got it but I lunge for the door and slam it behind me. We careen off the steps and sprint straight across the snow-covered lawn, stumbling as the crust shatters in toothy triangles, freezing snow scraping our ankles, but then we reach cleared sidewalk and sprint away.

Behind us, the door bursts open.

"HEY, COME BACK!"

Val is pulling her hoodie over her head. I risk one look back and see a man built out of barrels and logs but also barefoot and only in boxers and a T-shirt, standing on the front steps.

"He's not coming," I say through heaving breaths, each one an icy dagger into my chest.

"Keep going," says Val. Her cross-country muscles are probably reactivating, whereas my haven't-done-sports-things-since-JV-volleyball thighs feel like they are going to seize up.

We round the corner, and Val leads the way in a new direction.

"He's got a motorcycle," she pants. "We need to get inside."

Two blocks later we reach stores and run into a bank. Everyone glances at us like we may be there to rob the place.

We stand just inside the entryway, catching our breath. My lungs have gotten tight, each breath painful.

Sure enough, a minute later, the boyfriend, now in sweatpants, sneakers, and a helmet, cruises by on a black Harley, still in his T-shirt, screw the cold.

Val checks the train schedule on her phone. "We're going to miss the eleven forty-five. Next one isn't until one o'clock." She says this like everything's normal.

"What were you doing in their room?" I ask.

Val shakes her head. "Nothing. What was with you taking a photo?"

"There was a picture on the wall. I swear it's the same place as that little painting Eli left in his guitar case."

Val rolls her eyes. "My mom thought of herself as a photographer. You should have heard her go on and on about it when she was high. How that was her calling except then I came along and screwed it up."

"I just thought it might be important."

Val shrugs.

"Do you think he could tell who we were?"

"Who else would have a key to the house?" Val says. "But whatever. Mel will come home and he'll tell her but then they'll probably take a hit to clear their heads, and next thing you know it will be tomorrow morning and we'll be gone."

"Okay," I say, my heart still hammering.

"I hope, anyway." Val gazes up and down the street again. "Coast is clear. Come on."

We cross Princeton in clandestine spy fashion, stopping into every convenience store and shop, one time mere seconds ahead of boyfriend's cruise-by.

Finally, we make it back onto the train. I text Caleb to let him know we're running late.

Summer: We're idiots. Took the wrong subway line!! Now Val is insisting on slices at this place in NoHo.

I worry what his reaction will be until he says that he and the guys have made their way to Sam Ash guitars and are geeking out, which is a guarantee that they'll lose track of time.

We've been on the train a half an hour when I ask Val:

"So, what happened the night you left?"

She's been looking at the drawing of Garr, and the earlier ones, in the notebook. Some of the pages are ruled out into comic panels and filled with scenes, some are just loose sketches. There are also pages of handwritten script.

Val sighs, like she's considering whether or not to tell me. "You'd think it would be some big dramatic thing, but it wasn't. It was Christmas Eve. Normally we would have gone to Grandma's up in Connecticut but Mom had spent the entire fall calling Grandma 'that rat bitch.' I think because she tried to check Mom into rehab. At the time I felt like I was on Mom's side. It wasn't like she couldn't heat up frozen food for dinner, or make it to work mostly on time. She got her hours in, was maybe even a pretty good nurse. She had a temper, and probably needed counseling. But not rehab. And it was sorta like Grandma to see the drug thing but not the emotional thing. Sorry, I'm going on."

"It's okay."

Val flips back to that last drawing of Garr. "It was the stupid trash," she says. "Tuesday night is trash night, but it was Christmas Eve so, duh, no trash pickup on Christmas. But Mom comes storming into my room, lit up and not thinking it through, and starts yelling at me like, why haven't I put the trash out and why am I so lazy and why do I have to listen to the radio so loud. And I started yelling back like, do you even remember it's Christmas, and she was like yeah, but then she said I didn't deserve Christmas because I took away the one gift she ever had."

"Oh no. Did she mean Eli?"

Val nods. "Such a nice thing for her to say. That was

always the punch line, when any argument got big enough."

Val's finger runs over the blood drops on the drawing. "She threw my clock at me. Grabbed it off the desk and hurled it. Hit me right in the side of the head. . . . But . . ."

"Val . . ." I put my arm around her. She convulses, and tears come out silently. "That's awful. And it's not your fault."

"No," she whispers, "you don't understand . . . ." She taps the page. "This isn't my blood."

"What do you mean?"

"I . . . I hit her first. I was so mad and she was screaming and looking like a demon and she tore the notebook out of my hand and was all *What's this?* Because I'd never shown her any of my drawings. And I snapped, I jumped up and just . . . swung. Punched her right in the nose. Well, not like a real punch. Like a hand-half-closed, think-I-sprained-a-finger punch. Blood started pouring from her nose. Then she shoved me back on the bed, and threw the notebook at me and then the clock, and we were both like cornered animals at that point. She stormed out and I just shoved a bunch of things in my bag and took off. Started driving and didn't look back. A neighbor called the cops, I guess. But . . . I don't know if I was scared or ashamed."

"You were protecting yourself."

"Maybe. But I hit her. Sure, she'd smacked me a time or two, but I felt like I was going to kill her. Even more than she might kill me. I was just as much a monster, and I

242

needed to save her from *me*. That's why I ran."

"You weren't, though. Not really. You were scared, and you had every right to be."

"I don't know."

Val slaps the notebook closed and leans against the window.

We are silent for the rest of the trip.

She dozes off, and I open my phone and look at the photo I took. It's more blurry than I hoped. I zoom in on the corner where the words are. There's what may be a number . . . 13? And then some other text, but I can't quite make it out. There's a blurry word that maybe says *Avenue*.

I try a sharpening feature but it doesn't help. I could find an app with more rendering tools, but I see my phone is already down well under half battery.

We get back to Penn Station and beat it for the subway up to the Hard Rock. There's no service in the tunnels, and so when we finally pop up above ground, I've got a home screen full of texts again.

Caleb: on our way to the Hard Rock. You? *(1hr ago)*

Ethan: at the MoMA solo. This place never gets old! What are you up to? *(1hr ago)*

Ugh!

Maya: I'm a little bit sorry. But not too much. Just so you know. *(23min ago)*

For what?

(424) 828-3710: You don't want to miss the show there

tonight. *(16min ago)*

Spam?

Caleb: We've been waiting outside for like a half hour. What happened to you guys? *(11m ago)*

Summer: We're almost there!

Caleb: Come to the front of the line.

We jog the two blocks to the Hard Rock. Beneath its giant marquee, a line of people extends up the block, corralled by felt ropes. I feel their eyes on us as we rush past them and through the main doors.

The tiny entryway is awash in blaring Green Day. Caleb and the boys are standing by the glass doors with a young guy in a collared Hard Rock shirt.

"Man," Caleb says as we hug. "I missed you all day."

"Me, too," I say, and even though I'm relieved to be holding him I'm tensing up at the thought of dancing around the details of our trip.

"Hi, I'm Manny," the guy in the Hard Rock shirt says. "If everybody's here, then let's head inside. Right this way." We follow him into the restaurant, weaving through the rooms, their walls covered in rock memorabilia: guitars, clothes, platinum records, photos. He leads us into a room with a bar in the center. There is an area roped off with yellow twine. Inside are six chairs in a semicircle.

"We're going to have you sit here," says Manny. "Our curating manager, Lara, will bring out the guitar for you to see. We'd like to film you seeing it and holding it, and then,

244

if you agree, we'd love to get you playing a song, perhaps?"

"You mean out here?" Caleb says.

"Yes," says Manny. "It will feel like an impromptu concert. We'll let the other diners know what's happening and we'll get a great little crowd."

I grip Caleb's hand. "You can do it," I say by his ear.

He nods tightly.

A security guard pulls back the little twine barrier. We are just getting seated and a crowd is already starting to mill around. I hear the words *Eli* and *Allegiance* sneaking around the onlookers.

"We should have brought the rest of our gear," says Jon. He doesn't look thrilled with this whole situation. He and Matt and Val will just be sitting there with nothing to do.

"Okay, here it is." A professionally dressed woman with dark features and rectangular glasses emerges from the crowd. "Hi, I'm Lara." In her hands is the relic: Eli's sea foam green Jazzmaster. It has a sticker for the Posies on the white pickguard, and a long strip of paint chipped away along the side. One of the knobs is missing. She carefully hands it to Caleb.

I can practically hear his heart pounding.

"So amazing, right?" says Lara. "Caleb, how does it feel to be reunited with your dad's guitar? This must be some moment for you."

Manny is already taping, the red light glowing on a handheld camera.

Caleb runs his hands over the strings. "It's a lot," he says. He strums it quietly.

"Now," says Lara, "we understand that you have a band of your own . . ." She glances at notes on her phone. "Dangerheart."

"That's us," says Caleb, indicating the rest of the band.

"Very exciting." Lara doesn't actually sound like she thinks it is, but like it's what she should say for the "video." "So, want to play us a song?"

"Play some Allegiance to North!" someone calls from the crowd.

"Do you have instruments the rest of the band could use?" Caleb asks.

"Ah, no," says Lara. "But it could just be you?"

"Um . . ." Caleb glances down the line.

"Go for it," says Val, speaking for them, though based on his scowl, maybe not for Jon.

A black-clad tech guy appears and places a microphone in front of Caleb. Another tech wheels an amplifier around and runs an instrument cable to him. "Here you go, sir," he says.

Caleb plugs in, but when the tech turns on the amp, he gets no response. "Is the volume up?" he asks Caleb.

Caleb checks the knobs. "Yeah, it's up."

The tech catches Lara's eye. "We're getting nothing. Should I check the guitar's circuitry?"

"Actually . . . ," says Randy. "I think it might be missing

some parts. That's . . . what I heard anyway."

"Oh, um . . ." Lara glances worriedly at the assembled crowd. "Can you do an area mic and we'll go unplugged?"

"Sure." The tech talks into his phone, and a minute later, another girl appears with a cylindrical silver mic on a short stand. He places this a couple feet in front of Caleb.

"Great. Ready?" Lara asks Caleb.

"Okay," he says. The mic picks up his voice, and the amplified sound quiets the crowd. "You probably want to hear me play one of my dad's songs—"

"Yeah!" someone shouts.

"But I think if my dad were here, he'd want me to play one of my own. This is my band, Dangerheart, and this is our song called 'On My Sleeve.'"

I fire up my phone to record as well. Caleb starts to strum. The unplugged electric makes a tinny little sound. The tech cranks the volume, and I see Lara sending a waitress away. Moments later the house music ceases. Caleb has been vamping on the opening chords, and now he starts:

"You never knew, what you left behind . . ."

The fact that the song is about Eli is clearly not lost on the crowd. They hang on every word, and some are singing along by the second chorus. Caleb starts out nervous but he settles in, and by the end he's lost himself in the song, eyes closed, his voice smooth and confident. I give Val a nudge as the second verse starts, and she joins in with her harmonies.

Phones are out all around us. This is amazing. They sound perfect. The crowd is rapt. It couldn't have gone better.

No matter how much light shined on you

You took it with you . . .

Caleb and Val sing in unison and he lets the last chord hang.

There's that excellent pause that happens when band and crowd have arrived at the end, as the silence grows louder than the fading sound, when to clap is to end a moment that no one yet wants to leave . . .

But then someone breaks the ice and the applause becomes an uproar.

I stop the video and give Caleb a thumbs-up.

"What's your band called again?" someone calls.

"Dangerheart," Caleb says.

"A-band-called-Dangerheart dot com," I add. And damn I wish I had my bag because I had a spare stash of buttons in there.

"Play another!"

"Nah," says Caleb. "We're playing over in Williamsburg tonight at Needlefest, though, if you want to check us out."

Some people start to leave but others push forward, adults and some kids and teens who want autographs on Hard Rock napkins, on their arms. I flash Caleb a pen. An employee shows up and hands Lara a stack of Hard Rock T-shirts. "Buy a T-shirt and you can get it signed by the band!" she announces. It's a frenzy.

"Get the other band members, too," says Caleb, waving his hand toward us.

I look around and find Matt and Val. . . . Wait, where's Jon?

Randy sees me looking around. "He left the second you were done. Said he'd meet us at the club . . ."

"Is he mad?"

Randy shrugs sort of sheepishly. "Maybe? I think he's got a case of underappreciation."

I wish I'd noticed! Things had seemed better on this trip. Then again, there have been a lot of distractions.

Caleb and Val and Matt stand with two young girls, sisters, as their parents take photos. Others are still watching and milling around.

Randy leans in beside me. "Time to try . . ." I motion to the band and we make our way over to Lara.

"I'm Caleb's uncle and Eli White's old band mate," says Randy. "Listen, this is going to sound crazy, but before Eli died, he left Caleb a note that said he'd hidden a gift for Caleb inside that guitar."

"Right," says Lara. I can't tell if she sounds like she's interested or is dismissing this outright.

"We were wondering—again, I know this sounds crazy—but would it be possible to take off the pickguard and quickly look inside?"

"Yeah . . . ," says Lara. "I spoke with my boss about

that after you called this morning, and he said it's fine given your concerns about a possible felony."

"Wait . . . ," says Randy. "Spoke this morning? I never called you."

"Oh . . . Was it another member of your team?"

"Yes it was," says a voice from behind us.

My heart falls through the floor. I don't even have to turn to know who it is.

"Hi, friends," says Jason, appearing beside us, smiling smugly. "That was an excellent moment. Nice work, Caleb." He holds up his phone. "I got a great video."

I feel like I probably already know the answer, but I find myself asking anyway: "How did you know where to find us?"

"Maya told me that you guys were headed to New York," says Jason, sounding delighted to share, "and that she suspected you might be on the hunt for more lost songs. Such a good intern. And that got me thinking . . . Denver . . . New York . . . What linked those cities in Eli's past? A quick call to Kellen and it was obvious: the Jazzmaster."

He makes it sound so easy. I remember Maya's text, the one that I barely processed in our rush to get here in time . . .

I'm a little bit sorry. But not too much. Just so you know.

Jason holds out his hand to shake Caleb's. Caleb leaves him hanging but Jason doesn't care. "Seriously, outstanding

250

performance. You are a one of a kind for about five different reasons. But on top of all that, these moments just seem to find you."

I feel like pointing out that it was the other way around. That *we* found this moment, but I'm still too stunned to speak.

Jason introduces himself to Lara. "So . . ." He looks hungrily at the Jazzmaster. "Shall we get all Indiana Jones with this guitar?"

"We'll open it up in the back room," says Lara, holding the guitar and leading the way like a tour guide.

As we follow her through the restaurant, I sense the air deflating from all of us. Can see the disappointment on everyone's faces. I can't believe we got this close, only to have everything fall apart.

We push through double doors and immediately our surroundings change from kitschy rock and roll to slick corporate. We pass offices and meeting rooms and enter a small workshop. There are half-finished display cases on a large wooden table, tools everywhere.

One of the techs clears a space and lays down a piece of black felt. Lara gently lays down the guitar. "We need to open the pickguard," she says to the tech, pointing to the large white panel.

"This is so exciting!" says Jason grinning. "Was it like this finding the other tapes, too? Were they all this expertly hidden?"

I just look away. No one else answers, either. I feel dead, standing there watching. And my heart is pounding and suddenly I'm thinking about the lies to my parents, the interview missed, all of that . . . for this. I take Caleb's hand, still damp from the sweat and nerves of the impromptu performance. He squeezes back but doesn't look at me. He's drained, too, defeated. His chance to know his father slipping away.

"All right . . ." The tech takes an electric screwdriver to the panel, zipping off the screws. He carefully removes the knobs, then the plate, sliding it under the strings.

I don't know what I expect to see inside, maybe wiring and electronics, but instead a thick ball of white puffs out. Balled-up paper suddenly released.

Lara gingerly pinches it and lifts, and a mass of small cocktail napkins flutters down over the guitar. They all seem to have the same oval-shaped logo on them. I pick one up. Ten Below Zero. It's the same club name I've seen on Eli's guitar case and on his gig bag. A place he played, long ago? These napkins have an address below the name: 10 Avenue A, New York NY.

"What else is in there?" Jason says, brushing at the napkins and peering over the space in the guitar.

"Some of the wiring is disconnected," says the tech, "but that's it."

Lara looks up at us all. "Unless your gift was these napkins, I'd say there's nothing else in here. Sorry."

Everyone is silent. We all take turns peering into the guitar, and then the tech reattaches the cover.

"Maybe there's something on these napkins," says Jason. He flips over each one while we all just stand there dumbly, but aside from their time-yellowed edges, the napkins are clean.

"So, um . . . is that it?" Lara asks. "Anything else we can do? This was going to be a great story."

"It sure was," says Jason. "Could you just give us a sec to talk among ourselves?"

"We actually need to get to our gig—" I start.

"You can talk here," says Lara. "Can I take this back?" She indicates the guitar.

"I think we're done with that," says Jason.

Lara leaves with the guitar, and it's just us and Jason around the workshop table.

"I'll make this brief," says Jason. His smiling, cocky exterior dies away, and just like these back rooms, what's behind it is pure-grade business. "We went out of our way to make you an offer that, quite frankly, you barely even deserved. I don't know what you found in Denver, but I do know this: you have until you get back to LA to turn over the tapes or songs, anything you've found, or we're pulling our deal. And it's an offer we won't be making again. Everybody clear?"

"But we didn't find anything," I lie. "We don't have any tapes."

Jason gives me a pitying look. "Well, then, you'd better make some between now and then." He checks his watch. "My car's waiting outside. See you guys over at the show tonight!"

He walks out, leaving us standing there, still stunned.

We sit silent on the subway nearly all the way to Williamsburg.

"Maya?" Matt asks at one point.

"Yes, dumb ass," I say. "Does that surprise you?"

"I guess not."

Caleb and I are slouched against each other, our heads back against the rattling subway window. I don't know what to say. Don't even want to move.

"What are we going to do?" he asks.

"I don't know. What do you want to do?"

He shrugs. "Why wasn't the tape there? Not that I'd have wanted Jason to get it. But still . . . It should have been there."

I don't know what to think about the tape *not* being there. For the last two days this whole crazy search has felt so certain. Like we were really going to find it. If Eli went through all the trouble to be so specific, why not deliver in the end?

I stare out the far window, at the dark blur of tunnel slipping by. I wonder if there was something we missed in the letter from Eli, but that's back in Caleb's stuff at the place they're staying. I'd do some searches online, or, now that the secret's out, send some tweets about tonight's show, but I can't even do that because I have to save battery life. Val and I already realized we don't have time to go back to our place, which means no charged phone, not to mention no cool black shirt and boots and actually brushed hair for the show.

"Can we copy the other tapes before we turn them in?" Matt wonders.

"Who says we're turning them in?" I reply.

Val huffs. "We don't have another choice now."

"We have Jet City Records," I say, but even I think it sounds so lame compared to what Candy Shell is offering us.

"No," Val says stiffly. "We don't." I wonder where this new certainty is coming from, but don't ask.

"Let's just focus on the show," says Caleb, and this tugs a grunt of agreement out of everyone. "All we have for sure right now is the band. If none of this tape or label stuff works out, we can just keep being ourselves, Pluto strong."

He's right. At least we have each other.

The thought seems to buoy us all . . . that is, until we get to the club. We walk in while Postcards is soundchecking . . .

And see Jon is onstage with them.

Postcards slams to the end of a song.

"Fantastic!" Jason is standing alone on the floor in front of the stage, clapping dramatically and grinning back at us. "Not bad, right?"

None of us respond.

Jon glances up and notices us, but turns back to the members of . . . *his new band?* I see him share a smile with Mark, hear Pete say, "Nice, man," and I wonder.

Ethan hasn't seen us yet. He always was very insular onstage. Like he assumed all eyes were on him, and he couldn't play favorites. "Do we have time for one more?" he says into the mic.

"Yeah," the sound man replies.

"What's left in your charts?" Ethan asks Jon.

Jon reaches to a music stand, flipping through pages.

"Charts?" Caleb murmurs beside me.

Charts sounds like a plan.

Was Jon really upset at the Hard Rock or did he just leave early to get to this? Or both? And I find myself glaring at Ethan. I wonder about everything these past few weeks. I mean, when did they make this arrangement? Was it a conversation in Denver? But now I remember Ethan's comment way back at school: *From what I've read, Dangerheart already has Mount Hope's best guitarist.* Was this Ethan's motivation for joining us at these shows all along?

"Did you know Jon was playing with them?" Caleb asks me as we head to the side of the stage and down a narrow hall to the greenroom.

"No idea," I say.

"Did anyone?" Caleb asks Matt and Val, but they didn't either.

The more I think about it, the further back it goes. Even when I just so happened to run into him over bath salts . . . Was that the start of this long con? If it was, then I am some kind of idiot.

The greenroom is spare with cracked concrete walls and a sloping concrete floor. Every inch of the walls is covered with stickers or scrawled band names. There are three sagging couches, a mini-refrigerator full of cheap beer and sodas, and it smells vaguely like the toilets down the hall.

We all collapse on the couches with not much to say.

Nobody wants to talk about Jon onstage, about there being no tape.

"This sucks," I say to Caleb. I feel like I want to melt away to some alternate reality.

He shakes his head. "One minute, we're grinding the Hard Rock to a halt, the next we've got nothing . . . I seriously can barely take it anymore."

"It's a lot," I say, and Caleb doesn't even know about Val's day. . . .

There is very little that is not a total mess.

Jon walks in a few minutes later. Nobody speaks as he leans his guitar case in the corner and visits the fridge for a soda. Ethan, Mark, and Pete come in as he's sitting down.

"Hey, Summer," says Mark. He was always my second favorite in that band, and the one who was most apologetic when I was left behind. I kind of avoided them in Denver with everything else going on, but now I get up and give Mark and Pete hugs.

"Good to see you again," Pete adds.

"You too," I admit, swallowing a moment of hurt for these old friends, who I used to think of as my band of pirates. But rather than strike up a conversation, I sit back on the couch beside Caleb. It's a move meant to keep the past and present in their places.

And also so that Ethan doesn't get the impression that there will be a hug for him, ever.

"Sounded good," Caleb says diplomatically.

"Aww, thanks," says Ethan. "Really glad Jon was willing to sit in with us."

"What a lucky break," I mutter because I can't resist.

Ethan salutes me with a soda. "Worked out pretty great, I have to say."

I hate him for his bullshit, and I want to accuse him of playing me right here in front of everyone, and yet I hesitate because part of that play involved our snowy gyro walk in Denver . . . an event I never actually mentioned to Caleb. Man, I should have! There was nothing to hide, but we were so far from Denver by the time Caleb was awake, and there was so much else to talk about, and I didn't want it to be weird with everything else that was weird . . . but suddenly now it has become another secret, one that binds me to Ethan right when I want to burn all connection to him. The feeling makes me want to barf.

The sound man appears in the doorway. "Dangerheart?" he reads off a clipboard. "You guys are on for soundcheck."

While the band sets up, I take the merch out and claim a space on the table by the main doors. I arrange the postcards and EPs, the mailing list and the buttons. At least it's always satisfying to set up the merch. To look at the little stack of CDs and feel that irrational hope that you might sell them all. It almost takes my mind off our current theater of suck. It reminds me that we still have a chance tonight: all this backstage bullshit will sting a little less if the band can just play one good drama-free set.

They start with "Knew You Before." I'm playing with arrangements: CDs in front, in a fan shape, straight up stack, buttons in line or in a mess, best spot for the list, when I hear "Catch Me" grind to a halt. Now that I'm paying attention, something had sounded off.

"Sorry," Jon says, kneeling down and tweaking knobs on Mission Control. "Delay's all different."

As he fiddles, Caleb huffs. "Come on, man, we only get ten minutes."

Jon offers him a quick glare. "I know."

I hope Caleb just leaves it alone . . . "Maybe you should have fixed that after your set with your new band."

Or not.

"Wow . . . ," says Jon, standing up. "Hey, maybe we'd have longer than ten minutes to check if you hadn't been busy playing rock star at the Hard Rock."

"You know what, fuck you, Jon!" Caleb explodes. "I'm sick of your shit."

I'm moving toward the stage as fast as I can.

"Calm down," says Val, getting there first and grabbing Caleb's arm.

"I'm sorry I happen to have a famous, dead dad," Caleb says anyway, nearly shouting. "It's *so* much cooler than having a living parent like you have."

"It doesn't mean you have to act the way you do," says Jon.

"I— Wait, that's right, I forgot how terrible it is being in a band that's getting tons of notoriety! What a burden!"

"Caleb—" Val urges.

"Guys!" I reach the front of the stage.

"You know what?" Jon is nearly shouting. "Maybe you could just once look at things from somebody else's point of view besides your own!"

"What do you care? It looks like you've found a new band anyway!"

"Hey!" Val screams. "Can you both please act like professionals for five more minutes so I can check my vocals?"

Jon and Caleb glare at each other, but then both nod to Val. I half expect Jon to walk off, but he stays and they finish "Catch Me." Utter silence between songs . . . They wrap up soundcheck with a sterile version of "Starlight."

After, we eat at the Mexican joint around the corner, all of us together but silent: everybody taking shelter in their phones. It's terrible sitting there, stuck in the Red Zone, feeling like if we open our mouths at all, the whole thing might explode. And that, on top of the failure at the Hard Rock . . . The tension is suffocating.

We head back to the club and it's nice to see a line out the door. It lifts everyone's spirits a touch, out of the gloom we've been in.

Caleb and I linger outside while everyone else goes in. We stand in the dark and cold on the corner, by a glacier of trash-strewn snow. I put my arms around him. He doesn't react at first, but slowly thaws. His hand starts to rub up and down my back.

"How are you holding up?" I ask him. As I say this I have to stifle a yawn. The lack of sleep this week is catching up to me hard. I want to crawl into bed for a month.

"Fine, I guess." He looks up past the streetlights. Apartment windows glow in yellow and blue. The sky is a featureless wash of orange. It's supposed to snow again, later. "I'm bummed about Jon," he says. "About the tape. This trip is starting to feel like a huge waste."

"I know . . . I can't believe there are no points for crossing the country, rocking a party in Denver, or playing an impromptu show in a Hard Rock."

"Excuse me, are you Caleb?"

We turn to see a young woman and a guy standing behind us. They are both wearing black coats and scarves that are so similar they could be part of the same military unit.

"Yeah," says Caleb.

"I'm Tessa from Jet City. This is Sam."

We shake hands. I introduce myself.

"How was your trip out?" Tessa asks.

"It's been an adventure," says Caleb diplomatically.

"We had a great show in Denver," I add, "packed. Good buzz." As soon as the words are out I feel like kind of a rookie. Like I'm bragging.

But Tessa beams. "Awesome. Can you guys hang out

after the show? One of our bands is on first, so we want to get in there, but we'd love to chat later."

"Definitely," says Caleb.

"Great. We'll find you backstage after." Tessa smiles and they head inside. Man, I like her already. *Do you have a half million bucks?* I feel like asking her.

"They seem nice," says Caleb sadly, and I know he's thinking the same thing.

The show starts almost an hour late, as so many shows do for reasons I can never quite figure out. Tonight, it's something to do with the wristbands that attendees get, and also an issue with the house speakers. The bands are supposed to have thirty-minute sets but the very first one goes forty and that seems to set the tone for the night. We are on fifth out of nine and somehow a set that was supposed to start at ten is instead pushed back to nearly midnight.

Caleb and I watch the earlier bands from out in the crowd, saying little. As a band called Slip into the Void plays, Matt wanders out to us.

"How's it going back there?" I ask.

"You should probably come talk to Val."

We find her draped on the side of the couch, chatting up the keyboard duo called Dalliance that just played. And passing a slim glass bottle of red-colored liquor back and forth between them.

"Val," says Caleb.

"Hey, bro," she toasts and takes a swig.

263

"That's enough. We're on next."

"I'm already on," she says, laughs, but then she passes the bottle back to the Dalliance boys without drinking more. "Relax, I'm fine."

"It's been a big, crazy day," I say, trying to empathize with her without blowing the secret of our day trip.

"What would you know about it?" she shoots back at me. Maybe she's doing that to keep our cover. Maybe it's the drink. Either way, I'm worried that we're losing her again.

"Come watch the set with us," Caleb says, tugging gently on Val's arm. "Please. For me."

She looks like she might fight, but then she smiles at Dalliance. "Sorry, gents, duty calls."

As we are leaving the greenroom, Ethan, Mark, and Pete walk by.

"Oh, hey there," Ethan says, like we're buddies. "We were just going to get some food. You guys want to join?"

"Dangerheart is on in fifteen minutes," I say coldly. He probably knew that. And yet, here's that hierarchy among bands again, only this time, we're the band getting skipped for dinner.

"Oh, right," says Ethan. "We'll be back for it."

No, you won't, you sooooo won't, I think, but I let it go. He gets nothing.

Out in the crowd, Val nurses a soda and sways a little between us.

"It's okay," she says when she notices Caleb and I glancing

at each other. "I'll be fine. Just keeping the demons at bay."

I want so badly to tell Caleb about our day, but I can't risk setting Val off. Who knows what she'd do at this point, half drunk with her nerves already frayed from being here.

The Void plays their last song.

"Showtime," says Val.

"You sure you're okay?" Caleb asks.

"I got this, bro, I got this."

"Good luck," I say, kissing Caleb.

"Thanks. We're gonna need it."

Dangerheart takes the stage. There is the moment where I wonder if Jon will even join but then he does. And while I can tell that they are all feeling off and cold and distant in their own orbits from one another, the crazy thing about music is that this translates completely differently out in the crowd. Out here, they end up coming across as relaxed and almost a bit indifferent, like they're going to do their thing and they don't particularly care if you like it. And that of course makes you want to find out more about it. It's one of the great mysteries of bands: the internal tension can look like strength from the outside. Which is funny because they will be lucky to survive the night.

That said, the set is kind of amazing. Caleb is solid. Val digs in and brings it. She's sloppy, but as the set goes on you can see her sweat her way out of it, the alcohol wearing off. Now if we can just keep her away from it afterward. Matt has a particularly good night. Head down, playing louder than ever, his arms a blur. As if he's pouring the mess of the last two days into the drums. And Jon is great as always, but definitely keeps a shoulder turned toward Caleb the entire set. He's the only one whose affect crosses the line from disinterest to boredom. Though maybe I'm the only one who notices that. Otherwise, the band is channeling their rubbed-raw emotion and turning it into stage fire.

The crowd is into it. I've sold five CDs before the set is over. The applause grows for each song. "On My Sleeve" actually generates more quiet listening than disinterested talking, which is rare for any room with a bar in it.

They are about to play their last song, the applause dying down while Caleb tunes, when I hear a shout that catches my attention:

"Cassie!"

Before I'm even sure of what word I've heard, alarms are ringing inside. The timbre of that voice is too familiar.

I crane up on my toes.

"Cassie!"

I'm already moving toward the side of the stage when I see Val backing away from the crowd, doing her best not to look toward the voice.

Caleb is noticing this and Val nods at him urgently.

"This last song is called . . ." Val races over and gets in his ear. I think they were planning to play Val's song, "The Spinelessness of Water," but now Caleb returns to the mic and says, "This is called 'Artificial Limb.'" One that Caleb sings, which allows Val to stand back near the drums, look-ing everywhere but toward the edge of the stage.

I head backstage and climb the staircase to the side of the stage. Peering around a heavy red curtain, I can see the faces of the crowd on that far side. . . .

It's him.

Melanie's boyfriend. A giant among the skinny kids. And if he's here . . .

Val spends the song beside the drums, head down and thrashing. She blows a couple notes, never looks up except to lock a death glare on Matt now and then. The second they're done, she unplugs and starts across the stage.

"Val, is that—" I say.

"Gotta go." She hurries past me, leaps down the stairs, darting toward the greenroom.

I am barely down the stairs when she runs past me in the other direction, slipping on her coat. She must have left her bass behind.

"Val—" I try again, but she's already out the backstage door and bolting into the crowd.

"What's going on?" Caleb is rushing toward me.

"Val's mom is here."

I hurry to the greenroom for my coat, and then chase after her, pushing through the crowd.

"Summer!" Jason suddenly appears from the crowd. "Really impressive—"

"Shut up!" I snap at him, pushing right past and not

slowing down until I emerge outside. The sidewalk is cluttered with kids taking smoke breaks. No sign of Val.

Caleb appears beside me. He scans the scene and his couple inches of height make the difference. "There."

We weave through the clusters of people and find Val a half block down, just beyond the club's lights.

She's not alone.

Standing in front of her is a girl of similar height, with straight hair dyed red. Until you are a few feet away, you might think they were sisters.

Her face is deeply lined, her hands jittery with a cigarette. She's wearing a tan faux-fur coat.

Caleb and I instinctively move to either side of Val.

"What are you even doing here?" Val is saying.

When Melanie sees me, she points her cigarette at me. "You the other one that broke into my house?"

The boyfriend stands beside her. He's even bigger than I remember. His face is scraggly and unshaven, his eyes bloodshot.

"Mom, it's not breaking in if it's my own house!"

"It hasn't been your house since you ran off and worried your mother sick for a year," says the boyfriend, his words heavy and menacing.

Melanie's eyes fall on Caleb. She takes a drag from her cigarette. "You're Eli's son."

"Yeah," says Caleb, and his polite instincts kick in. "Nice to meet you."

Matt appears beside us. "Everybody okay?" he asks breathlessly.

No one replies.

"So, what?" says Melanie, turning her glare back to Val. "Did you run out of money?"

Val laughs incredulously. "No! What are you talking about—"

"My checkbook!" Melanie snaps. "I found it with a check missing. I keep track of the numbers. You probably didn't think your mom had that much of a brain left but she does."

I don't know what to think. That's what Val went into Melanie's room for? To steal a check?

"You could have just asked for money," says Melanie. "You could have just called."

"Yeah, right," Val says, laughing but with tears in her eyes.

"You don't want me as your mother, but you'll steal my money—"

"I wasn't stealing your money!" Val yanks a folded piece of paper out of her pocket and throws it at Melanie. Tears are pouring now. "I was going to GIVE you money, Mom! For your treatments!"

As the boyfriend snatches the check from the sidewalk, Melanie's eyes go wide.

"Yeah, I know about your illness, and I know you don't have much money and whatever you do have I know you're just going to waste on drugs and booze and so YES, I wanted your bank account number so I could wire you money! We're about to get a huge record deal and I could pay for your treatments."

Melanie's eyes are wet now, too, but she waves her cigarette at Val. "I don't want your guilt money," she spits.

"Mom, you're going to need it—"

"I want you to come home!"

Val sighs to the sky. "I'm not coming home, Mom. Ever."

"Cassie . . . ," Melanie sniffs. "I want you there. I'm doing better. Darryl is helping me." She reaches for Darryl's big hand.

I see Val scowling at this. "I don't want *you* and *Darryl*, Mom. I have a life now at Caleb's house. I'm in a band, finishing high school, and I have a safe place to sleep. . . ."

"It would be safe at home," says Darryl.

Val sort of chuckles. "I was there today. I saw the *paraphernalia* or whatever right there in the living room! You're still fucked up, Mom—"

"Hey . . . ," says Darryl menacingly.

"And I'm not coming back. I'm not going to feel guilty anymore about how you had to raise me on your own, or that you miss me now, and I'm not going to take the blame when *this*"—she waves her hand at Melanie and Darryl—"falls apart!"

"It's not like that!" Melanie shouts, wiping at tears. "I never wanted you to leave. I've been trying to find you.

270

Left messages with all your old friends . . . Now that I'm sick—"

"No! No." Val holds her fists to her temples. "You don't get to do this! You don't get to play the sick card. It's always some kind of pity with you! It's not fair. But you know what? Don't worry, I'm still going to send you money like a good little daughter. Just spare me the manipulative bullshit!"

"Watch your mouth, Cassie," says Darryl. He looks at Melanie, a wreck now, and grabs Val's wrist. "Enough of this. You're coming home."

"Let go of me!" She strains the other way.

"Let her go!" I shout.

"You're coming home to your mother like she asked!"

I grab Val's arm and try to pull her away. Caleb puts his arm around her and helps, but Darryl is tugging hard. Val's coat tears as she struggles to get free of him.

And then it's Matt, of all of us, who is suddenly darting in front of me, his arm swinging.

"Let her go!" he nearly screams, and he punches Darryl in the jaw. There's a hollow crack. I don't know if it's jaw or hand or both.

Things happen fast.

Val stumbles and falls back onto her butt.

Darryl spins, doubling over and grabbing at his face.

Matt looks dazed as he turns to check on Val.

"Stop it!" Melanie yells. She grabs at Darryl's arm.

He's already back up and spinning and his fist is flying through the air.

"Matt!" I barely get out.

Matt looks up but he'll never move in time. Darryl's fist slams him in the temple and ear.

I see his eyes unstick from time and space. He falls forward like a piece of wood.

Bystanders are closing in on us now.

Caleb jumps at Darryl, but Darryl's big hands slam him in the shoulder and send him sprawling onto the plow pile.

"Hey, knock it off!" Bouncers from the club reach us and grab Darryl.

I drop to my knees and pull Matt to me. He's holding his nose and blood is pouring out all over his hand.

"Stop it, dammit!" Val yells. "Every day I've been without you has been better, not having to feel sorry for being alive! Look at this!" She throws up her hands. "This is life with you! Now leave me alone!" She turns and takes off through the crowd.

"Cassie . . . ," says Melanie, her voice slurring and fresh tears running.

"Hey, come back here, Cassie! Don't you talk to your mother that way!" Darryl shouts, fighting at the two guys who are holding him. He's fired up now and looks like he just needs to hit something.

Caleb scrambles back to his feet. "Val!" he calls, scanning the crowd.

"That way," I say, pointing over my shoulder.

"Dammit, I'll get her." Caleb takes off.

Melanie grabs Darryl's arm. "Forget it, come on. Forget her, I just want to go home."

"All right, fine. I'm fine," Darryl says to the bouncer. He puts his arm around Melanie and they stumble away down the street.

Suddenly Matt is getting up, trying to shake my hands free as he staggers after Darryl.

"Let me go . . . ," he mumbles.

"Matt, no . . ."

He pulls away from me and breaks into a run but he's weaving sloppily from side to side. I catch up with him by the end of the block and grab him by the shoulders. "Stop!"

"I'll kick his ass," Matt sputters.

"Matt . . . come on, calm down," I say into his ear. I notice a stream of blood that's trickling out.

"He doesn't get to—" Matt's eyes roll back and he falls again.

I barely catch him. I lurch toward a nearby stoop and collapse to the cold cement steps, Matt's body limp in my arms. I turn him over so his head is on my lap.

I glance back toward the club. One block seems like a mile. "Hey!" I call, but we're just far enough away that my voice can't compete with the sound from the band inside.

"Shit. Matt, wake up."

Matt's eyes stir, but stay shut.

"Stay with me, Matty." I wrench my phone out of my coat pocket.

A message informs me that I'm below 10 percent on the battery. There are texts, too.

Ethan: Where'd you guys run off to? We're going on in a minute.

Caleb: I can't find her anywhere.

Summer: Matt's hurt bad. I need help.

I watch the send bar fill agonizingly slowly, and when the text finally registers delivered, I switch to the phone and dial 911.

"Hello?"

"This is 911 dispatch. Please state y—"

"Hello?"

A hiss, and the screen goes blank. I stare at the phone, as if it's going to shrug and apologize. All this power, to speak to any other human on the planet via a quick space walk, to like what they're having for lunch from thousands of miles away, and still . . .

The battery goes dead right when you need it.

"Ugh!" I want to throw the stupid phone I—

"Summer . . . ," he groans from my lap.

I bite my lip and squeeze back the tears and shove my phone away in my jacket pocket. It's not the phone's fault, not the phone company's conspiracy to build batteries that start sucking after two years. It's not the 911 operator's fault or the fault of the inventor of the steam engine that made the human dream of long-distance travel even possible in the first place.

It's my fault.

A pack of adults stumbles by. A couple of them eye me mid-laughter. Twentysomethings with liquor-glazed eyes. Their cheeks are rosy above their fashionable scarves.

"Are you okay?" one of them says, nearly serious, her eyes starting to clear.

"Girl, you are *not* getting any there," another says, appraising my situation, and this trips the alcohol-loosened triggers and they all start giggling and leaning into each other and the almost-lucid girl sinks back into the pack and they stumble on.

"Can I borrow your phone?" I ask quietly after them.

He coughs in my lap, a thick sound. I wonder if there is internal bleeding I don't know about. Probably not. But still . . . His body starts to shiver.

I take off my coat and drape it over him. My own shoulders won't stop trembling. My ears and toes are starting to feel numb. My butt is long gone from sitting on this ice-slicked staircase. I should get up and head back to the club, get someone to help, but I don't want to leave him. Or risk hurting him by trying to drag him inside.

I don't want to move at all.

Hasn't there been enough? Three thousand miles of wild plans, lies, and dreams that soared like magical leaps to the stars and back. . . . Maybe my battery is dead, too. We tried, though, didn't we? A for effort? But it doesn't matter. This is what I get, deserved or not. Everyone's gone. Everything's ruined. No band, and no future. Just pain, loss, and a dead cell phone.

This time the tears come. I wipe at the snot on my sore, freezing nose and look desperately up and down the street. Williamsburg at one a.m. You would think there'd be no shortage of people. But not on this street, not in this weather.

Something stings on my already frozen cheek.

A snowflake.

They drift down through the yellow streetlight, large and solitary and sentient-seeming, floating to earth like little paratroopers, making tiny whispering sounds as they land on the pavement.

"Nnnn."

"It's okay," I whisper to him, but once again, I am a liar. Nothing is okay.

"Summer!" I look up the street and see Randy hurrying toward us.

"Yeah."

"Hey, I was looking for you guys backstage—what the hell happened?"

"Val's mom and boyfriend."

"Where's everybody else? Well, besides Jon. He's onstage with Postcards."

"Val ran off. Caleb went after her."

Randy kneels in front of Matt. "It looks like he got punched, hard."

"Yeah. It's bad."

"Wow, okay. Um . . . let's get to the corner and get a cab. We'll take him to the ER. Better to be safe."

I just nod. Push Matt to his feet. We put his arms around our shoulders and slowly make our way back toward the club, through the crowd and to the corner past that.

"Any word from Caleb?" Randy asks me.

"My phone's dead." I feel like a robot in my responses.

Randy waves his arm and a cab starts to pull over. "Oh, but, crap," he says, glancing back at the club. "The gear."

"I can stay with it."

Randy grimaces, straining as he carefully lowers Matt into the backseat. "Okay. I'll tell Caleb you're here. Oh, and . . . hold on."

He digs in his coat pocket and holds out a charger. "Please tell me we have the same one."

"Yeah, that's it. Thanks. Keep me posted."

"Roger." Randy jumps in the cab.

I make my way back inside. Back into the loud, unaware club. Up onstage, Postcards are rocking out. Man, it sounds great with Jon. He's jumping around more animated than I've maybe seen him since the first Dangerheart gig. Like he's free of some big sulk that was hanging over him. I feel like saying to him, *You're choosing Ethan over Caleb? Just you wait* . . . but screw Jon if that's the choice he wants to make.

Right now he's the last thing I've got time to worry about.

Also, Postcards are in the midst of one of their most epic songs, "The View from Saturday," and the song reminds me of long ago in a weirdly direct way that makes a lump form in my throat. Suddenly last summer seems immediate. This is not at all the moment when I want to think about the past, but it's like my immunity to all things tragic is critically low.

So I don't break stride. Just head backstage. The green-room is full of other band members. There's an animated conversation in progress about the best clubs to play in Philadelphia, which ones have food, good weed, and so forth.

"Do you mind if I sit there?" I ask a fishnet girl with bubblegum hair who was in an earlier band called the Meat Dilemma. I hold out the phone charger and nod to the power strip that's hanging off the couch arm, both to indicate my intentions and to ward off her scowl.

"Scooch," she says to her neighbor, and they make a sliver of sunken couch for me to slump into.

I plug in the phone and wait. Nobody recognizes me. Their currency is stage time. And that's fine. What could I possibly talk about right now? I'd just be a downer. I lean against the side of the couch and make myself as small as possible, and feel utterly insignificant but at least anonymous.

"Ya, we've played Philly five times. We're selling it out now," says the Meat girl. "Have you guys ever played DC?"

"Oh, totally," says a stringy boy in a Neutral Milk Hotel

T-shirt. I think his band was called Yesterday's Kill. "DC? You wouldn't think it would be cool? But then it is?"

I listen to them and the failure that is our own band starts to really sink in. Jon is probably gone. Especially given that soundcheck fight and how happy he looked up there just now. What will Val do now that she's been found? Will she run again? Oh, and Matt's in an ER. That's not exactly going to warm his parents on the idea of touring. And the tapes . . .

We were so close.

Twenty minutes pass before my stubborn battery agrees to even turn the phone on. There's a buzz and I see it starting to power up. I have been staring blankly at the ceiling, half listening to the vibrations of Postcards through the wall.

A minute later my phone starts to chirp with alerts.

Caleb: No sign of Val. I went to Neeta's but she wasn't there. Heading back on the subway now. She'll turn up. I hope.

Randy: At the ER. Long wait but they've checked to be sure he's stable.

(424) 828-3710: Did you get my message before? Be at that show.

Missed call and voice mail: Home.

My gut freezes at the sight of this last one. It's one in the morning. Only ten back in LA, but still . . . why are my parents calling? There is no scenario where this is good.

I tap the alert, and the voice mail starts to play.

"Summer, this is your dad. We just got home from dinner and a movie. There's a message from an Andre Carleton. He said he'd had a change in his schedule and as it turns out he could fit you in for a Stanford interview on Saturday if you could get back early. He says the deadline is Sunday. We . . . well . . ."

I nearly die in the pause.

"I've gone ahead and bought you a plane ticket home," Dad says. "You leave out of JFK at seven a.m. tomorrow."

I start to cry. There's no stopping it now.

"When you get back," Dad continues, "we can talk about your choices . . . prior to this. But for now we . . ."

Another brutal pause.

"Just, that plane tomorrow morning. You'd better be on it. The confirmation should be in your email. We let Andre know you could make a one o'clock interview. Okay, please let us know when you get this. We'll be in bed but send a text. Love you . . . Bye."

And there it is.

Failure complete.

I turn my body away from the chatting crowd, stuff my face into my shoulder as the tears increase.

When I was lying to them, when I was dodging the interview, I never imagined I'd feel like this. Well, I never imagined them finding out. But I also felt like I knew what I was doing, what was important for me. I felt like a character in a story, a big person doing a big thing. But no, I am just a girl who told a lie and got caught. The universe, the fates, they don't give a fuck how important you think you are. Andre will still call on a Friday night—a very nice thing of him to do, by the way, so nice I never even remotely planned for it—and everything will finally fall apart.

Oh man, I am so done for. I ball my fist but I can't punch anything in this greenroom. I'm not going to be the drama queen having a big freak-out in front of everyone. But what else am I going to do?

I'm going to take that flight.

That's the only option, now.

And suddenly I get it. Why not getting Eli's final tape has been bumming me out more than almost anything else. More even than it seemed like it was upsetting Caleb. Because the tapes felt like a sign. Like fate. We would find them and *that* would be the future, done and done. Like, in effect, I wouldn't have to make a choice about next year because the choice would be made for me. No one could deny such a crazy, magical thing as those lost tapes. They'd far outshine my other options, and everyone would see that I'd *have* to follow them, to be Summer with her band.

God, listen to me. I sound so selfish.

But there are no tapes. There is no magic key to the future. There is only a plane ride home and the disappointment on my parents' faces. There is only our broken band scattered across a vast, freezing city.

I don't know how I could be so confident in my own

abilities and yet so afraid of dealing honestly with the choices they create. Having a future like mine is a gift. I'm so lucky. And yet I've been treating it like such a burden. Running scared when I should be standing tall.

I feel gross.

Distantly through the walls, there is huge applause out in the club.

And I realize that the absolute last person in this universe or the multiverse beyond that I want to see right now is Ethan.

My phone buzzes again.

(424) 828-3710: The show ends at 2. You need to be there before then.

Okay, that's the same caller from earlier tonight. I wonder if I should reply and tell them they got the wrong number.

(424) 828-3710: That's where you'll find the answer.

Wait. How does this person seem to know that up until very recently I've been searching for something? I look at the time. 1:25. In six hours I'll already be in the sky . . .

I write back.

Summer: Who is this? And what show are you talking about?

(424) 828-3710: You already know. You found the clue under the sea.

Under the—

He just quoted Eli's letter. The clue we found . . .

I open my browser and search.

Ten Below Zero has a show tonight. A series of performers, and then an open mic that lasts until two.

Holy shit.

Summer: Tell me who you are.

(424) 828-3710: You need to be at that show.

I map Ten Below Zero. It's in the East Village. Not too far a cab ride from here if I can get one. . . .

But wait.

Summer: How do I know I can trust you?

(424) 828-3710: I'm the one who gave you guys Eli's guitar case. Now hurry!

My heart is racing. I jump to my feet, jostling band kids who leer at me. I unplug the phone charger with one hand, texting Caleb with the other. The phone is only 60 percent charged, but hey, I'll be on a plane home soon anyway.

Summer: Sending you an address. Meet me there as fast as you can. I'll bring the guitars.

He won't get that until he's out of the subway. It will probably be too late.

Postcards have launched into an encore. I rush up to the side of the stage, find the sound man who's running monitors, and ask if it's cool to leave Matt's drums until the next morning. He says he'll move them to the corner and make sure they stick around at night's end.

I grab Caleb's guitar and Val's bass and hurry out.

I hail a cab. Luckily the sight of me weighed down with two guitars must inspire sympathy, because I get one faster than the other corner dwellers outside the club.

In the cab, my head is spinning. Who is this texting me? 424 is an LA area code. How did whoever this is have Eli's guitar case and deliver it to us on Christmas?

We cross a high bridge. The streets are more populated over in the East Village. Groups stumbling here and there or standing around making small weather patterns of smoke and breath.

Ten Below Zero is on a corner, in the basement. The stairs down are steep and covered in ice and beneath that are blots of gum like little jellyfish. The club's sign has scripted neon letters, cool blue and chipped and probably actually old, as opposed to a fashionable eighties revival. A board on the railing lists "Tonight's Lineup" but the acts have been erased. The only words remaining are: "Open Mic Every Friday 11 p.m. to 2 a.m."

I trudge down the stairs and nearly slip to my death on a slick patch. Add another scuff to Eli's case. Maybe he got one here before.

The door opens out and I have to lean and hook it with my elbow. Finally I stumble in and find myself in a narrow bar with brick walls. The row of tables is empty. There are two guys at the bar. They look like regulars. The sound of guitar drifts out from somewhere in back.

"Good morning," says a woman behind the bar. She's middle-aged with a magenta wrap around a thick pile of dreadlocks.

"Hi . . . ," I say tentatively.

"It's okay, hon. Were you looking for the open mic?"

"I'm meeting someone . . . ," I say. "I think."

"Do you want some food? I just closed the kitchen but there's a few things left. Free of charge. I'm throwing it out otherwise."

It also occurs to me that I'm beyond starving. "Thanks, that would be great." As I talk, I pinpoint the source of the guitar sound: a doorway at the back of the room.

The bartender waves her hand at the empty tables. "Sit anywhere you want, or go check out the open mic. Play a song if you like," she says, nodding at my guitars. "There's no list, just whoever's next."

286

I take another look at the two guys at the bar. They are talking quietly. They don't seem to care a bit that I'm here. I head for the back room.

"I'll bring your food out in just a minute."

This room is a bit bigger, with an actual stage, but still with a low cramped ceiling. The stage is narrow with a brick wall along the back. A black curtain runs along the left side, leading to what must be a pretty meager backstage area.

The current performer is sitting on a stool. He has bushy brown hair that sprouts from beneath a cap like what you'd wear hunting ducks or something. He's playing a beat-up acoustic, its pickguard worn away in places. Sunglasses, the aviator style that is one part retro and one part pilot. Black wool sweater. Faded jeans. Work boots. And singing what I think is an Alice in Chains song.

There are three other people back here. One well-dressed and very tipsy-looking couple at the far corner table, murmuring quietly with the occasional bubble of giggling, and an older woman by herself at a central table, reclined in her chair, both hands around a mug. She's staring transfixed at the performer. Is she here for a clandestine meeting? She seems like the only potential candidate.

Except then she feels me looking at her. "What?" she snaps.

"Nothing." I take a table along the near wall. I've barely sat down when the bartender arrives with soup, a plate of tempeh squares in brown sauce, a basket of bread, and silverware rolled in a napkin.

I watch her hands for a tape, a note, anything . . .

"Want a drink?" she asks. "I've got soda, a couple kinds of tea . . ."

"Maybe a Coke?" I say.

She leaves and my phone buzzes.

Caleb: Just got off the subway. Like three blocks away. What is going on?

Summer: I'm not sure but at least I have food. Hurry.

And then I reply to that phone number:

Summer: Why exactly am I here?

I check my email and find a confirmation for my flight. Delta JFK to LAX 7:05 a.m.

I check the time. Nearly two.

I dig into the food, shoving bites down, barely chewing.

My phone buzzes . . . but it's nothing I want to see.

Ethan: Jon is starting to wonder where you all got off to. Aren't the bands going for pancakes?

God, fuck that guy. If I could smack him through the phone I would. Instead, I just put it down. Can't reply to him. And I can't believe he thinks everything's fine. That he has the gall to keep texting me.

Ethan: cool if we keep your boy for tomorrow's show at the Mercury? He said he's okay with it. Leaves you down a driver though.

288

I don't reply to this either. The theft of Jon is now complete.

The song ends onstage. The lone woman claps. The couple has started making out and doesn't notice. I manage to get a few claps in once I wipe the tempeh's sesame sauce off my fingers.

"Thanks," the performer says. His voice is raspy and worn. "Gonna do just one more. Kind of a long-distance dedication. Another oldie . . ."

He starts to strum a quiet but steady rhythm. It sounds like Elliott Smith or maybe he means real oldie, like Nick Drake. Something in that vein.

I watch him hunch over the acoustic. His chin gets so low to his body, I can only see the top of his head. The motion of his hand with the pick threatens to hit him in the face. He bobs, tapping his heavy boot. The song sounds vaguely familiar. I look down to inhale some soup, but his singing pulls me back up.

I made the hard choice
I took the easy way out

He's better than you'd expect of a two a.m open mic but it's more than that. Captivating. He has presence. And that melody is so familiar but I can't quite place it. My brain is mush from tonight, from the week on the road, from life. I keep glancing back at the door, glancing at the couple at the far end of the room. Looking for a sign . . .

But when I say
I'm all better now

Wait a minute.
These words.
This melody.
I look at him, head still down, except now I am seeing the similarities in posture . . .
The cheekbones beneath that beard . . .
The shape of his face so similar oh my god oh my god oh my god—
And suddenly, completely and utterly, I feel time stop and focus and the corners go dark and—

So replace my circuitry
With memories of you
And I'll play an encore

I am hearing the impossible.

To an empty room

But now there are footsteps behind me and a voice says:
"Never pegged you as the open mic type."

I spin and see Jason standing above me.

And I hear the guitar stop.

My eyes flash back to the stage. There is a little clicking and I see that the pick he was holding has slipped from his fingers. It catches the light as it hits the floor.

And then for the briefest moment I am locked in a stare with a ghost.

It can't be. But it is.

Eli White.

Right there.

"Oh, sorry," Jason says to the stage.

He doesn't know.

But Eli knows him. I can tell. His gaze seems to flick back to me. It's hard to tell with the sunglasses—

And before I can even think it through I mouth a single word to him:

Run.

"No problem," Eli says to Jason, just another random coffeehouse performer on a lonely basement stage. I can hear now how he's faking the low voice. "I was done anyway." He stands quickly.

"No, it's okay," says Jason, sounding legitimately apologetic. "You can keep playing."

"Nah." He checks his wrist. There's no watch there. "It's late anyway. Time to fly."

He drops the acoustic guitar back on a beat-up stand, checks his hat and sunglasses, and walks quickly to the black curtain at the side of the stage.

"Look what you did, you idiot!" the drunk old woman yells at Jason.

He scowls at her but turns to me. "So, I can't think of any reason why my people would observe you coming to this strange little spot at this hour that *doesn't* involve theft of tapes that legitimately belong to us."

My heart is slamming, my breath racing. There he goes. Eli. Pushing aside the curtain. Leaving . . .

"They have great tempeh," I say, my words barely more than a whisper. It's all I can do to keep my eyes off Eli, to hide my racing pulse.

He reaches the curtain and doesn't look back. It flutters behind him in a ghost breeze. I hear a door groan open, the din of street noise, then it squeals shut.

And he's gone.

The bartender pops in and hits the lights. "Thanks for coming, folks."

"Should I grab a seat?" says Jason. "It seems like we're waiting for someone."

"No . . . just eating."

"Hey." And Caleb arrives. The sight of Jason stops him in his tracks.

"What a coincidence, right?" I say, faking sarcasm, faking breathing. "He was jealous of our date."

Jason studies the room again. "I'm not leaving until I figure out what you're up to."

I stand up. "Well, have a great time, because we're going. Right?" I lock eyes with Caleb.

And it kills me to look at him.

Oh God. He has no idea what's happening. And now that's a bigger understatement than ever before.

"I just want to get a picture of this place," I say, fighting desperately to stay calm, "before we go. To post."

"Is this the moment when you pick up whatever you came here for?" Jason asks suspiciously.

"No," I say, but I take two steps around in front of our table. And when I crouch to take the shot, I glance down and see the pick by my foot. It's navy blue and says Regent Sounds. I snap the photo, then put my hand down as if to steady my balance. It's not hard to fake since I feel like the universe is completely out of balance.

I pinch Eli's pick between my fingers, and curl it into my fist.

It's still warm. As I stand up, I slip it into my pocket along with my phone.

"Well, we're going to go," I say. "You can stay if you want."

Jason is still peering around, trying to figure out what he might have missed. "Remember what I said," he warns. "When you get back: tapes, or no deal. I'm not playing this game."

"Neither are we," says Caleb, taking his guitar while I get Val's bass.

I put my arm around him, but I have to wonder what game we are playing now. With what I just saw, what could the rules possibly be?

For the moment, I just focus on putting one foot in front of the other, and on not looking back, even though I want to stare at that stage and tell myself over and over that I wasn't hallucinating.

"How are you?" Caleb says quietly to me as we make our way through the bar.

"Okay," I say, not, *HOLY SHIT, I JUST SAW YOUR DAD*.

Caleb hugs me hard with one arm as we walk. "I got here as fast as I could. What was up with meeting here?"

We navigate the slippery steps, and once we're up on the cold, snowy street, I say, "I got a message from someone to meet here."

"And Jason was following you?" Caleb asks.

"Yeah."

"And whoever was supposed to meet us didn't show?"

"Well . . ."

I feel my phone vibrate. There's a new text.

(424) 828-3710: We tried. Didn't realize they were onto you. It's too dangerous for him to show up again.

(424) 828-3710: Don't tell Caleb. It will only hurt. Maybe another day . . .

"What's up?" Caleb asks.

"It's . . ." My head is spinning. "It's Randy. Making sure

294

we're good. I'll let him know our status."

I type back:

Summer: Don't do this. It's not fair. Tell me where to find him.

"So, this place," I say, trying to change the subject. "I don't know. It was an LA number that said to meet here. And since this was the same place as those napkins in Eli's guitar, it seemed promising, but . . ." I check my phone again. Nothing. "I don't know."

"Maybe Jason showing up scared them off," says Caleb.

"Maybe."

We start to walk. I am imploding, shivering, barely breathing and two voices are warring in my head at once. *Tell Caleb. Tell him now!* While the other voice shouts, *It will wreck him! And for what? Are you even 100 percent sure what you saw?*

God, was it even real? It's already blurry in my mind, so short and intense.

And still no reply. No new spot to meet, to make it real.

What the hell do I do?

But more than anything: Eli . . . ALIVE. There are so many questions. Millions. Starting with: what happened on the night he died and, even bigger . . .

Where the hell has he been?

I don't just mean for sixteen years. That's one thing. But I mean for his son's whole life? How could he let Caleb grow up without a dad?

"I can't believe you guys went to Val's mom's," Caleb

295

says, moving on, as any person who doesn't know their dead father is somewhere nearby might do.

"I'm sorry I didn't tell you. Val made me swear not to. I mean, I was going to tell you eventually, but . . ."

Caleb kisses my head. "It's okay."

I'm going to explode. And I realize I haven't even told him the *other* stuff yet. "I— I'm going home in the morning." Because, OH HELL, there's that, too, on top of everything else.

"Wait, what?"

"My parents found out about the Stanford interview." Suddenly the tears are pouring out of my face again, and I don't know if they are because of my parents or Eli or all of it. "They completely lost it," I say between sobs. "Bought me a plane ticket and everything."

"For when?"

"In like four hours."

"Wow. You . . . but we—"

"Don't worry about me," I say. "I'll head home and take the heat."

"Of course I'm going to worry about you." Caleb reaches out and takes my hand. "I love you, Summer."

I sniffle like a big idiot. "I love you too, Caleb."

"And . . ." He puts down his guitar and takes both my shoulders. "I've been thinking about it and I don't care if you go to Stanford or wherever or not. I mean, I care, but like, I'm going to be happy for you to do what you really

296

want to do. To be who you want to be. No more sulking when we talk about next year. Whatever happens next year will be amazing no matter what we do."

This only makes me cry more. I throw myself into him. He's so honest, so sensitive. He deserves honesty from me, to know what I now know.

Except then what? It's going to tear him apart. Knowing is only going to lead to so many more tough questions, and none are worse than: Why?

And God I'm back to Eli again: Caleb says he wants me to be happy. That our future will be amazing. What the hell made Eli think that his son's life would be better without him? What has he been doing? *WHERE IS HE?*

I have to keep Caleb safe from this. From all these questions. Not forever, but at least until I have some answers. He's barely had time to come to terms with what we've learned already. But now this . . .

"It's okay, Summer," Caleb says, rubbing my shoulders, thinking he knows what my tears are about. "It's all going to be okay."

I nod into his shoulder, but all I can think is:

No. It's really not.

Pluto

I leave him at the door to Dave's. We kiss for as long as we can, the minutes ticking by, and I hang on to him even when he's telling me to go because I can't shake the feeling that on the other side of this plane flight, nothing will be the same.

And yet, plane flights don't wait.

"I should come with you," he says.

"You should check on Matt and look for Val. I'll be fine." Maybe it's the exhaustion or the impending storm back home, but part of me just wants to be alone.

He watches me until I am at the corner. Until a cab has stopped and I am in it and collapsed against the cold vinyl.

Caleb: I'll miss you so much.

Summer: You too.

298

Caleb: Two days.

Summer: Yeah.

It feels like a countdown. I've got to find out something more by then.

Caleb: I love you, Summer.

Summer: I love you too, Caleb.

Neptune

Summer: I hope your set was good. Please don't contact me again. Not tonight. Not when you're back in Mount Hope. Not for a long time. I'm sorry but it's how I need things to be.

The cab bounces through the vacant streets, alone with its kind, hurtling up and over a magnificent bridge. The city sparkles with possibility.

Ethan: Set was great. Um, this is a bummer. Are you sure?

Summer: Yes.

I am sure.

Cold and blue as ice and dead to me. You and your manipulative bullshit. You are the furthest planet now, Ethan.

I delete our conversation. And his contact info. Again.

Uranus

I knock for a while. Just when it seems like there will be no reply, the door squeals open. It's a magazine-hot guy, a couple years older, shirtless and wearing only boxer briefs.

He clutches his almond-colored, all-too-adequate chest and looks up and down the street. "Who are you?"

"Friend of Val's. I just stopped by to get my bag."

Super chest looks me over but only like I'm a curiosity. "Cool."

I follow him up the stairs, trying to keep my eyes off him. I'm not turned on or anything. It just feels indecent at this hour. And I'm too tired to process anything.

When we get to the apartment, he heads to the couch, flickering in the light of SportsCenter. Pulls a blanket back over him and returns Neeta's sleeping head to his lap. Resumes eating a bag of SunChips.

My bag has been carelessly shoved to the wall. My toiletries have spilled out. As I replace them, I see the blankets where Val had been sleeping.

Empty.

"Do you know where she is?" I ask the guy.

"Who?"

"Val, who was staying here."

"Mmm," he says around chips. "Somebody left like a half hour ago. Gave Neeta a hug."

Oh no.

Val, who spins on a horizontal axis when all the other planets are vertical. Val, who has faint rings, if you look close enough. Val, who may live a thousand years and save us from our sorrow.

Have we lost her for good this time?

Outside, the cab honks.

I gather my things and slip out.

Saturn

The sky begins to gather a cold blue as the cab rattles back over a wide bridge toward Brooklyn and JFK.

I have been dozing off but now find an email in my inbox.

From: Tessa Cruz (tcruz@jetcityrecords.com)
To: Dangerheart's Mailbox (info@a-band-called-dangerheart.com)

————————————————————

Impressive!
February 21 at 3:50am

————————————————————

Summer!
Sam and I were really impressed with the band's set tonight. Was everything all right afterward? We were hoping to chat with you guys. We also saw footage from the Hard Rock. That was something! We'll let you guys get back home, have some fun on the road, but we look forward to talking with you next week. Sound good?
Tessa and the Jet City Team

At least there's this. All is not lost.

If we still have a band when we get back.

Jupiter

I print my boarding pass and make my way through the bustling airport. Cold sideways sun streams through all the windows, catching the tail tips outside.

It never ceases to amaze me how many people are at the airport at five in the morning.

And I find myself glancing at every face, watching them all for . . .

It would take 1,321 Earths just to equal the volume of Jupiter.

How can he be alive? How can no one know? How can he not have *told* anyone?

But he did tell someone. Whoever texted me. The LA number. The one who sent us the guitar case . . . then sent me there to see him. Was all that on Eli's instructions? Did he plan to reveal himself to Caleb and me?

That must have been his plan. There wasn't a third tape. We were going to get the man himself.

But now he knows that we're being watched.

Will he get in touch? Or was that our one chance?

What does this mean for . . . everything?

Mars

I trudge to the gate in a blur. Space out in a vinyl chair until boarding. Afraid to sleep and miss the flight.

My last-minute seat is in the second-to-last row next to a mom with a four-year-old in the seat beside me and a few-month-old in her lap. They are not happy. And so my penance begins. I put in my earbuds and turn up Cold Hearts Play with Fire, even though I only have a little battery left (again). I consume a stale bagel and bitter coffee, and lean against the window, watching the Northeast race and recede beneath me. The brown swaths of trees, the narrow twisting highways, the white-frosted lakes.

I think about the sight of Eli onstage. I consider using the credit card my parents gave me for emergencies to buy the in-flight Wi-Fi. I want to reread the articles about his death. Was there a body? If not, how could there not have been more speculation about whether he was alive or not? Elvis-style stuff. Not that Eli was that famous.

But given the state Carlson Squared is in, I don't dare risk the fifteen-dollar charge.

Besides, I will be home by noon. I will see Andre at one. We are going straight from the airport to his office. Apparently, he and I are getting coffee.

The thought of it leaves me blank. Part angry, part relieved. Mars is the god of war, and inside I battle back and forth. The fact that this interview is really going to happen is possibly some sign of a larger meaning to the universe, just the kind of thing I was hoping for, but that discounts how I behaved, how my parents are essentially rescuing me at the last minute.

I've been mad at them at points over the last few hours. But I'm probably the better one to be mad at.

How can I be eighteen and not yet know what I want?

Correction: how can I not be able to say what I want most out loud?

So far, it's been a slaughter.

Earth

The in-flight movie is a lighthearted romantic comedy.

The baby spits up on the four-year-old, who slaps his cup of soda all over me.

Turbulence keeps the seat belt light on, and I spend an hour having to pee so bad, I consider just letting it go and blaming the resulting smell on the kids.

My seat doesn't seem to recline as far as it's supposed to.

The person behind me keeps bumping it with her knee.

There are too many humans.

There are too many babies.

There is too much technology and too much trash and there should only be a few of us, nomadic across the Bering Strait, and there would be no time for bands or colleges or fake deaths or airplane rides. There would just be foraging and hunting and elk skins and huddling close around campfires against the unknown dark and we would have none of these problems.

And also, how can there be only two drink services

on a five-hour flight? My need for ginger ale knows no bounds.

Venus

Before my phone dies out again, I look through my pictures and find the selfie I took of us all, Dangerheart by the food table in Denver. It seems like a year ago that the five of us were standing together, arms around each other, smiling.

I hitch up and start to cry.

And I wonder: Why does any of it matter? Record deals, lost songs, gigs and college and money and any of it. I love these four. We are a thing. Or maybe were. And only now do I feel like I realize how completely rare that might be. We will never be eighteen and in a band and chasing a dream together again. Even just the coming jobs and college will forever change what it is right now.

Venus, spinning backward, the sun rising in the west. Would we get these days back again, if we lived there?

How can we spend any time frustrated or angry when life is this fast and fleeting?

How can we not just be blindingly happy for what we do have?

My phone is off for most of the flight, and the moment the plane's wheels touch the LAX tarmac, I restart it and type a quick group message.

Summer: Guys. I miss you all already. Remember this? This

is all it needs to be, right? Love you all. XO

I attach the photo from Denver and hit send.

Halfway through sending, my phone dies.

Mercury

You thought it was Caleb who was mercurial. Ha.

But Mercury is only as hot as it is frozen.

Catherine forever in the dark.

Summer with her face to the searing sun.

Or vice versa.

Always stuck all one side or the other. Scalded or frozen.

No harmony.

No balance.

23

I stagger off the plane and trudge through the terminal. It's a long walk, and my bag is weighing on my shoulder. Dad said they'd be waiting just beyond security. I walk a bit slower, use the bathroom, stop for a couple minutes to charge my phone, and then get a doughnut. Delaying the inevitable, I know.

The doughnut is Bavarian cream and turns out to be messy, so I have to stop again and manage that situation. Across the hall is a wall of monitors, four by four wide screens, listing the arrivals and departures. I look for flights back to New York. Trace down to the Ps and look for Palau. No dice, but there are so many other places, so many worlds. Before I return to reality, reenter my own time and space through the opaque security doors, a world that is going to suck hard, I want one more moment of possibility. All these places one could journey to, that a band could tour to . . .

"Time to fly."

The words echo in my head. Eli's last words . . .

I gaze at the alphabetical flight listings.

Reach into my pocket and pull out the guitar pick.

Regent Sounds.

I type it into a search.

Regent Sounds is an independent guitar shop based at no. 4 on the famous Denmark Street.

In London.

I race through my phone again . . . To the picture of the brownstone from Val's house. Like the little painting in Eli's guitar case.

It's not in New York, is it?

It's not even in this country. Eli called that tape the Summer Soho sessions. But he didn't mean SoHo in New York.

All the pieces suddenly fit. Well, except for all the pieces that don't, like how could someone dead be alive, and who knew, and who texted me last night, and on and on, but . . .

Eli White.

Alive, and in London.

Is this a picture of where to find him?

I find the mystery number and send a message.

Summer: You may not want us to find him. . . but guess what? We're going to. Whether you like it or not.

I don't wait for a reply. And I don't get one, either.

24

Formerly Orchid @catherinefornevr 8m
ICYMI, Dangerheart was on tour last week! Amazing shows in Denver and NYC. Pics coming soon!

Monday I am back at school.

The interview was nice. Really promising, actually. Andre made his law experience sound cool, and I came across as intelligent and world-weary about music and business and such. He said he thought I was "Stanford material," echoing Dad. And then I went home and accepted the terms of my grounding.

I lost phone and social privileges for a week, which is absurd but I didn't argue. There was no point. Also, my allowance is going toward the plane ticket until it's paid back.

My parents did listen when I explained to them about Caleb's dad and the tapes. They sort of knew about the

Eli connection (turns out they went to an Allegiance show once, back in the day) but we'd never really talked about it and they didn't want to pry into my business. I didn't tell them about Eli being alive. I have a feeling they'd think that was pretty messed up.

As in, criminal, both morally and legally.

I can't say that I disagree.

Caleb updated me by email as they drove nonstop to make it home by late Sunday night. Matt's head is okay. He slept a lot of the ride.

Jon did stay to play the next Postcards show.

Val didn't show up for the drive home.

No one's heard from her. Cassie Fowler has run again.

And now all too soon here I am, standing on the front steps, watching everyone make their way inside. I am thinking about going in circles. Starting over. I remember wondering, once upon a time on the first day of school, if I wasn't just going around but also spiraling down into a black hole.

"Summer."

I turn to find Maya approaching me. As if to prove my theorem, the buoyant, peppy smile I remember so well from our first day has been exchanged for a stone-cold scowl.

"Hey," I say. I'm not sure why she's talking to me. The whole Jason thing seemed like the equivalent of putting our friendship in the microwave.

"I'm sorry about how things went in New York," she says clinically.

"How nice for you." I can't help it.

"I have a future to protect at Candy Shell. Anyway, Jason wants to know your answer about the tapes."

My first instinct is to explain to Maya how the boys just got back, how half the band is missing, and how we haven't had a chance to figure out our next move. And of course the tapes seem like ancient history, given what I know now.

But, no. She doesn't get to know any of this. We're not friends anymore.

Maybe that's mostly my fault. Maybe I did use her, took her for granted. Or maybe she was the one who should have been more observant about her boyfriend's behavior. Ah hell, maybe a million things.

What ifs.

They're kind of a waste of time.

"Tell him I'll be in touch soon," I say, and it comes out cold, Summer the Bitch, but that is where we're at. "Directly."

Maya glares at me with pure fury. "Fine," she says quietly, and storms away.

I watch her go, and it hurts. We aren't going in circles. Ever. We're always moving forward. No matter what wreckage we leave behind.

I don't see Caleb until we're in the Green Room during free period. I have americanos waiting when he arrives.

"How's the reentry?" I ask after we kiss.

"Fine. I feel good actually. Except my ass is still sore from the van. How's yours been?"

I shrug. "Fine. Brutal. No word from Val?"

"No. Charity sent a message to Melanie, too, but no luck there either." We kiss and sip our drinks. "So . . ." Caleb looks around the busy room, kids noodling on guitars, tapping drumsticks on walls, sitting in clusters. "Should we begin the search for Dangerheart's new guitarist?"

I'm squirming inside. "Actually, I was thinking Taquitas."

"Oh, now? Breakfast burritos?"

"Well, yeah."

Caleb checks his watch. "We only have thirty minutes until class."

"There will always be class."

He smiles. "Well played."

We slip out the glass doors by the Green Room and make our way across the parking lot. I can feel Caleb wanting to hurry, but this time I am the one who is walking slow, silent, holding him back by his hand.

"Everything all right?" he asks.

"Yeah," I lie. Waiting. I trace the smooth line of his cheek and jaw with my eye. Watch the way his lashes catch the sun. Things I want to treat so gently for just a few minutes more . . .

Until we have our breakfast burrito to split and a horchata to share and we have made our way to the center of the universe and taken a seat in the grass, in the shadow of the giant metal sun. The circle complete.

"So I was thinking," Caleb says around his first bite as he passes the burrito to me, "for guitar, what about—"

"Caleb," I say, and when he sees how much I'm trembling, he stops.

"What is it?"

I pause . . . but only to remind myself what I am sure is right.

We can take this thing to the end.

We can make everything whole.

But first, Caleb has to take one more shot he doesn't deserve, that he could never see coming.

I hate that I have to do this.

But if someone has to, I am glad it's me.

I take his hand.

"There's something I have to tell you."

Stay tuned for the conclusion in

FINDING
ABBEY ROAD